That One Heartbreak

CARRIE ELKS

Edited by Rose David

Proofread by Proofreading by Mich

Cover Designed by The Pretty Little Design Company https://www.theprettylittledesignco.co.uk/

This book is a work of fiction and any resemblance to persons, living or dead, or places, events or locales is purely coincidental. The characters are fictitious products of the author's imagination.

CHAPTER
One

"I'M NOT GOING on a date with your neighbor's son," Kate Connelly told her mom over the phone. She had it jammed between her shoulder and ear, freeing up her hands to yank open the kitchen cupboard and pull out the cereal boxes for breakfast.

Granola with added protein for James, because at fifteen years old he had a thing about not having big enough muscles. Frosted Lucky Charms for eight-year-old Ethan – Kate hated the things but she'd long since given up the fight for him to have at least one meal a day without added sugar – and boring old cornflakes for Addy who at six was the fussiest of them all and hated anything that wasn't plain.

"Why not?" her mom asked, sounding put out. "He's single."

Kate would have laughed, but she knew her mom was deadly serious. And this was one of the many reasons why she was thankful that she'd moved far, *far* away from her hometown. "Because he has six kids," she pointed out, grabbing the milk from the refrigerator. Dammit, she'd forgotten to switch on the coffee maker. They were going to be late.

"So? That just shows you he's the settling down type," her mom countered.

"That would make nine kids between us." Addy lumbered into the kitchen wearing her Sunday dress. At least one of her kids was up on time.

"And? People have big families all the time."

Yeah, but Kate could barely cope with her three. Between school and the after-school activities, the housekeeping, and holding down a job, she was never quite sure what day it was, let alone which kid it was time to pick up.

Thank goodness the end of the school year was in sight. She couldn't wait for the warm days and the long evenings.

"Mom, it's not happening. Anyway, he lives two hundred miles away." She could still remember Ray from when she was a kid. Ten years older than her and a momma's boy. Not that there was anything wrong with that. She had two of her own momma's boys, after all.

But a man wasn't what she needed right now. Unless he was willing to do school drop-offs and pick up cereal from the grocery store when the boxes were empty and do something about the backyard, then she wasn't interested.

"But if you two fell in love you could all move back here," her mom said, sounding whiny. Kate checked her watch. They'd been talking for exactly two minutes. That was usually all she could handle. She loved her momma to pieces, but damn, if she didn't get her own way she let you know it. "It's been two years, Kate," her mom added softly.

And there it was. The reminder that twenty-four months had passed, because yeah, she hadn't gotten out of measuring the time in months yet. Funny how people expected that to mean something. And funny how little time two years felt when you'd spent most of it in some kind of weird half-life.

"Mom, I have to go. The kids need breakfast," Kate said quickly, needing this conversation to be done. "I'll talk to you soon, okay?"

"But what about Ray?"

Kate ended the call without acknowledging her mom's question right as James walked into the kitchen, wearing a pair of old sweatpants and a t-shirt. He already looked so much like his father it caused her chest to tighten. "We're leaving in twenty minutes," she told him. "Where are your Sunday clothes?"

"I'm not going to church," he mumbled, grabbing the granola and pouring it into a huge bowl. She winced, knowing the price of the stuff, but didn't say anything.

"Of course you're going to church. It's the one day of the week that we're all together. Now go get changed."

He poured milk into his bowl. "I'm going to the station. They have some space for new junior firefighters."

And just like that her heart felt like it was doing a loop-the-loop. She was so not ready for this. Even less ready than she was to think about dating again.

She should have known he'd want to go. James had always hero worshipped his dad, after all. And since Paul had been a firefighter, James wanted to as well.

But she couldn't stand the thought of it. Which was probably why he was trying to blindside her. Because if he'd asked, she would almost certainly have said no.

"Not this week," she told him. "We need to talk about it first." When she was ready. Which would probably be never, if she was being truly honest.

"When?" he asked.

"Soon," she promised.

His lips were tight as he looked up at her. He could be as stubborn as his dad was, too. If Paul was here, he'd bark at James and that would be the end of it.

If Paul was here, they'd both be at the station for fire training.

"Mom, I can't find my pants," Ethan said, running into the kitchen in his shirt and boxers and nothing else.

"Can you put it away? I'm trying to eat here," James muttered, pretending to gag.

"And I'm trying to get dressed," Ethan huffed. "Mom, where are my clothes?"

"Check the pile in the laundry room." She really had meant to sort and fold all those dry clothes last night.

She really needed some coffee. And that's when she realized that she *still* hadn't turned the damn machine on. Rubbing the heel of her hand against her eyes, she groaned when she pulled it away and saw the smudged mascara on her palm.

"Fifteen minutes," she shouted, loud enough for them all to hear, finally switching the machine on. She'd have to take her mug to go. She pulled out the stainless steel vacuum one she bought when the kids were little.

When she was mom of the year. Before she became a widowed mom of three.

"This milk tastes weird," James said. He'd already eaten half of his bowl of granola. Kate sighed and picked up the milk jug.

The best by date was two days earlier.

"Does it taste weird to you?" she asked Addy, trying not to sound worried. Addy shrugged. James took her bowl from her and she started to protest.

"I'm getting you a fresh one," James muttered. "Before we all end up with food poisoning.

And there he was. Her buddy. Her bestie. He came out occasionally, when he managed to fight his way through the teenage hormones and the anger.

The boy she'd met when he was barely two years old and as cute as a button. The one she'd legally adopted when he was three after she'd married his dad and they'd become a family. He was as much hers as Addy and Ethan, and she loved him so fiercely it hurt.

He loved her, too. She knew that. They'd kept each other going over the last two years since Paul's death.

"Thank you." She shot a smile at James as he pulled out a fresh carton of milk and bowls, then made him and his baby sister breakfast again.

He even splashed some into her stainless steel mug before putting it back in the refrigerator.

"No problem," he muttered. "Now, can I go to the fire station?"

"No." She shook her head. "Not this week. But I'll think about it. Soon."

"Why don't we have any photos from Daddy's funeral?" Addy asked Kate as they walked up the steps to the First Baptist Church. Kate was holding Addy's hand, the other gripping her coffee. Could you even take a coffee cup into the church?

Surely they wouldn't turn her away because she needed a caffeine hit.

Just to be sure, she lingered outside to finish, watching as James and Ethan caught up with them.

"People don't take photographs of funerals," Kate told her. Kids came up with the strangest questions sometimes. After losing Paul she'd thought she'd heard them all, but this was a new one.

And she had no idea where it had come from.

Grief was a strange thing. It ebbed and flowed like the ocean. Sometimes the tide would be so low you barely thought about the loss at all, and then it would come rushing back, a tsunami of remembering.

She knew that Addy couldn't remember Paul as much as she used to. She'd been four when he'd died. Ethan had been six and James – her poor James – had been thirteen.

More than once he'd held her as she broke down, much to her horror.

"Why don't they take photos?" Addy asked. "I wore a special dress, didn't I?"

"Yes…" Kate frowned.

"My friend Annabel was a flower girl. She has pictures she brought to school. She's such a show off. She said she was a princess for a day."

"That's because you take photos at weddings, dummy," Ethan said. "They're happy things. Funerals are sad things."

"So we can't take pictures of sad things?" Addy asked. "We have pictures of dad in the house. Isn't that sad?"

Kate let out a long breath. "Those pictures are happy. That's how we remember Daddy. That's how he wanted us to remember him." She drained her coffee cup. "Now can we go in?"

"I want to take a photo in for show and tell," Addy said.

"Of what?" Kate asked.

"Of Daddy's funeral."

She ruffled her daughter's hair. "I don't think your teacher would like that much."

"Why don't you take in something of Dad's?" James suggested. "His helmet or a photo of him in his uniform?"

"Hey, remember when Dad came into my school to talk about fire safety?" Ethan asked. "I must have been in Pre-K then."

Addy's lip wobbled and Kate knew exactly what was coming. "Did he come in to my Pre-K class?"

Kate swallowed hard. "No, honey, he didn't. He wasn't with us then, remember?"

"That's not fair." Addy pouted. "Did he go to James' Pre-K class?"

"What's going on here?" a female voice cut through the beginnings of Addy's tantrum. "Are you all gonna hang around out here or are you coming in?"

The sound of Shana Wilson's voice was enough to make Kate relax. She turned around, smiling at her. She and Shana had been friends for years.

"Hey Aunt Shana," Ethan said. James nodded at her.

"So, are we going in or what?" Shana asked. "Because the quicker this finishes, the quicker we can get to the diner. And I'm determined to get a booth this week. I'm not going to be beaten." She slid her hand through Kate's arm. "Go ahead and choose the best pew. Save us a couple of seats."

Kate watched as her kids hurried in through the church doors.

"You okay?" Shana murmured.

"I'm fine." Kate nodded. Because mostly, she really was. Yes, there were bad days, but there had been some good ones too. And as time wound on, the good was starting to outweigh the bad.

"You sure?"

Kate smiled. "Apart from my mom wanting me to be the stepmother to six additional kids, even though I almost poisoned my own three with bad milk this morning. Oh, and I'm also the worst mom ever because I won't let James go to Junior Firefighters, and Addy wants to take a photo of her at Paul's funeral for show and tell."

Shana blinked. "What?"

Kate squeezed her friend's hand. "It doesn't matter. I'm fine, I really am."

"Not as fine as that sight," Shana said, looking over Kate's shoulder to the town square beyond.

It was only natural to turn around and see what her friend was staring at. But when she did a mixture of pain and longing washed over her. Because the good men and women of the Hartson's Creek Fire Department were on their pre-training run.

She usually got into church before they ran past. Not just

because it hurt to watch them run without Paul. She was getting used to that.

But because she'd pushed every single one of them away after Paul died. They'd tried to help her, but she'd refused their offers. It had hurt to see them, and she'd found it almost impossible to deal with their grief as well as her own, and most importantly, her kids'.

Her throat felt thick just thinking about it. There was a divide there now that she couldn't quite bridge. They didn't know how to deal with it, so they just got on with their lives.

Or most of them did.

She went to look away, but then she saw him.

Marley Hartson's eyes caught hers and she felt every cell in her body tighten up. He'd been Paul's second in command. His closest friend. The man who was with him when he died.

And the one man she'd pushed so far away she could never see a way back from that.

And it hadn't been because he had anything to do with Paul's death. Her husband's passing had been a freak of nature. That's what everybody said. Unexpected, and completely sudden.

It was because Marley had been with him. Holding his hand. Seeing the life pass out of her husband's body. It was too painful to think about.

And yes, there was a certain jealousy there, too. That he'd been there and she hadn't. When it happened, Kate had been happily filing books away at the library, thinking about what to cook for dinner and where she and Paul would go for their date night.

She took a deep breath and watched as Marley's jaw tightened, his gaze still on her. The intensity of his stare made her chest feel so tight it was hard to breathe. And she hated that, hated feeling anything. So much better to be numb.

Like the rest of the crew and juniors, he was wearing a blue t-shirt with FDHC embroidered on the left-hand side.

There was a tattoo on his left arm, peeking out from his sleeve. That was new. And yeah, she noticed the way his biceps looked bigger than before because she might feel dead inside sometimes but she was still, apparently, a woman.

He had the easiest gait of any runner she'd ever seen. It had to come from his constant activity. Outside of volunteering for the department, he was a construction worker. He worked with his twin brother on real estate developments all over the county. And on the weekends they played in a local band. Like her, he was always busy. And yet she knew for a fact that every evening he ran past their house just to check on them.

Because yes, she'd made it clear she didn't want his help. But he checked on them anyway. He didn't know she knew. But she could time her watch by the man.

It felt like a relief as the group of firefighters ran past the church, toward the far end of the town square, to the road that led to the firehouse. She inhaled raggedly as the organ started to play inside the church.

"We should go in," Shana said.

Kate nodded, pulling her gaze away from the disappearing squad of firefighters. "Yeah, we should."

"And the kids better have chosen seats at the end of a pew," Shana added, completely unaware of Kate's reaction, thank goodness. "Because we'll need to make a quick getaway if we want to get that booth."

"Six kids? Wow. And I thought three were hard enough to handle," Shana said as they sat in the diner. "Doesn't your mom love you?"

Kate grinned. Now that church was over she could relax. Sure, she had a list of chores as long as her arms to do when she got home, but right now she knew all of her kids were safe, and she had a cup of bottomless coffee in front of her.

They hadn't gotten here fast enough for a booth, much to Shana's disgust. Instead, they were at a table by the window overlooking the town square.

James had said he wasn't hungry and headed out to throw a ball with some friends, and Ethan was pouring what looked like half of a bottle of maple syrup onto his pancakes. Addy was coloring furiously, her crayon blunting on the paper.

None of them were listening to Kate and Shana talking, which wasn't a surprise. Her kids had long since learned that grown up conversations were mostly boring.

"My mom's problem is that she doesn't think any woman can survive on her own," Kate admitted. Her mom was the poster child for moving on after bereavement. She'd remarried barely ten months after Kate's dad had died.

"Maybe she's right though," Shana mused, taking a bite of bacon.

"What do you mean?" Kate frowned because Shana never agreed with her mom. After Paul died and her mom flew in to 'help' – which meant proclaiming that Kate's life had ended and she'd never be the same again – Shana had practically frog marched her to the airport as soon as the funeral was over.

"It's been two years. How long are you going to wait until you start dating again?"

"Forever."

"Mom, can we go play outside?" Ethan asked, looking through the window. There were a bunch of kids from school in the grassy town square.

"Have you finished your food?"

"Yep." Ethan shoved the last of his pancake in his mouth and swallowed it down in double time.

"Okay then. But stay within my sight. Between the bandstand and the oak tree."

"Of course." Ethan nodded.

"Can I go too?" Addy asked.

"No, you need to stay with me."

"That's not fair." Addy pouted, and it made Kate's lip twitch.

"Honey, Ethan is two years older than you."

Ethan sighed, looking like he was eighty, not eight. "I'll look after her. And James is over there."

Shana caught Kate's eye. She knew how protective Kate felt, especially toward her youngest.

"Why don't you message James?" Shana murmured. "See if he'll keep an eye on her, too?"

Her chest felt tight, because she hated this. Hated her kids growing up. And yes, Addy was still young, but James wasn't.

Paul was supposed to be here to help her navigate through this, dammit.

Within a minute James had walked back into the diner to grab his brother and sister, nodding patiently as Kate instructed him to keep an eye on them at all times, and to come get her if there were any problems at all.

"I'm a big girl, Mommy," Addy said, shaking her head. "You gotta learn to let me go."

That set Shana laughing, which was probably what they needed at that point. Kate's own lips started to curl, right until the diner door open and Marley walked in, his long strides taking him straight to the counter.

Twice in one day. Kate took a deep breath and lifted her coffee cup, praying for him to leave quickly.

But then he turned and saw her staring. Oh God. She tried to relax her expression but he held her gaze a moment too long.

There was no smile on his face. She let out a low breath and nodded at him, thankful that Shana was too busy watching Addy and Ethan cross the road to the square with

James to notice that the town's hottest firefighter had just walked in.

No, no. Not hot at all. Just a friend of Paul's. Or ex friend, whatever you wanted to call it.

Her chest felt weird, like she'd just run a hundred yard dash.

"What can I get you?" the server asked him at the counter. She heard his low voice as he put in an order for a coffee and pastry to go. Watched as he leaned on the counter, his thumb running along the length of his jawline. Felt herself flush like a teenager.

God damn it, what was wrong with her? She blamed her mom and all this talk of needing a man.

She didn't need anybody. She was fine as she was.

"So come on," she said to Shana. "Tell me about your date last night." Because now that the kids were out of earshot, her friend could give her all the gory details.

Shana's dating life was always diverting. And she sure could use some of that.

CHAPTER Two

SLIDING his feet into his running shoes, Marley Hartson quickly laced them up and checked his watch. Almost nine in the evening. He'd spent most of the day at the fire station. Firstly, helping to run the training and Junior Firefighter drills. And then he'd headed over to his parents' place to meet up with his family.

His brothers had been there. Including his twin, Pres, who he worked with. Along with Pres' wife and kids, ten-year-old Delilah and his twin sons, who at two-and-a-half years old were out of control in the cutest way.

And though it was fun, he still couldn't get Kate Connelly out of his mind.

The way she'd looked at him as he ran past. The way her stare had felt like a punch in the gut.

The way he always felt like he'd let her down. Let her kids down.

Broken the promise he'd made to Paul as his friend laid dead on a gurney.

He let out a long breath. He'd go on his run and then he'd try to get some sleep. Because working in construction always meant an early start. And juggling his day job with volunteering as a firefighter meant he was always on the go.

He was lucky because his brother owned the construction company and Pres had always been supportive of Marley's volunteer career.

The cool evening air wrapped around him like a blanket as he stepped out of the front door of his small house. He'd bought it years ago, close to the fire station because that's what volunteers did. They lived close so they could get there fast when there was a call out, because time could mean life or death.

And it was weird, because as soon as he started to move, he felt better. He always did. Standing still meant way too many thoughts rushing through his mind. According to his mom, he'd always been overactive, even as a kid. But as an adult – and especially in the last year – his need to always be doing *something* had become more of a compulsion.

He ran past the fire house. It was quiet, empty, which was always a good sign. He'd been part of the twenty-person strong volunteer force since he'd come back to his home town after college, at the age of twenty-two. Before that, he'd volunteered as a firefighter in his college town, and as a teenager he'd been a junior firefighter here in Hartson's Creek.

That's when he'd met Paul Connelly. His best friend.

The man he'd seen collapse in front of him and die within minutes.

There were no cars on the road as he made his way to the town square. All the shops were empty with the lights turned off save for the Moonlight Bar. He could smell the sour notes of beer as he ran past it, heading to the road out of town.

As he reached the edge of town the houses thinned out, until there were only a few here and there. The fields that surrounded the town stretched out toward the burning orange horizon.

He planned to run to the house then back again. Just check that all was well and then he'd be able to sleep.

Kate and her children had moved there a year ago, out of the house that was near the station where her husband had died. It had been easier when she'd lived there. To keep an eye on her. To check on her.

It was harder here, because he knew he stuck out like a sore thumb when he ran past. Maybe that's why he waited until night had fallen every evening before he ventured out.

There was a light shining in her upstairs window. One of the kids, probably. And on the porch there was a light, illuminating the plant pots full of dead flowers that had turned a brilliant shade of brown due to lack of watering.

He would have watered them but he knew Kate wouldn't accept help. She'd turned down everything that the fire department had tried to offer her.

He was about to turn back again when he saw it. At first he thought it was a crack in the pathway leading from the driveway to the house. But then it moved and he almost jumped.

A damn copperhead. It was early in the year for them. The thing must've just woken up from hibernation, but it had been a warm day and it must've enjoyed bathing in the brightness of the sun, but now it was trying to find somewhere warm to sleep overnight.

Marley sighed as he watched it begin to slither toward the house. Because now he was going to have to do something about it. It wouldn't be his first encounter with a snake. They had plenty of calls from frightened tourists and locals alike over the summer months, especially out in the fields where the snakes preferred to make their homes.

Hell, he'd been called out a few times for ones that had found their way through the holes in brick walls and into houses. And he wasn't certain that this snake wouldn't do the same thing.

The house was warm. The outside air was not.

Looking around on the ground, he found a stick. The copperhead wasn't too big – only ten inches long. He could easily lift it and move it far away from Kate's house. Holding the stick out, he walked carefully toward the snake, sliding the end of the stick beneath its body and lifting.

Thankfully, the snake lifted up with it.

There was a field about ten yards away, so Marley carried it carefully over, letting the snake down and watching as it slithered away. Sure, there was a possibility it could be back, but most snakes he'd encountered were more than happy to be left alone and far away from human scrutiny.

"What's going on?" Kate called out from her front door. He hadn't even heard her open it.

"I was running past. Saw something on your driveway." It wasn't a lie. And he knew she'd hate it if she knew he was keeping an eye on them all.

He turned around to look at her. She was wearing a pair of yoga pants and a t-shirt, her dark hair swept up to reveal her slender neck. There was some dirt on her cheek, like she'd been cleaning. But it couldn't disguise the attractiveness of this woman.

It hit him like a Mack truck. He felt his pulse – already fast – starting to throb in his neck.

Fuck, no. She was Paul's wife. He wasn't going to be attracted to her. He pushed the thought away, hoping it would never come back.

"What did you see on my driveway?" she asked. Her voice was low, like she didn't want to wake up her kids.

Marley hesitated, because he knew that some people freaked out over snakes. Imagined that one little visit meant an infestation. "It's dealt with."

She put her hands on her hips, her head tipping to the side. "What's dealt with?" she asked him. "I saw you pick something up."

Of course she wouldn't let it go. He let out a sigh.

"A snake," he said, his voice low.

She blinked, her lips pressing together. "What kind of snake?" She sounded less certain now. Less in control.

"Just a rat snake," he lied. "I took it over to the field."

Kate let out a long breath. "Was it poisonous?"

"Rat snakes are fine." There, that wasn't a lie, just a little stretch of the truth. "But if it's okay with you I'd like to inspect the outside of your house when it's light."

"Why?" she asked, looking confused.

"Just to…" He shrugged. "Make sure everything's okay."

"You think the snake might come back?" Her voice lifted and he winced, because he was making things worse.

"No." But it was a good excuse to make sure her house was secure.

"Then it's fine. I'll take a walk around the property tomorrow to be sure." She lifted her gaze to his, her jaw jutting out. "And you don't need to run past here every day. We're fine."

So she knew about that. Damn.

"It's my favorite running route," he told her.

A ghost of a smile pulled at her lips. "Sure it is. Just like your old favorite running route was past our house in town."

"It's a small town," he pointed out. "It's not exactly full of places to run." And he couldn't give this one up. He'd made a promise. He intended to keep it.

"You don't need to check on me. I can take care of myself. And the kids," she told him, her voice firm. Because yeah, she knew exactly what he was doing.

Of course she did. She was an intelligent woman. Pretty. He could remember the way she used to smile so easily. Before.

"I know you can. I know you do." He lifted his hand to his brow, brushing away some of the sweat he'd gotten from running. "I'm not trying to make your life harder." He looked at her carefully. She still seemed a little freaked out by the snake. "Kate," he said softly.

"Yes?"

"If you need anything at all, you just let me know, all right?"

The light of the moon caught her eyes. He could see how shiny they were. "I don't need anything," she told him. "I'm fine. I'm just trying to live my life the best way I know how."

He nodded, hating that he'd upset her. "Well good night then," he murmured.

"Good night."

And then she was gone.

CHAPTER *Three*

"MOM, have you thought about me joining junior firefighters yet?" James asked the next day after school. Kate had finished work early and was walking around the outside of the house, her phone in her hand. She'd googled 'how to secure your house from snakes' but apart from looking for holes in the brickwork and for pipes that didn't have mesh in them, she wasn't exactly sure what she was doing.

All she knew was she didn't want anything creeping in that shouldn't be there. The thought of it made her shudder.

She stopped what she was doing and looked up at him. "I have," she said, stealing herself for the worst. "I just don't think you're ready for it yet. Maybe next year, if your grades are a little better."

"Next year I'll be a junior. And you'll say I have to concentrate on my schoolwork and that I won't have time."

Kate winced, because that was exactly what she was planning to say to him. Because the truth was, she didn't want him to be part of the scheme at all.

Because then he'd want to volunteer as an adult. And she'd be as afraid for him the same way she'd been afraid for Paul every time he got an alert.

Because being a firefighter wasn't an easy job. Before moving to Hartson's Creek to manage the volunteer team, Paul had been a captain in a big city force. The stories he'd told her made her feel panicky and anxious. And it wasn't just that – even being a small town firefighter was dangerous. People got injured. People died.

She couldn't bear for that person to be James.

She'd be waiting for the day somebody rushed in to fetch her from the library. And her heart couldn't take it. Not with her son.

"I thought you were going to try out for football," she said, trying to change the subject.

"I'm no good at football. I've never gotten picked for the team." He stuck his hands in his pockets, his jaw jutting out. "I just want to do something that will make Dad proud."

Her heart tightened. She stood up and turned to face him. This boy that was turning into a man in front of her eyes. Surely he couldn't be this old. It felt like only a few months ago when he used to climb into her lap and hold her tight, his little chubby arms wrapped around her neck as he told her he wanted her to marry his daddy.

That he wanted her to be his mom.

And she was. In every way except biology, this boy was hers.

"Your dad would be proud of you," she told him, her voice tight. "He is proud of you. He's looking down on you and I know he sees what I see. You're a kind, strong boy, James Connelly. You take care of your brother and sister and you take care of me. And you get good grades at school. In a couple of years you'll go off to college and you'll make us all even prouder."

"What if I don't want to go to college?" he asked her. "What if I want to become a firefighter like dad?"

"Dad wanted you to go to college," she reminded him.

"He saved up all that money. He wanted you to have choices, the kind of choices he didn't have."

"I have enough choices," James told her.

"Oh sweetheart." She smiled softly at him. "It's a big world out there. And you'll get to see it all. You'll meet new people, learn so many things. Visit the places that your dad only dreamed of." He never wanted James to be stuck in one place. Not like he had been.

"What if I want to stay here with you? You need help with Ethan and Addy." He lifted a brow. "God only knows how much worse they'll get when they're teenagers."

She wanted to laugh because suddenly her boy sounded so grown up. "I'll cope," she told him dryly. "The same way I did when you hit the dreaded thirteen."

"Yeah, well I was a good kid."

Reaching out, she cupped his face with her palm. "You still are."

He grimaced, stepping out of her touch. "If I'm that good, why won't you let me join the firefighters?"

And they were back to *this* again. He wasn't letting go. But neither was she.

"Next year," she promised. "I'll think about it then."

James pressed his lips together and nodded, then turned around and walked into the house and Kate let out a long breath.

She'd won the battle. But she'd long since learned that didn't mean anything with teenagers.

She turned back to the house and recommenced her inspection, because dealing with snakes was so much easier than dealing with her son.

And she had a feeling that this discussion wasn't over.

The Hartson's Creek Memorial Library was a low modern brick building a few roads away from the town square. Kate had been working here for the last ten years, only taking time off when she had Ethan and Addy.

It was in the same strip as the police department and town park, and behind it were lush green fields that families came to picnic at in the summer months.

But today wasn't about families. It was about bracing herself because it was Thursday, and Thursday were Stitch and Snitch days.

Okay, officially the Thursday morning club that met at the library was called the Hartson's Creek Sewing and Knitting Club, but for as long as she could remember they called themselves Stitch and Snitch.

And the chief snitcher – Mary Cooper – was walking through the double doors, carrying her knitting bag that Kate knew for a fact contained the same sweater she'd been knitting since last November. It was a vermillion color that made Kate blink every time she saw it peeping out of the bag.

Not much stitching went on as far as she could tell.

"Kate, tell me, did you remember to put the chairs out this week?" Mary asked.

Kate took a deep breath and tried not to let her smile falter. "Yes, of course." She'd forgotten once. Two months ago. And had yet to hear the end of it.

"Oh, and has anybody come about those birds on the roof? They made such a noise last week I couldn't hear myself think."

Couldn't hear the gossip more like. Kate shrugged. "I put a call in to county, but there's a backlog on their bird removal service."

"Damn." Mary frowned. "I guess we should try a little poisoned seed."

Over Kate's dead body. "I'm sure they'll come eventually. In the meantime, I've made sure all the windows are shut."

"Good plan." Mary nodded, about to turn away. Then she tipped her head and looked Kate dead in the eye.

"You look different."

"I do?"

"Hmmm." Mary's overgrown brows pulled tightly together. "Have you changed your lipstick?"

"No." Mostly because she wasn't wearing any.

"Done your hair then? Is it a different color? You look…" Mary pressed her lips together. "Attractive."

Oh God, she wasn't going to laugh. How could somebody make a compliment sound more like an accusation?

"Thank you."

"It wasn't a compliment, dear."

Of course it wasn't.

"Maybe it's time you started thinking about dating again," Mary said to her.

"I'm sorry?" Kate's brows pinched together.

"We were talking about it while we were knitting last week. There are a lot of eligible men in Hartson's Creek. And a woman shouldn't be on her own for too long."

Kate frowned. "Have you been talking to my mom?"

"No, why? Should I?" Mary pressed her lips together.

Absolutely not. Having her mom trying to set her up was bad enough. Having Mary taking an interest in her lack-of-dating life was something that wasn't going to happen.

"I'm still deep in grief," Kate said, leaning forward, putting on her best sad looking face.

"A good man will get you out of that, dear," Mary said, patting her hand. "I read an article in a magazine the other day. Sex is good for sadness."

Okay this was going too far. Dating was one thing. Talking about sex with the head honcho of the Stitch and Snitchers? No thanks.

The door opened and Shana walked in, carrying two Styrofoam cups of coffee, followed by a huddle of ladies carrying sewing cases, already talking loudly as they walked in. Luckily, their arrival diverted Mary's attention, and Kate used the opportunity to walk back to the counter where Shana was standing.

"Quick," she said, her voice low. "Ask me something about the Dewey Decimal system."

"Stitch and Snitch getting you down?"

"Something like that."

"Good thing I bought you a coffee then," Shana said, grinning. "I got them to put an extra shot in it. Figured you'd need the caffeine."

"Have I told you lately that I love you?" Kate said, taking the coffee gratefully.

"Stop quoting Van Morrison at me. You know it always makes me weak in the knees." Shana watched as the Stitchers filed into the recreation room. "So what gives?"

"Mary asked me when I was going to date again." Kate rolled her eyes. "Why is it that everybody wants to know that?"

"It's the year thing," Shana said. "They feel like they've given you some grace. Now it's time to meddle again."

"I wish they wouldn't." Kate shook her head. "I swear snakes are easier to deal with than them. Did you know that sex is good for sadness?"

Shana laughed out loud. "Who told you that?"

"Mary."

Shana laughed louder. "Oh God, tell me she didn't."

But Kate just lifted a brow.

"Well, the woman is wrong about a lot of things, but even a stopped clock is right twice a day," Shana said. "Sex is pretty good for everything. Maybe you should try it."

"No thanks. I'll stick to reading books in bed."

"At least choose some raunchy ones." Shana winked. "Have you checked out the latest Meghan Quinn book?"

"No," Kate lied, because of course she had. She may not

ever be ready to date again, but it didn't mean she was dead inside.

"That's good. Because it'll make you want to have sex with every gorgeous, rugged man in town. Ask me how I know."

But she didn't need to ask. And there was only one gorgeous, rugged man she thought about when she read romance books.

And he was the one man she shouldn't be thinking about.

CHAPTER
Four

"THERE'S a kid over there asking for you," Nate, one of the new carpenters they'd hired called up to him. Marley was on the roof of the house, rolling out roof felt, getting ready to fix the shingles on top. "Says his name's James," Nate added.

Putting his power nail gun down, Marley looked over in the direction that Nate was pointing. Sure enough, there was James Connelly standing right outside the wire fence they always erected around their construction sites. He had his hands jammed in his pockets, and what looked like his school backpack at his feet.

Nobody had let him inside the gate. Good. Marley had spent enough time lecturing the crew about only allowing authorized personnel inside the fence. And even then they had to have a safety briefing and wear construction hats inside the fence. He'd seen enough building accidents to know that careless safety led to injuries.

Climbing down the ladder, Marley nodded at the new guy. "You guys can take a break. Grab a drink."

"Thanks." Nate smiled. "Want me to get you a coffee?"

"I'd kill for one." He'd spent two hours last night on a call out. Nothing major, thank God – a small electrical fire that they'd managed to put out within minutes. But then there'd been the paperwork and making sure everything in the station was tidied up and ready for the next call, which meant he'd crawled into bed at two am.

And of course he'd been up at six, the way he always was. Tonight he was going to sleep like a baby.

Just as soon as he'd done his evening run.

There were always fewer volunteers available for the night time call outs. Most of the fire crew either had kids that they needed to be home for, or they had working hours during the day they couldn't change. So Marley was always one of the first on a scene after the clock turned midnight.

He was just glad that last night had turned out not to be a big one.

The one they always dreaded. The one they trained week in and week out for.

He pushed that thought out of his head as he pulled open the mesh gate and walked out.

"Hey," he said to James, pulling his hard hat off and running his fingers through his hair. "Is everything okay?"

"I need you to talk to my mom," James said, shifting his feet.

"Why? Is there something wrong? Is she hurt?" He frowned, because that thought made his stomach knot.

James shook his head. "No, she's just refusing to let me join the junior firefighters and train with you on Sundays. I need you to tell her to let me."

Marley let out a mouthful of air. "I can't do that," he told James. "She's your mom. It's her decision."

"But it's the wrong decision. Dad wanted me to join. He always said he did. You know that. And it's not like there's a long line of volunteers lining up outside the fire house." James looked at him pleadingly, his blue eyes clear and bright. "Please talk to her. I need to do this."

Marley's stomach felt tight. He felt a responsibility to this kid. Not just because he was Paul's son and Paul was gone, but because he'd known James since he was toddling around in diapers.

And now James was the one struggling. And despite knowing that Kate would be pissed if she knew James was here, he couldn't turn him away. He just couldn't.

If you decide to start running another route, I'd be absolutely fine with that.

If that wasn't a brush off, he wasn't sure what was.

"I guess I could ask her…" he said, trying to think it through. Let's face it, she already seemed to hate him. Things couldn't get any worse.

"Please do," James replied quickly. "I know you'll make her see sense."

"Now hang on there," Marley said, his voice low. "Your mom already sees sense. She must have her reasons for not wanting you to join. I said I'd talk to her, not that I'd be able to make her change her mind."

But James was already smiling. And looking at Marley like he was some kind of God covered in gray construction dust.

"Thanks, I really appreciate it." It was the hope in his voice that almost killed Marley. "You're the best."

"I'm really not."

But James was already walking away.

"Ethan, honey, I need to wash that t-shirt," Kate said to her son as he walked out of the bathroom in his pajamas, carrying the dirty clothes he'd been wearing all day. On top was Paul's old Hartson's Creek fire department t-shirt, which Ethan had insisted on wearing to school, even though it was stupidly big on him.

But she hadn't had the heart to argue with him this morning.

"No, I like the smell," Ethan protested. "And I want to wear it tomorrow."

As if a day dealing with the Stitch and Snitch brigade wasn't tough enough, now she had to deal with her son's fixation with his dad's t-shirt. They didn't teach you about this in the life after grief books.

"You can't wear it to school tomorrow," Kate pointed out, trying to keep her voice even. She was frazzled but she wouldn't let it show. "You wore it today. You have plenty of clothes in your closet that you can wear. Let me clean this one."

"No." Ethan frowned, turning around and gripping the clothes tightly. "I'm wearing it."

There were some fights worth fighting. And others you had to give into gracefully. "We'll talk about it in the morning," she conceded, fully planning to sneak into his room once he was asleep and grab it. "Now get into bed. I'll be in to kiss you soon."

Thankfully, Addy was already in bed. She was a tired little puppy now that she was at school every day.

As for James, he was studying at a friend's house, which was a minor miracle. She'd given him strict instructions to be home by nine-thirty.

And to top it off, Addy's class had a bake sale tomorrow and she'd somehow missed the email the class parents had sent out last week. So, now a batch of very boring, allergen friendly cupcakes were in the oven, ready to be iced when they cooled down, probably at midnight if her luck continued this way.

When the knock at the door came, it made her jump. Assuming James had forgotten his keys, she rushed down the stairs to pull it open.

Only to see Marley Hartson standing on the stoop.

He wasn't in his usual running gear. Instead, he was wearing jeans and a gray Henley, the fabric tight on his torso, revealing the powerful set of his chest muscles.

She blinked. "You're wearing too many clothes."

Okay, that came out the wrong way. But it didn't seem to faze him. Maybe he didn't hear her.

"I meant you're not in your usual running gear," she added, trying to make it better.

A smile pulled at the corner of his lips.

"I'm not running tonight," he told her. "I just finished band practice."

She'd forgotten he drummed in a local band. Did the man have any spare time? Well, quite clearly he did – enough to check up on her every evening.

But he was early tonight.

"If you're worried about the snakes, I checked the outside of the house," she told him. "No entry points. And no more snake sightings."

"I wasn't worried about the snakes," he murmured, but there was still a hint of relief in his voice. "Can I come in?" he asked. "There's something I want to run past you."

"What is it?" she asked, looking up at his face. She felt hyper aware of this man. Of his height, his strength.

Having him so close made her feel dizzy.

"I just wanted to talk to you about James," he said. "Give me five minutes, and I'll be gone. Promise."

Curious, she stepped aside and let him in. If she'd thought he was overwhelming before, now it felt like all of her senses were being overloaded. The hallway was small and he felt too big for it.

She couldn't remember the last time a grown man had been in the house, other than her stepfather. Maybe last fall when they had the furnace serviced? Either way, it made her feel off kilter. A little tingly.

"Come on into the living room," she suggested, mostly

because that was the only room that didn't look like a hurricane had rushed through it.

The room felt cold when they walked inside. She pointed at a chair and he sat down and leant forward, his elbows resting on his long legs. She followed suit, sitting opposite him.

"Is James in trouble?" she asked, because she couldn't work out why he was here.

"No. But he came to see me at work today."

She blinked. "James did?" Why would he do that? She felt dizzy, like she was losing control. She didn't like it.

"He wanted to talk to me about the junior firefighters."

Of course he did.

"He shouldn't have interrupted you at work," she told him. "I'm sorry. I'll speak to him about it."

"He really wants to join, Kate. And we really want him there." Marley ran the pad of his thumb across his chin, capturing her face with his eyes. "And I hate to say it, but I think it's what Paul would have wanted, too."

"Paul wanted James to go to college," she said, trying to keep her voice even. "It was his dream."

"He can still go to college and be a firefighter," Marley said softly. "I volunteered all through my four years."

Suddenly, her heart felt tender. Like somebody had taken it out and pulverized the muscle. The thought of James in a uniform made her want to be sick. "I already told him no," she said. "And I meant it. He needs to concentrate on his schoolwork. His grades haven't been great since..." She let out a low sigh.

Marley's gaze didn't waver from hers. She felt exposed in a way she didn't like at all.

"Why not just try it?" he asked her gently. "See if he can combine it with his studies? If it doesn't work, no harm no foul."

Every word he said made sense. And yet she couldn't

agree to this. She wouldn't be able to cope if James got hurt. And yes, she knew they were careful with the junior firefighters. But she also knew that as soon as he turned sixteen he could join the official volunteer team. He would go on call outs, do almost everything a firefighter could do.

A ragged breath escaped her lips. "I'm sorry, I can't."

Marley's face was full of compassion and she hated that. She'd have preferred he fought her, made her angry. Because she was so full of damn emotions she wasn't sure she could keep them all in.

And then the screaming started from upstairs. Not the scary kind. The sort that told her that Addy and Ethan had both gotten out of bed and in the middle of an angry spat that only six- and eight-year-olds could have. She squeezed her eyes shut. "I need to go."

Addy screamed again, and it was blood curdling this time.

"Sorry." Kate ran out of the living room and up the stairs, all too aware of how this must seem to Marley. He must think she had no control over her kids. One of them was sneaking out to complain about her. And the other two sounded like they were starting World War Three.

She'd pay a million dollars for a drink and a spa day right now.

"Mommy," Addy called out as Kate stomped into Ethan's room. "Ethan won't give me Daddy's t-shirt."

Oh, damn that t-shirt. Why had she ever pulled it out of the closet in the first place?

"It's mine," Ethan said, baring his teeth at his sister. "Get out of my room before I push you out."

"I hate you," Addy screamed at him. "Daddy hates you too."

Kate reached for her daughter. "Come on now, that's not true. And you should be in bed."

"I want a t-shirt. Ethan has one."

Of course she did. "Come with me," she told Addy,

reaching for her daughter's tiny shoulders. "We'll go find one." She looked at Ethan, who'd gone completely quiet. Tears were falling down his face.

"Oh, honey." Her heart clenched for him. "Come here."

He shook his head.

"Tell him you're sorry for what you said," she whispered in her daughter's ear.

And because they were good kids, even though they'd been through so much pain, Addy croaked out an apology.

"Please don't cry, Ethey," she whispered, throwing her arms around her brother. "You can keep the t-shirt."

"Kate?" Marley called from downstairs.

"Who's that?" Addy asked.

"Marley Hartson. He just popped in to ask me about something."

"Something smells like it's burning," Marley shouted, his voice louder now. "Do you have something in the oven?"

Oh crap. The cupcakes. Could anything else go wrong tonight?

"Can you get yourselves back into bed?" she asked her kids, praying that this time they'd listen. "We'll talk about t-shirts tomorrow."

"I want a firefighter one, too," Addy said.

Of course she did. And Kate knew for sure that she didn't have another one of those.

She ran out of Ethan's room and down the stairs. Marley was already in the kitchen, pulling out the cupcakes. Smoke rushed from the oven, and as it dissipated she could see that the tops of the once yellow cakes were ash black.

For a moment she couldn't react. It was like she was struck dumb. Is this what her life had become? Bouncing from one little disaster to another?

Her shoulders slumped because some days were just too hard. She wanted to crawl under a stone and never come out.

"What do you want me to do with these?" Marley asked, glancing at the blackened cakes in his hands.

"Throw them away." Her voice was thick. And that's when the tears started to roll down her cheeks. Because there was only so much she could take.

She was strong. Or she tried to be. And yes she knew she wasn't exactly winning any mom-of-the-year awards, but she loved her kids. She was trying so hard to make them happy.

Marley pulled open the trashcan and slid the charred cakes in before putting the tray on the stovetop. And then he walked toward her, his brows knitting, reaching out to wipe away her tears.

"Hey," he said softly. "It's just some cupcakes. They don't matter."

That just made her cry harder.

"Yes they do. They're for Addy's bake sale. I'm going to have to cook more. Or I would, but I'm out of flour." And let's face it, no local store was still open for her to get some new stuff tonight.

And then it kept coming. "And my youngest kids are in some kind of battle to the death over Paul's old t-shirt, and James hates me and is going behind my back because I can't bring myself to let him join training."

Why was she telling him this? He didn't care. And she'd spent the last year and a half making sure he had no idea how hard her life was.

Without a warning, Marley folded his arms around her, pulling her against his chest. She was surrounded by him; her face pressed against his gray Henley, her body way too close against his. With one hand he stroked her back, while the other cupped the back of her head.

When was the last time she'd been held like this? She could smell the soft fragrance of whatever laundry soap Marley used, could feel the heat of his skin through the thin fabric of his top. It made her feel light-headed.

And yet she didn't pull away. Instead, she cried into his shirt, letting him soothe her, his voice soft as he whispered words she couldn't quite hear.

She wasn't used to this. To being held for so long. By a man that wasn't her husband. Or related to her. But it felt good. Too good.

There was a little flutter deep inside her belly. Like something waking up from a long sleep.

"Mom?" The front door slammed shut. "Is something burning?"

The sound of James' voice was enough to bring her to her senses. Within a heartbeat she was stepping back, breaking Marley's embrace, and lifting her hand up to wipe the tears away because she couldn't have her eldest son seeing her like this.

"I burned some cupcakes, nothing to worry about," she shouted back to him, right as he walked through the kitchen door.

Marley's shirt was damp in the center of his chest. And he was still standing there, this mountain of a man who felt like comfort and fear at the same time. Looking at her, his lips pressed together.

"Hey," James said to him, walking into the kitchen and grabbing an apple, biting into it without even taking a breath. "Saw your truck outside. Everything okay?"

"Everything's fine," Marley said. "I'm just heading out." He looked at Kate. "And your mom is going to take a bath and go to bed."

She wanted to laugh because there was no chance of that happening. She was sure she still needed to calm Addy and Ethan down, and then she needed to get to bed early so she could rush to a bakery first thing and pick up a dozen or two cupcakes.

"Okay." James nodded, giving Marley a pointed look. "You two been talking about anything interesting?"

Marley looked back at him, calm as anything. "No. Nothing important at all."

CHAPTER *Five*

KATE WASN'T sure what she expected to see when she opened the front door the next morning, but it definitely wasn't the two boxes on the stoop.

She felt exhausted. She'd barely slept all night. Unsettled by Marley coming to the house.

And the way she'd felt so… strange after he hugged her.

"We got a delivery," Addy said, jumping up and down, because to her boxes meant toys. "Come on, let's open them," she said, her voice full of excitement.

The lids of the boxes weren't taped together, just folded. Addy pulled open the flaps of the closest one and peered inside. "Look, Mommy! Cupcakes!"

"What?" Kate frowned. But Addy was already picking up a cupcake and holding it, the frosting glinting in the morning sun.

"Can I have one?" Ethan asked.

"Wait." Kate put her hand up. "Let me see." Opening the box fully, she could see there were at least thirty cupcakes in there. All expertly frosted.

"Who delivered these?" Ethan asked. "I didn't hear the doorbell."

"Are there more cupcakes in the other box?" Addy asked, her eyes widening as she turned her attention to the second box.

Ethan was already pulling the other box open. Addy bumped him with her shoulder so she could look in, too.

"What are they?" she asked, sounding disappointed. "They look like rags."

"There's a note," Ethan said, pulling out a white letter. "It's got your name on it," he told Kate.

She took it from him and read it.

Kate,

Hopefully these cupcakes will be okay for the bake sale at school. My aunt is a heck of a baker and was happy to help. And the t-shirts are from Paul's locker. I couldn't bring myself to let them go when you asked me to empty it.

And if you ever need anything, please ask. We want to help.

Marley Hartson

She blinked at his words, willing herself not to cry again. Because this was so damn sweet she could taste it. She hated the fact that she'd needed his help. That she hadn't been able to manage her kids' needs alone.

"Mommy, what does the letter say?" Addy asked, rolling onto her tiptoes to try to read it.

"Marley dropped these off." She let out a breath.

"Are they Dad's t-shirts?" Ethan asked, staring at them.

"Yeah." Kate nodded. Her throat felt tight.

"Can I have one?" Addy asked. "Please?"

"I'll go through them later," she promised them. "See what we have." She could remember Marley asking her what she wanted him to do with Paul's locker. He told her they'd keep it at the station for as long as she needed. But she'd been so overwhelmed and had told him to clear it out.

She guessed Marley couldn't quite bring himself to toss it all.

Sliding the box of t-shirts into the hallway, she pulled the front door closed and locked up. James had caught the bus to school half an hour ago, so it was just the young ones she needed to wrangle today.

"Come on," she told Ethan and Addy, because now she had another stop to make before she headed to work. "Let's go."

"You got another visitor," Nate said, bumping Marley in the ribs with his elbow. He was standing at the makeshift table, staring at the plans the architect had redrawn for them after they'd encountered a problem with some drainage at the back of the lot. "She's pretty hot, too. That your girl?"

Marley looked up, blinking. And sure enough, there was Kate, standing by her car, looking wonderful in a skirt and silk blouse that showed off her soft curves to perfection.

His throat tightened. "No, that's not my girl. That's Kate."

"Kate?"

"My friend's widow." He grunted it out. And hoped that'd put an end to Nate's questions, because he really didn't want to answer anymore.

Nate blinked. "Oh, sorry, man." Then, because he was clearly an asshole and Marley was already wondering why they'd given him the contract, he added, "So is she single?"

"Get back to work," Marley said, rolling up the plans and walking over to the gate, annoyed by Nate's question.

"Hey," he murmured to her as he walked through the mesh closure. "Everything okay?"

"I just wanted to thank you for the cupcakes and the t-shirts." She looked completely awkward and stupidly adorable. "You didn't have to do that." She reached her hand up to cup the back of her neck. She had her hair in a messy bun that revealed the slender curve of her throat.

He pulled his eyes from her. He wasn't going to look at her that way. He wasn't Nate, the asshole. Nor was he going to do anything to rock the boat. Not when she was finally talking to him again.

"I know I didn't have to do that," he said, walking over to where she was standing. "But it wasn't hard. My aunt likes baking. I had the t-shirts."

"Paul's t-shirts." Her voice was low.

His chest tightened. "Yeah."

"Did you keep anything else of his?"

He lifted a brow. "His whole locker. Anything left in his desk drawers. I have it all."

She let out a low breath. "I told you I didn't want it."

"I have space in my garage. It isn't a big deal. I just didn't want you to make any rash decisions."

Her jaw jutted out and he knew he's said the wrong thing. He didn't know anybody with as much pride as this woman.

And yeah, she deserved to have pride. Not everybody would have been able to keep it together after losing their husband. But she had, and she'd done it well. Her kids were a testament to that.

"If you want anything else, you can come take a look."

"I don't want anything else." She shook her head. "I just…" She let out a long breath. "I was in a bad place last night. I overstepped the mark. I'm sorry."

"You overstepped the mark?" He was confused now. His

gaze dipped to the base of her neck, where her skin dipped before it met her sternum. Fuck, it looked soft.

Eyes away, Hartson.

"I shouldn't have let you hug me."

She was worried about him trying to console her? He wanted to roll his eyes, but this conversation felt too precious.

"You were upset. It was a simple hug. Nothing more." His voice was low. "You don't have to worry about that."

She took a deep breath, her chest rising beneath the silk of her blouse. "I don't want you thinking I'm some kind of weak woman, burning my daughter's cupcakes and having my kids screaming at each other. Because I'm not."

There was that pride again. And fuck if it wasn't the most enticing thing he'd seen.

"I've never thought you were weak, Kate," he told her. "Never."

"But other people do." A fleeting smile pulled at her lips. "Some people think I can't cope."

"Then fuck them."

Her eyes met his. "I think you might be one of them."

"What gives you that impression?" he asked gruffly.

"Because you run past my house every night."

"I told you, it's on my route. I need to keep in shape." Yes, it was a fucking lie. But he couldn't sleep if he didn't know they were okay. Not that he'd ever tell her that.

Her gaze dropped to his body, then shot straight back up again. And then her phone started to ring. She lifted it from her purse and looked at the screen and sighed.

"Bad news?"

"My mom." She gave him that hint of a smile again. "So kinda."

He remembered Paul talking about his mother-in-law. *"High maintenance doesn't even describe it, man."* Marley blinked at the memory of them talking about her over a beer at the station late at night.

God, he missed his friend. So much so that sometimes he didn't know what to do with the emotions. Except push them away and run until he forgot them. The department had pushed him to have therapy after Paul had died in front of him. He'd lasted three weeks.

He wasn't a talker. He was a doer. Action was his therapy.

"I have to go," Kate said. "I need to open the library. I just wanted to stop and say thanks and… you didn't have to. You don't have to."

"I know that."

"Okay then." She shot him the most fleeting of smiles. And yet it felt like he'd just won the lottery. "I guess I'll see you around."

Yeah, she would.

It wasn't until just before lunch that she finally listened to her mom's voicemail. Mostly because they'd had a mother and toddler group come in this morning, and she'd had to get her full quota of cute sticky baby hugs, as she read them a story about a cat who lost his mittens.

One of the little boys had taken a liking to her, and had kissed her cheek constantly as she read, much to his mom's embarrassment.

But truth be told, she loved it. She missed her own kids being little. Even Addy, at six, felt grown up compared to these little ones.

It made her heart hurt a little to think about how fast her own children were growing.

But now the library was quiet, and from experience she knew it would be until school was out and the older kids wandered in to do their homework or find a new book to read, followed by the younger kids and their caregivers who would do anything to keep them amused until dinner.

It wasn't a surprise that her mom's message was every bit as un-urgent as she thought it would be.

She put the phone on the counter, listening to her mom's breathless explanation of how her best friend's niece was having Botox injections. And had Kate ever thought about it, because apparently it was best to start in your early thirties, and since she was already in her mid-thirties she'd be playing catch up.

Pressing delete had never felt so satisfying. She'd call her mom over the weekend, the way she always did. And she didn't need Botox, did she?

She turned on the camera of her phone and stared at her reflection. Sure, she had a few extra wrinkles. But who didn't? She wasn't a kid anymore.

Wait. Was that a gray hair?

Before she could look any closer, her phone started to ring again. She almost expected to see her mom's name on the screen, but instead it was James'.

So of course she answered.

"Hey honey, is everything okay?"

"Hi, Mom. One of my friends asked if I want to sleep over tonight. Is that okay? I'll head home after school and pick my things up then go straight to his."

"What friend?" she asked.

"Cal."

"Do I know him?" she asked. There was a time when she knew all of his friends. All of their parents, too. They'd call each other up, make plans for playdates, stay and gossip while the kids played on the swing set or – when it was raining – tried to beat each other playing video games.

And then he'd gone to middle school. The students were bussed in from all around, and his friends were more scattered.

Now that he was at high school she barely knew any of the kids he interacted with. And James had left a friend group last year, anyway. She never got to the details of it, but she long since suspected it was some kind of grief response.

"He's new," James told her. "It's Friday night and I don't have any homework. So can I go?"

"Where does he live?"

James let out a little sigh. "Near school."

"Wouldn't you rather I pack up your things and bring them to you?" she asked him. Because yes, she found it hard to let her eldest go. She also didn't like the idea of him spending the night with people she hadn't met. How the hell she'd deal with him going to college, she didn't know. But she'd face that problem when it got here.

"It's fine. You don't get off work until five. I'll get my stuff and head out. Ethan and Addy are in after-school club, right?"

"Yeah, that's right. Just send me the address. I'll pick you up in the morning."

"I'll catch a ride home."

"No, you won't," she said quickly. "Send me the address, please." And yeah, she was totally going to check the house out on Google Maps. Just for her own peace of mind.

"All right, Mom!" He sighed. "The bell just rang. I gotta go."

"Okay honey. Have a good evening. I'll see you tomorrow."

"Sure."

Before she could say anything else, he'd hung up. She slid her phone into the pocket of her skirt. Damn, she loved skirts with pockets.

Why did nobody tell her that children got harder when they got older instead of easier? She thought of the little boy who couldn't stop hugging her this morning. He reminded her of James when he was little and how every time she saw him he'd throw his arms around her neck and never let her go.

She missed that. She missed him. Why did teenagers not come with a manual? Maybe she should complain to the library about that.

"I hear you spent last night pretending to be Santa, delivering gifts all over town," Pres said, passing a burger to his brother. They'd worked late tonight, even though it was a Friday. Then they'd stopped for dinner in the diner on their way home, because Cassie and the kids had already eaten with their mom, and neither Pres nor Marley had had time for lunch.

Marley lifted a brow. Word spread fast around here. "I delivered one thing. And I was just doing a friend a favor."

"Don't you want to know how I know?" Pres asked him.

Marley planned to eat dinner and head home to crash for the night. Not that he ever managed to sleep until the morning.

"Nope. I'm pretty sure it's some convoluted story involving mom, Cassie, and the grapevine."

Pres smirked. "Something like that. Is Kate doing okay?"

Marley nodded. "She's fine. Her kids were just a bit overwhelming last night."

"I didn't realize the two of you were so close."

Marley took a bite of his burger. Damn, that was good. His stomach gurgled in appreciation. "We're not," he said simply once he'd swallowed the mouthful down. He could explain the whole situation — about James and the junior firefighters. But he was tired and cranky and needed to eat. "I just happened to be around when she needed help."

"So you got Aunt Becca to whip up a batch of cupcakes?" Pres grinned. "Man, I wish you'd brought some of those to the site."

"Get your own cupcakes," Marley told him, wondering how he could change the subject.

The truth was, he didn't really care if people were in his business, but Kate would. He knew that. And last night was the first time she'd actually let him help her.

It was like he'd found the tiniest chink in her carefully constructed armor. He didn't want that to change.

"Are you okay?" Pres asked, bringing Marley out of his thoughts.

"Yeah. Why wouldn't I be?"

Pres shrugged. "You just went quiet. Is there more to this thing with you and Kate than you're letting on?"

A flash of annoyance rushed through him. "No, there isn't. And I'd appreciate it if you didn't start blowing your mouth off about that. She doesn't deserve people gossiping about her."

Pres lifted a brow at Marley's sudden outburst. "Okay, man. I was just wondering."

"Yeah well now you can stop. Can we change the subject, please?"

"Sure." Pres gave him a grin that was a little too knowing for Marley's liking. "Let's talk about next week. We still doing that fundraising thing next Friday?"

Marley was trying to raise money for the Junior Firefighter program. They always needed money for equipment, clothes, and training. This year, Pres had suggested the band they played in held a concert with all the money going to the cause.

"Yeah, as long as you and Cassie are okay with it."

He shrugged. "We're good."

Pres and Cassie were both in the band, Altered Reality, along with Alex, the bassist who never knew how to shut up.

"Even though it's at *Chairs*?" Marley asked, a smile finally pulling at his face. Because he knew Presley disliked *Chairs*. Most of the men of the Hartson family did. It was a strange name for a strange tradition. Every Friday in spring and summer most of the townsfolk of Hartson's Creek would gather together in the grass alongside the creek. They'd bring food and drinks and their own chairs to sit in and gossip for a while. The reason for the gathering having its name.

As kids, they'd loved running around by the water until the sun slid down under the horizon. Their parents would sit and chat while they played football or built forts.

And then they'd grown up. As teenagers, there'd been nothing more uncool than hanging out with your parents and grandparents on a Friday night.

But recently, now that he was a dad of three, Pres seemed to be hanging out with his wife and family there every week. Another sign that life for his brother was moving on.

He was happy for him, but he missed him, too. It was a strange feeling.

"Yeah, Mom and Dad said they'd keep an eye on the kids. Though of course Delilah wants to be on stage with us." Delilah was Pres' oldest, his daughter with his first wife, who'd sadly passed. She wasn't far off from starting middle school, whereas Pres' two other kids were still babies. Cassie, his wife, had adopted Delilah shortly after they married.

"Of course." Marley smiled. This was better. He felt like he was back on an even keel. And after last night, he needed that. More than he'd realized.

CHAPTER *Six*

MARLEY WAS HALF-ASLEEP when the shrill sound of the fire alert echoed out of his phone. For once he'd managed to go to bed early. He blinked his eyes open as the high-pitched sound continued and instinct kicked in. He grabbed his phone and opened up the alert app the fire department had been using for the last few years.

Time was the biggest factor when it came to call outs. That's why most volunteers lived close to the station. Before the first minute was up he was already dressed, pulling his shoes on and running down the stairs. He grabbed his keys because sure, he only lived a five-minute walk away, but it was a one minute drive to the station and every second counted.

By the time he parked, there were five other volunteers already there. Enough to send out the first truck. The second one would follow, just as soon as the other firefighters arrived, along with the EMT if medical assistance was needed.

As soon as they were in their protective clothing and in the truck, Tayto, their driver, pulled out and took a left. According to the alert, there was a fire in the cornfields right

outside of town. He winced because his uncle was a farmer. He knew how destructive fires could be in a tinder dry field full of crop.

"How bad is it? Anybody know?" he asked. Adrenaline was buzzing through his veins.

"Can't see much smoke," Tayto, the driver told him. "But it's kinda cloudy. And dark."

"Who called it in?" Sian, their youngest volunteer, looked at Marley. She was twenty-three and lived three doors down from the station. Along with Tayto, she was always the first there.

"Some neighbors," Marley said, reading the details on his app. "Sounds like there's some kind of party going on. Kids, they think."

"Fuck, I hate kids," Tayto groaned.

"You have three of them," Sian pointed out.

"Exactly. Why'd you think I prefer fighting fires to being home with them?" It was a joke. They all knew that. Tayto loved his kids. He was always showing off photos of them and telling the crew about their accomplishments.

The road was clear – thankfully. From leaving the station to arriving on scene had only taken them eight minutes. By the time they were climbing out and unloading their equipment the second truck was pulling in behind them.

The fire wasn't in the fields, which was a good thing. It was in an area of scrubland around a hundred yards from the nearest farm – presumably the neighbors who'd called them out.

It was the kind of land where long-abandoned rusty old trucks took up residence, and people threw their trash because they didn't have the good sense to take it to the waste management center.

The fire was big – but not out of control. There were people standing by it, though, and that was their first priority.

Teenagers, by the looks of them. About thirty of them.

Some were drinking. He could tell that from the bottles on the ground. Someone was playing music from Bluetooth speakers.

A fucking party where they thought lighting a bonfire would be a great plan. Jesus, didn't he spend enough time at the local schools educating them about the danger of fire?

"Who's in charge here?" Marley asked loudly. He pushed his way through the crowd of partying kids to the small speakers set up on a pile of logs. Flicking it off, he turned around, trying to keep his cool. He wanted them out of here before they put the fire out. So much easier to do your job when thirty drunk teenagers weren't milling around, making problems.

"He is," a girl said, pointing at a boy kissing a girl over by an old Ford truck. "Or he was…"

Marley didn't recognize the kid, but that wasn't a big surprise. "Hey!"

The boy didn't even look up from his girlfriend.

Jesus. Marley was just about to walk over to him and drag him away from the girl when he caught a familiar face in the crowd.

James Connelly. What the hell?

He was standing on the other side of the fire to Marley, his face flickering orange from the reflection of the flames.

For a moment Marley was so shocked he faltered. But then the training kicked in. He looked back at the one girl who was at least able to form a sentence.

"The party's over," he said roughly. "You all need to go home. Your parents know you're here?"

"Kinda," the girl said, her feet shifting.

Hmm. He'd worry about that later.

He looked back at where James was standing. And the kid was staring at him, his eyes wide. And they should be. The little shit. James started to walk away, but Marley was having none of it.

"Connelly!" he shouted out. "James Connelly."

James stopped walking, busted. Marley felt a rush of annoyance flow through him.

"Get over here right now," he yelled, because that kid wasn't going anywhere.

James looked like he was sighing as he turned back around. Marley beckoned him over, and the kid finally started walking toward him.

Marley looked at the girl he'd first talked to. "Either you all leave or I call the cops. What's it to be?"

"We're going," she said quickly.

"You got a ride home?"

"A few of us aren't drinking. We have enough cars."

"Good. Make that all of you next time." He would have given them hell, but most of them weren't in any state to receive it. And they had a fire to put out.

But every parent in town whose kids weren't home tonight would hear about it in the morning. He'd make sure of that.

The girl turned to the crowd. "Time to leave," she yelled. "The cops are coming." Marley lifted a brow because she'd obviously added the last part to make everybody move.

And it worked. Tayto and Sian stood in front of the bonfire, making sure the kids kept well away from it as they swarmed like ants toward the cars parked on the side of the road.

James had finally arrived to where Marley was standing, his face sullen.

"Get in the truck," Marley told him.

"My ride's over there. I'm leaving," James said, not meeting Marley's eye.

Fury washed through Marley. "Get in the damn truck and stay there. Don't touch anything. Don't go anywhere. You hear me?" Fuck, he was furious. What was the kid thinking?

James nodded and walked over to the firetruck, sitting in the front seat.

"Connelly's kid." Tayto shook his head. "He should know better."

"Yes he should." Marley gritted his teeth as the kids left, standing guard by the fire to make sure it didn't start growing. Whoever had built it up knew what they were doing, but by the looks of it that was an hour or more ago. The logs they'd used were blackened and the fire was starting to wane. If they'd come here an hour later the flames would have almost certainly burned themselves out.

It took them ten minutes to fully extinguish the bonfire. Mostly because it clearly wasn't going to cause any danger to anybody. There was no rush, they could take their time.

And yeah, he wanted James to stew, too.

When there were only smoking black logs left, they began to pack up the equipment.

"Not such a bad one tonight," Tayto said. "Could have been worse."

"You see anybody you know?" Marley asked. "Apart from Connelly."

"Yeah. A couple of kids from my son's football team." Tayto lifted a brow. "Don't worry, I'll be calling their parents tomorrow. And I'll find out who the rest are, too."

Some departments would have called the police. Not just because of the fire and the underage drinking, but because the kids needed to learn a lesson.

But the truth was, they didn't get a lot of trouble from the youth around here. And experience had taught him that getting the parents involved was always better than calling the law. Not least because the police department was so small and they had better things to do than chase stupid kids.

"Thanks." Marley nodded, because that was one less thing he needed to do.

"We taking him home?" Tayto asked, looking at James.

The kid was still sitting silently in the cab of the truck, watching them. He looked sick, but Marley couldn't tell if it was from the alcohol or the fact that he'd been caught doing something completely idiotic.

"Yeah, I think I should probably talk to him and Kate."

Tayto slapped his arm. "That's the right thing to do. I guess it was always going to happen. The kid lost his dad. He's gonna act up."

"He's lucky it wasn't anything worse than this." Marley pulled his helmet off and unfastened his coat.

"For sure," Tayto agreed.

"Get in the back," he told James when they reached the truck, his voice letting the kid know just how annoyed he was. James sullenly climbed down from the front seat, his sneakers thudding on the hard ground.

"Please don't tell my mom," James muttered as he walked around to the back seats. He really did look nauseated.

"How much have you had to drink?" Marley asked him, because the last thing they needed was to have him throw up in the cab. It can't have been too much, not since he could string a sentence together. But still, if needed he'd get him some medical attention. It was Marley's job to make that happen.

James blew out a mouthful of air. "Just one beer."

Thank God. It could have been so much worse.

"And how old are you again?" Marley folded his arms across his chest as James scooted across the seats and did his belt up without asking.

"Fifteen," James mumbled.

"And what's the legal age for drinking?"

James looked down at his feet. "Twenty-one."

"Exactly. So you can be damn sure I'll be telling your mom."

James winced. Good. The kid needed to feel bad.

"I'm disappointed in you," Marley told him. "One minute

you're begging me for help to be a firefighter. The next you're setting fires where they could get out of control."

"I told them not to do it," James said quickly. "It was only supposed to be a bit of fun. I told them a fire was stupid."

"You shouldn't have been here in the first place," Marley said. "Does your mom know about this?"

Tayto had started the engine up. Sian was sitting in the seat beside him, and the others had gone in the second engine.

"No she doesn't. I won't do it again. Please don't tell her, it'll kill her."

Marley winced, because he knew that. Or at least he knew it would hurt her. And the last thing Kate needed was to be hurt.

But she was James' mom. She needed to know. It wasn't his place to hide something like that from her.

"It'll be okay," he told James as Tayto pulled up outside the Connelly house.

"No it won't." James' face fell.

"Want me to wait here for you?" Tayto asked as Marley pulled the door open.

"Nah you get back to the station, I'll walk." He wasn't about to make the whole crew wait up on him.

"I'll make sure everything's taken care of before I leave," Tayto said. "You just get home and get some sleep after this. We can meet at the station in the morning."

Marley hopped out of the truck and turned to James. "Come on then," he said. The kid followed him, his jaw tight as they walked up to his front door.

"Time to face the music," Marley told him, ringing the bell to the front door.

Kate sat bolt upright in her bed, her heart racing as she tried to work out what had caused her to so suddenly awaken.

And then the doorbell rang. A glance at the clock beside the bed told her it was almost one in the morning.

Her first thought was James. He wasn't home. Was he hurt?

She grabbed her robe, wrapping it around her as she rushed down the stairs. *Please let him be all right.* She'd sent him a message before she went to bed, wishing him good night, but he hadn't responded.

She'd assumed he was too busy playing video games or whatever it was that teenage boys did at sleepovers.

But what if something had happened to him? What if it was the police at the door telling her he was in the hospital? Or something worse? She should never have let him go for a sleepover without talking to the parents first.

Panic pulled at her stomach as she opened the door.

And then she saw James standing there and relief washed over her.

"What are you doing here?" she asked him, her brows knitting as she pulled him in for a hug. She sniffed at him. His breath smelled sour. "Have you been drinking?"

Then she realized they weren't alone. A pair of deep blue eyes were looking at her, concerned.

"Marley?" she said, confused. "Why are you here? What's going on?" It was way too late for him to be out for a run.

"Can I come inside?" he asked. That's when she realized he was wearing his firefighter uniform. The familiarity of the heavy black pants made her chest tighten. How many times had Paul come home wearing the exact same uniform?

Until he hadn't.

"Have you been at the station?" she asked James. He shook his head but said nothing. There were two pink discs on the apples of his cheeks. And he still wouldn't meet her gaze.

Marley pulled the door closed behind him. "We got a call out to a party in some fields to the west of the town. James and his friends were there."

"What?" She looked at James, who was staring determinedly at the floor. "Is this true?"

"Yeah." His voice was little more than a breath.

"You'd better come into the kitchen," she said, because she couldn't just stand here. "Would you like a drink?" she asked Marley.

"A water would be great." He pulled at his t-shirt. "Sorry if I smell. It gets a little sweaty under the gear."

"I can only smell smoke," she said softly. "Was there a fire?" She pointed at the kitchen table and Marley took a seat. James hovered in the doorway, as though all he wanted to do was bolt away. Trying to compose her thoughts, she grabbed a glass from the cupboard and filled it from the faucet before passing it to Marley.

"Sit down," she told James. Thankfully, he did what she asked.

"I'm sorry." His lip was wobbling. "I didn't mean for this to happen."

"Did somebody force you to go to a party?" she asked him. Why wouldn't he look at her?

James shook his head.

"Did somebody force you to drink alcohol?" Her voice was tight. She wasn't expecting to deal with this. Not yet. Maybe in a year or two, but not now. Not when he was only fifteen. He was too young, damn it.

"No. I'm sorry. I only had one beer."

"You're fifteen years old," she said, her voice louder now. "It's illegal. And idiotic. Do you understand what a bad decision that was?"

"Yes," he mumbled. Kate let out a long breath.

"I trusted you," she told him. "And you lost that trust."

"I know." His chin trembled.

He was a good kid most of the time, but she knew she couldn't let this go. Not even if he missed his dad and his whole world kept twisting upside down.

Why wasn't there a manual for this? Yes, she'd read books about helping children deal with grief. How to parent boys. Even how to talk to teenagers.

But right now she couldn't remember any of it. She was relying on instinct alone. And she trusted those as much as she trusted James right now.

"You're grounded," she told him. "For a month except for school, church, and anything else I decide is okay."

He nodded.

"And you won't be sleeping over at anybody's house for the foreseeable future. Especially not without me talking to their parents first."

James pressed his lips together.

"And if I *ever* find out you've drunk alcohol again, there will be hell to pay. Do you understand me?"

"Yes." His voice was small. And she was so grateful he wasn't talking back. Especially in front of Marley.

"Okay." She let out a breath. "Now go take a shower and go to bed. We'll talk about this more in the morning."

James stood up. "I'm so sorry." He looked at her and then Marley. "I won't do it again."

She tried to hide her sigh. "Go get some sleep."

He walked out of the room and pulled the door closed behind him. And for a moment the only sound in the kitchen was the thump of her heart and the drip of the faucet she needed to change the washer on.

Marley lifted his glass to his lips. She was so aware of his gaze on her face.

"Was I too soft on him?" she asked, because she had no idea what she was doing here.

The corner of his lip curled up. "I've no idea. I'm not a parent." He gave her an apologetic look.

"But you're a man who used to be a teenage boy," she pointed out.

"It's probably best not to talk about that." Marley gave a soft chuckle, and it was enough for the tightness to lift from her chest. His hair was mussed from wearing his helmet and she felt the weirdest urge to tidy it with her fingers.

"You've got me curious now," she told him, a smile playing at her lips. And God, it felt good to smile after what just happened. "Why is it best not to ask you?"

He let out a breath. "Because I was so much worse than James. There were two of us for a start. That makes for double trouble. The things Pres and I got up to were..." he trailed off. "Nah, you really don't want to know."

"But now I do," she said, grateful for the diversion. "What did you get up to?"

"We took my dad's car for a joyride when we were fifteen."

Her eyes widened. "No..."

"Yep. And got busted. Plus, there were the times we used to sneak out to see girls. And that summer when we made our own moonshine..."

Her mouth dropped open. "You're right. Maybe I don't want to know." Would James even know how to make moonshine? She had no idea, but she hoped not. "God, what have I got myself into?"

Marley laughed softly. "If it helps, I think you hit the right tone. James wasn't the ringleader, he was just there. And hopefully he's learned a lesson."

"He better have," she said grimly. "Oh God." She shook her head, her eyes meeting Marley's. "What must you think of me? Yesterday you saw me losing it over cupcakes. Today you're dragging my son home from an illegal party." Her eyes widened. "Wait, the fire. Was it bad? Did anybody get hurt? Any property get destroyed?"

"Just a bonfire on some abandoned land. Easily put out."

"Thank God." She let out a long breath.

"Yeah. As I said, if you're gonna learn a lesson, it's a good way to learn it. Nobody got hurt, no real damage was done." He ran his thumb along his chin. "And for what it's worth, I think a lot of you. I think you're a strong woman who's been dealt a shitty hand in life but you're playing your cards like a pro. Do you know how many kids I've taken home after something like this and their parents didn't even care?"

She shook her head. His words were making her throat feel tight.

"A lot," he said. "But that's not you. You care. A lot. More than anybody I know."

"I just want them to be happy…"

"And you're doing all you can to make them that way. But the rest… that's up to them." He reached out to take her hand, squeezing it softly. The warmth of his palm seeped into hers.

And she felt it again. That tingling sensation she only got when he was around.

It felt too good. She needed this to stop. Before she ended up embarrassing herself.

It's just because you're not used to a man being so close. Especially one as attractive as Marley Hartson.

She hated the way he made her feel safe and on the edge of a cliff at the same time.

"What if he gets worse?" she asked. "What if he goes off the rails?"

Marley ran his tongue along his bottom lip. Her eyes followed the movement.

"It might happen," he said, his voice full of honesty. "But if it does, it won't be your fault."

"I could just ground him for life." She was half serious.

Marley smiled again. He had the merest hint of crinkle lines around the corners of his eyes. She had no idea why she found them so attractive. But she couldn't look away.

She liked him being here. Liked him being close. Every cell in her body was reacting to him.

"No you couldn't. And you wouldn't want to."

She wouldn't, no. But she just wished she knew what to do.

"I have a suggestion," Marley said. "But I'm not sure you'll like it."

"I'll listen to anything right now," she admitted.

"Let him join the junior firefighters. Give him something to concentrate on. He'll be around grown men who know the dangers of making stupid decisions. We'll work him out until he's exhausted. We'll teach him how to deal with emergencies." He let out a breath. "You're doing your best, Kate. More than your best. But you don't have to do this alone. Let us help." He paused. "Let *me* help."

She couldn't say anything for a moment. Mostly because Marley's words made sense. And she hated that. Hated knowing that he was right and she was wrong.

"If I'd already let him join do you think he'd have stayed home tonight?" she asked him.

Marley shook his head. "No. Because he's a kid and he hasn't learned how to make the right decisions all the time. And I can't promise that we'll be a miracle cure for that. All I can tell you is that when I started volunteering, it changed me. It made me a man."

His thumb brushed her palm and she realized she was still holding his hand. She looked down, seeing the way his fingers dwarfed hers. Everything about him was big. Strong.

She took a deep breath.

"I'll think about it," she promised him. "When's the next meeting?"

"On Sunday."

"He's grounded," she pointed out.

"Yeah, I know. I was gonna suggest we make him sit and watch us go through the drills. A kind of punishment because all the other juniors will be joining in. No kid likes sitting on the sideline. But it'll do him good to know what he's missing out on."

His thumb brushed her hand again. And this time she could feel the thrill rushing straight to her core. It was just a physical reaction. She knew that. It didn't mean anything.

So why wasn't she pulling away?

"He would hate that," she said softly.

The corner of his lip curled up. "Yep."

And now she was smiling too. Not just because it felt like she wasn't alone in this. But because she could feel some hope rushing back in.

Yes, she was still scared of James joining the junior firefighters. Not least because the kind of danger he was in tonight was nothing compared to what he'd be exposed to if he graduated and became a full-fledged volunteer.

"You know he's a good kid. He just needs some direction," Marley told her. "Maybe we all do. But this feels good, you know? Like he's finally moving forward."

She nodded. "Yes, it does." Finally, she pulled her hand from his, already missing his touch. "Thank you. For bringing him home. For caring."

He glanced at her mouth then back to her eyes, his gaze holding onto hers for a moment too long. "Thank you for letting me."

CHAPTER
Seven

"OH MY GOD!" Shana said, her eyes lighting up. "You want to have sex with Marley Hartson?"

"Will you hush up?" Kate whispered, because Shana's voice was loud enough to wake up a bunch of hibernating bears. "And I don't want to do that."

"You said he gave you tingles." Shana took a sip of her coffee. They were sitting in the town square after eating brunch in the diner. This time, Shana had managed to score a booth and she was still gloating about it. Addy was playing with her friends on the bandstand, and Ethan was throwing a ball with a group of boys in the grass beyond.

And James was at the fire station. She was trying hard not to think about that. She'd wanted to drop him off but he'd insisted on walking over there first thing this morning. She hadn't seen him running with the rest of the juniors and the volunteers around the square before she went into church, though. Marley had promised her that he would have to sit everything out and he was being true to his word.

"That's not what I said," Kate told her friend, shaking her head. "I said maybe I'm not so dead inside after all."

"Because he gave you quivers." Shana wouldn't be

deflected. "You should definitely let him know you're interested."

"I'm not interested," Kate told her. "Not like that. I've been thinking about it, and I know exactly what happened."

Shana's smile widened. "Oh, this is going to be good. Tell me."

Kate rolled her eyes because she knew she shouldn't have said anything. But Shana had this way of getting secrets out of you. The CIA should recruit her. She'd be the best kind of torture device.

"You said yourself that maybe it's time to start thinking about the future," Kate said. "Maybe my body is telling me that I should try new things out."

"Like new guys?"

Kate sighed. Mostly because she hadn't slept for the past two nights. Not just because of James and worrying about him. But also worrying about herself.

It felt strange.

"Maybe. But not Marley Hartson. That was just me reacting to him being there. Any guy holding my hand would have caused the same reaction."

"Seriously? That's what you think?"

"That's what I know." Kate nodded. "I wouldn't date him even if he wanted to, which he doesn't. Not after everything…" Her eyes caught Shana's. "And I don't want to date a firefighter, that's for sure."

"Paul didn't die because he was a firefighter," Shana said softly. "It was a freak of nature."

Kate took a mouthful of coffee. Yes, thinking about that still hurt. But not as much as it used to.

Maybe life was moving on.

"I know. But now that I've experienced loss, I'd like to avoid going through it again. And dating a firefighter isn't a great plan." She caught Shana's eye. "What if it got serious? And Addy, Ethan, and James got attached?

What if they lost somebody else? I couldn't do that to them."

"What are you gonna do, put every guy through a physical before you date them?" Shana asked, her brows knitting. "Hell, Paul had lots of clear physicals but then..." she trailed off. "I'm sorry. I don't mean to bring up bad memories."

"You're not. It's okay. And you're right, I can't screen for everything. And Paul having an aneurism was nothing any of us could have foreseen."

That was one of her first questions after they lost him. How could nobody have known about the aneurism growing in his brain? The doctors said it had to have been there for years. And when it burst...

God, she needed another coffee.

"But anybody with a dangerous occupation is out," Kate said firmly. "At least I can control that."

"Maybe you should only go for guys that never leave the house. Never drive a car. Or cross the road," Shana said. "That'll lower the possibility of losing them even more."

"Stop it." Kate shook her head, smiling. "I'm trying. I thought you'd be glad about this."

"I am. Kind of." Shana pulled out her phone. "And I feel like this is the right time to tell you that I've made you a dating profile."

"What?" Kate blinked. "Why? Where?"

"On an app. Don't worry, I gave you a fake name. I was just curious to see what the response would be like."

"Show me." Kate held out her hand. "I can't believe you did this." She should be angry with her friend. But Shana didn't have a mean bone in her body. She was kind, caring, and she worried about Kate a lot.

"I was just testing the waters for you. Because you weren't going to try this by yourself. Remember what you said about there being nobody you'd date around here? Well, I set the area to Maple Cross and beyond. And honey, the waters are good. There are some nice guys there."

"You haven't talked to them, have you?"

Shana grinned. "No, of course not. That's the beauty of this app. The woman has to make the first approach to anybody she matches with. That way you get to keep the control." Her voice turned serious. "And I know you need that. I get it, I do."

She passed Kate the phone and she took it, looking at the profile Shana had made for her.

Amy, 35.

Shana had used Kate's middle name. And the photo was one she'd taken last year, when they'd gone up the mountains to the lake in Winterville. She was wearing a pair of shorts and a tank, her hair whipping around her face. She was laughing – you couldn't see at what, but Kate could remember.

James was throwing Addy and Ethan into the water and they were squealing with excitement. She could remember thinking it was the first time she'd seen them truly happy after losing their dad.

"You looked beautiful in that one," Shana said softly. "Annoyingly so. You got so many more hits than me."

"Did you add that I have kids?" Kate asked, scrolling down. And yeah, there it was. Three children.

And still she got matches? She was surprised. "The men over in Maple Cross must be desperate," she said.

"Shut up. You're a catch."

"Sure. With one kid fast becoming a juvenile delinquent, one who refuses to wear anything but his dead dad's t-shirt to bed, and the other who wants me to take a photo of her looking pretty in her funeral dress," Kate said, deadpan. "A real catch."

"Marley seems to think so," Shana pointed out softly. And Kate felt her pulse increase.

"He just sees a buddy's wife in trouble. And the last thing I need is a knight in shining firefighter uniform." Kate passed the phone back to her right as Addy ran up to them, dirt smeared on the knees of her dress.

"Mommy, Sammie's cat had kittens. Can we have one?" Addy asked, breathless from running from the bandstand.

Kate's gaze met Shana's. Her friend couldn't disguise her mirth.

"No honey, we can't. We don't have time to have a kitten."

Addy let out a sigh. "Thank goodness. I hate those things." Then she ran off again, leaving Kate and Shana shaking their heads.

"See?" Kate said. "My life is chaos. I'm nobody's catch."

"Can I have a word?" Chief Riley asked as Marley passed his office. It was Wednesday evening. He'd come in to pick up a pair of running shoes he'd left in his locker, because his other ones got soaked running in the rain yesterday.

"Now? Sure." Marley stepped into the Chief's office. Even after two years it was strange being in here and not seeing Paul sitting behind the desk. He didn't like it much, truth be told. A reminder that his friend was gone. That he wasn't coming back.

"Take a seat." The chief pointed at the chair on the other side of the desk. "I just wanted to talk to you about the Junior Firefighters.

Chief Riley had joined the firehouse a month after Paul's death, and was the only salaried employee in the station. He was a lifelong firefighter, had worked through the ranks to become a captain in Charleston, the state capital, before coming to Hartson's Creek. He was now a couple of years away from retirement. He was a hard man to get to know. He kept to himself, completely unlike Paul. And Marley didn't always see eye to eye with the man, even though he tried to respect him.

It was almost six. Marley had planned on eating some dinner as soon as he got home, then giving it an hour to settle before he headed off on his run. He hoped this wouldn't take long.

"Is there a problem with the juniors?" Marley asked.

Chief Riley lifted a brow. "I saw that James Connelly has officially joined. Do you think that's a good idea?"

"Why wouldn't it be?" Marley asked. And yeah, there was some defensiveness in his voice, because the juniors had always been his department. He ran it well. Had gotten commendations for it. And Paul had always let him manage it and handle it his own way.

"Because the kid could cause us problems," the chief said, his voice low. "I heard he was involved in that incident over in the fields last week. Unstable firefighters – whether they're juniors or not – aren't what we need. I think you know that."

"James isn't unstable. He's had a couple of rough years. We all want him here. For his dad."

The chief blew out a mouthful of air. "Paul isn't here anymore," he said, as though Marley didn't feel his absence acutely every time he walked into the station. "And yeah, maybe before he died his kid was different. But now? I don't want him putting any of my men in danger."

"He won't." Marley's voice was tight. "I'm sure of it."

"Are you? Because I'm not." The chief shook his head. "Our resources are tight. We don't have time to babysit a kid who can't keep his urges under control."

Annoyance rushed through him, but somehow he managed to keep it under control, thanks to years of being trained by Paul to manage his emotions. And yeah, he owed his dead boss. More than that, he'd made him a promise.

He intended to keep it. Whether the chief liked it or not.

"He'll be fine," Marley said firmly. "And I'm not babysitting him. I'm mentoring him. You saw him on Sunday. He did everything he was told to do in training. He's already agreed to the litter cleanup after the fundraiser next Friday. Give the kid a chance to prove himself, that's all I ask."

For a moment the chief said nothing. Just stared at Marley, who kept his expression cool.

And then he let out a long sigh. "Okay. But if he messes up once, he's out, understood?"

"Understood." Marley nodded. "But he won't. I'll make sure of that."

Kate was waiting for him when he ran past their house that evening. Sure, she was trying to hide it, acting like she was weeding the front yard, but the way she stood and walked over as soon as she saw him, coupled with the look of determination on her face made it a little too obvious.

He slowed down to a halt, all too aware of the sweat running off him. After the rain of the past few days the sun had come out with a passion. And even though it was setting now, the heat lingered like an unwanted lover, curling around his body and clinging on tight.

He lifted his hand to wipe his brow, watching her as she walked over. She was wearing shorts and a t-shirt, her hair pulled into a messy ponytail that made her look younger than she was. He remembered how thin she'd gotten in the months after Paul died. She'd put a little of that weight back on, and it looked good on her.

She lifted a hand to pat her hair back into place. He noticed she wasn't wearing gardening gloves. Nor were her hands covered in dirt. *Interesting.*

"Hi," she said softly.

"Hi."

"You want some water?"

A smile pulled at his lips. "I'm good. Is everything okay here? Seen any more snakes?"

"No. We're good. I just wanted to talk to you…" She glanced back at the house as though to make sure none of her kids were there. "About James."

"Sure." Marley nodded, all too aware he'd had more conversations about a kid that wasn't his today than anything else. "What's up?"

"He said the Junior Firefighters are supposed to be volunteering at *Chairs* on Friday night."

"Yeah, that's right. The band is doing a fundraising set. Playing some music. There's always clean up afterward and we've asked the juniors to be part of it."

Her eyes met his. Up close they looked like corn, just before it turned. Green with some yellow. Pretty.

"He's still grounded."

"I know. And it's up to you, but I can guarantee that the clean-up isn't the fun job you might think it is." Marley gave her a half smile. "I'll even make sure he doesn't have any fun. And at least you'll know where he is."

"I guess…" She didn't look certain. And he felt bad, because he was trying to help, not cause her more problems. God knew she probably had enough of them already.

"I'll even drop him home myself if you're worried about him getting back," Marley told her.

"I can bring him home," she said quickly.

"Are you coming to the gig?" he asked. It was strange how much he wanted her to say yes.

"I don't know." She offered him a small smile. "I'm not the biggest fan of *Chairs*."

"You should come," he told her. "You'll have a good time."

"Will I?" she murmured. And he wasn't sure if she was talking to him or herself.

"Yes."

Her eyes met his again and he felt it somewhere inside him. She was a beautiful woman.

But she was also Paul's widow. He was just trying to look out for her and the kids, that was all.

Her chest lifted as she inhaled slowly, her brows pulling tight as she thought it over. "I can't remember the last time I heard you play. Probably about seven years ago."

"We've only gotten worse," he told her and she laughed, the sound like nectar to his ears.

"Didn't you almost get picked up by a record company?" she asked him.

"Kind of. But that's an old story." He smiled at her. "So are you coming?"

She didn't say anything for a moment. Just looked at him, the setting sun lending her face an orange hue. In the distance, he could hear the rumble of a car, and – closer – the sound of a single bird warbling from the sugar maple tree at the edge of her yard.

"Yeah, I think maybe I'll come watch," she said. "Bring Addy and Ethan. Make an evening of it. Catch up on the local gossip." She widened her eyes and it made him grin.

"Good." He nodded. "I'll see you there then."

"Yeah, you will."

It sounded like a promise. A promise that hit him straight in the solar plexus. And when he nodded his head in goodbye and set off on his run back home, the smile lingered on his face.

CHAPTER *Eight*

ADDY AND ETHAN were already running ahead as Kate lifted up the trunk to get her chair and cooler out. The fields and roads at the riverside were mobbed with people. She was surprised. And a little overwhelmed.

"Slow down," she shouted, because there were way too many people here for her to feel comfortable with them running out of her eyesight. "Ethan, come grab the blanket. Addy, I need your help with my purse."

The kids were buzzing as they made it into the lush green field alongside the creek. The big houses that overlooked the water were further along. She could see people filling each yard. The fields were full of chairs, tables, and blankets. In the corner of the first field she could see the makeshift stage and the volunteers – one of them James – standing by it.

"Mommy, there's Noah from school. Can I go say hi?" Ethan asked.

"Can I go, too?" Addy said. "I want to say hi to him."

"He's not your friend, he's mine," Ethan said.

Here we go. "Nobody's going anywhere until we find somewhere to sit. And then we'll see," Kate told them firmly, looking around to find a friendly face.

"Kate." She felt a warm hand touch her arm and looked up to see Marley Hartson standing next to her. He took the cooler out of her hands. "Where are you heading?"

"I don't know." She offered him a smile. "Just trying to find a free spot."

"You want to join the others from the department or would that be weird?" There was no judgement in his voice. Just an offer and she took it as that.

She took a deep breath. "I don't think I'm ready for that," she told him. Once upon a time she would have sat with the fire department without a second thought. But now, it would feel too weird.

He nodded in understanding. "How about my family?" he asked. "They've got a little spot to the left of the stage."

"Can we put these things down *somewhere*?" Ethan asked. "My arms are getting tired."

"Okay." She nodded. "Near the stage sounds good." That way she could keep an eye on James, too, because that's where the volunteers were stationed.

"Come on, then." Marley took the folded up chair from her too and started walking. Ethan walked next to him, talking about the t-shirts Marley left the other week. Addy walked beside Kate, holding her hand now that she had them free.

The closer they got to the stage, the harder it was to weave in between the clusters of people sitting in circles. Kate kept Addy close, afraid she might lose her.

"Here okay?" Marley asked her, stopping next to where his mom was sitting. Maddie Hartson immediately stood up.

"Kate, it's lovely to see you." She reached out to hug her. "Oh my goodness, look at these children. How grown up are they?" She smiled widely at Kate. "Are you joining us?" she asked.

"If that's okay?"

"Of course." Maddie nodded as Marley put Kate's cooler

on the grass and opened up her chair. There were younger kids in the family group already – Marley's niece and nephews, plus some more of his extended family. Ethan and Addy were already walking over to them because they knew the kids from school. Marley leaned forward and whispered something in his mom's ear and she nodded.

"James is over there," Marley told her, pointing at the side of the stage. And sure enough, he was sitting on his own, sorting out what looked like fliers. He was wearing jeans and a junior firefighter t-shirt, under a bright yellow vest. "He'll go on litter duty every half an hour. Apart from that, he's been told to stay by the stage."

Her eyes met his. "Thank you."

"Any time."

"Shouldn't you go now?" she asked him. "Don't you have some drums to play?"

"In a while. Just wanted to make sure you're okay first."

"I'm fine," she told him. "Thank you. For everything."

He nodded. "Are you staying after the show is over?"

She looked at Addy and Ethan who were laughing at something one of the other kids was saying. "I'm not sure. I need to get those two into bed."

When she looked back at him, his gaze was on her lips. He quickly brought it back to her eyes, but she felt a strange pulse of excitement rush through her. It made her feel breathless.

Then just as she thought he was going to turn around and leave, he reached out, his fingers brushing her hair.

"You have a leaf," he murmured, pulling it out and offering it to her. A tiny green leaf was nestled between his fingers and thumb. She took it from him, her fingertips grazing his.

There was that pulse again. It made her breath catch. "Thank you."

This time he really did turn and leave. But the memory of his touch still lingered.

"Come sit down," his mom said. "And let me get you a drink. Tell me, are you driving or would you like some hard liquor to get through this?"

As soon as the first note echoed from the stage, Kate felt a shiver through her spine. Not just because they were so close to the speakers – close enough that Maddie was handing out ear plugs to the kids like they were bags of candy, insisting on all of them putting them on. But also because she couldn't remember the last time she'd sat down and really listened to music.

At first, after Paul died, song lyrics hurt too much to hear. And then it had felt wrong to enjoy songs without him. Sure, the radio could be on when she was driving to work, or when her kids would be playing something in the living room. But she rarely stopped and listened.

But now she was. Everybody had turned their chairs to look at the stage. Half of the people had gotten up and were dancing and swaying to the music. Pres and Cassie were harmonizing, as he played the lead guitar and she played the keyboards.

And next to them the bassist was rocking down like he was playing at Coachella instead of on a little stage in West Virginia.

But it was Marley who kept drawing her eye. He took drumming as seriously as he took firefighting. She could see the attention on his face as he listened intently to the tiny changes in tempo and depth in the vocals, and adapted to them as easily as he took a breath.

He ran his tongue along his bottom lip to catch a bead of sweat and she felt something deep inside her twist.

And then he looked up, his gaze catching hers and she felt her blood start to heat.

The song was building. She could hear the intensity in Cassie's vocals ramp up. Marley matched it beat for beat, and she could feel the vibrations coursing through her veins like he was playing just for her.

Her chest felt so tight she wasn't sure she could breathe. He was looking at her again, and she didn't want him to stop. Didn't want this to stop, whatever it was.

All she knew was she felt like she was alive. Like she was being touched, not by hands but by music.

By *his* music. And it felt like a drug. Making her soar.

She took a deep breath, trying to center herself. She shouldn't be feeling like this. He was Paul's friend. She was Paul's widow.

She pulled her eyes away, determined to get her heart rate back under control.

The next moment, Addy walked over with a muffin in her hand, poking at Kate's leg with the other. Kate lifted her daughter into her lap. It was the third sweet treat Kate had seen her eating. The kid was going to be on a sugar high or a plunge, she wasn't sure which.

But she stroked her hair and lifted one side of the ear plugs up. "You okay, honey?" she asked her.

"Mmm," Addy nodded. She had crumbs on her lips. "Tired."

A sugar plunge then. "Sit here with me for a while."

When Addy had cuddled up into her, Kate looked back at the stage and Marley was watching her again.

This time she didn't let her gaze stay on him. She brought it directly back to her daughter.

But it didn't stop her from feeling like she'd just gotten on a rollercoaster that was about to speed out of control.

CHAPTER *Nine*

"I'M GOING to take Addy and Ethan to the car," Kate told James when the concert was over and people were packing up to leave.

During the show the junior volunteers had weaved their way through the crowds with buckets and those card-reader machines to gather donations for the fire station. Now they were all holding black trash bags and little picker devices to clear away the remaining trash scattered across the field.

James had been given the front of the field – near the stage – presumably so Marley could keep an eye on him.

Addy had fallen asleep on Kate's lap halfway through the show with a muffin in hand, which was some kind of miracle. And then Marley's cousin, Grace, had made up a little makeshift bed with some blankets, and Kate had laid her daughter on them. Miracle of miracles, she hadn't even woken up.

"I'll wait for you at the car," she added, because once they were in the car, both Addy and Ethan would probably fall asleep again. "Come find us when you've finished here."

"You can go home without me if you want. I'll get a ride or walk."

She lifted a brow. "You're not walking home. And I'm happy to wait." The tone of her voice let him know she wasn't looking for a debate on this one. Yes, he'd been on his best behavior tonight, but she was also very aware that he was still grounded.

Or at least he kind of was. Damn, this parenting thing was hard.

"Okay." He nodded again. "I should get to cleaning."

"Go for it."

She turned around to walk back to the blankets and chairs where the Hartson family were all packing up. The blankets where Addy had been sleeping were gone. She looked around for her and then her heart did a little double take.

Marley was there with his parents. Holding a sleeping Addy in his arms. Her daughter had her own arms looped around his neck, her eyes closed tight as she nestled against his chest. Ethan was next to him, talking quickly, as Marley nodded.

And then his eyes caught hers. There was something wrong with her, she was certain. She felt a little dizzy, maybe a tad faint at the sight of her daughter in his arms.

She could hear the rustle of James' trash bag as he started to fill it. Could feel the warmth of the breeze coming in from the creek. Her ears were ringing, likely from the music.

But all she could think about was how perfect that looked. Addy being held by a man again. How long had it been since somebody other than Kate had picked her up? And to be fair, Kate was finding it harder and harder. Her little girl wasn't so little anymore, even if Marley made it look easy with his thick biceps and strong hands.

Somehow, she managed to propel herself over to where they were all standing.

"Mom and Grace wanted to clear up. We didn't want to wake Addy," Marley said softly. "This okay?"

Kate nodded. "I can take her now." She held her arms out, so aware of how slender they were compared to his.

"It's fine. I'll carry her to the car for you." His voice was soft enough not to wake Addy. "You lead the way, I'll follow."

She went to pick up her chair and the cooler.

"Leave them," Marley told her. "I'll come back for them. I can drop them over later tonight or tomorrow."

"Shouldn't you be packing up the stage?" she asked him.

"Pres and Cassie got it. Don't sweat it."

She opened her mouth to protest again, but she'd run out of excuses. The truth was she didn't have any. From a practical point of view, him carrying Addy made sense.

From an emotional point of view? She didn't want to think about that right now.

There were some battles you shouldn't fight. Especially the ones with yourself.

It took them another five minutes to get to her car, mostly because the people in front of them were walking so slowly. Kate grabbed the keys from her purse and opened up the back door, and Marley gently set Addy in her booster seat.

"Jump in," she told Ethan, because he could climb in himself. He ran around the other side and pulled open the door as Marley stepped back so Kate could fasten her daughter's belt.

When the door was closed she turned to look at him. "Thank you," she said. "For everything."

"I didn't do much."

"Yes you did." She swallowed hard. "And I appreciate it. It's not always easy being a single mom with three kids." It still felt strange saying it. *Single mom.*

But that's what she was. And it's how she lived her life. Juggling everything. Hoping she could catch it all on the way back down.

"Are you waiting here for James?" he asked her.

"Yeah. I just wanted to get these two strapped in. Then when we get home we'll put them straight to bed."

"You want me to help you?"

The offer was genuine. She could see that in his eyes.

"It's fine. I'll take one, James will take the other." Not that either of them would find it easy. Addy was hard enough to carry. At eight, Ethan was almost impossible. He was a tall kid for his age.

"It'll give James a good workout at least," Marley said and she grinned.

"And me. I keep forgetting to go to the gym," she told him. "It's been eight years."

He laughed. And it sounded good to her. Damn, she liked this man. The breeze was starting to pick up. It lifted his hair from his face, and she could see the start of laugh lines in the corner of his eyes. They suited him. Made him look grounded.

A car, driving too fast for the thin piece of road that was left between all the parked vehicles, veered way too close to where she was standing next to her Ford. Before she could think about moving, she felt Marley grab her and push her against her car, his body pressing against hers to form a barrier between her and the too-fast Honda.

The sudden impact of his muscles against hers winded her. She could feel the thickness of his thighs, the flat planes of his stomach. His body caged hers like a shield, his arms pressed against each side of her.

She looked up, her lips parted. And all she could think of was how good his body felt.

How solid he was. How strong. How it sent that electric pulse through her once again. In her neck, her wrists. Between her thighs.

No, that was more than a pulse. It was an ache. One that was growing inside her. Her breath returned, making her chest lift and fall fast. She licked her lips, trying to find some words but none came out.

She lifted her head to look at him, and their eyes connected. There was a darkness in his that made her heart beat so fast she was starting to feel dizzy.

"You okay?" he asked. "Damn kids. I swear he looked about twelve."

"Yeah." She nodded, her head still foggy. "I think so. Thank you for saving me. Again."

She lifted her hand to touch his shoulder. His skin was warm beneath his t-shirt. She could feel the hardness of his muscles. He let out the softest of breaths.

What was happening here? So many thoughts were rushing through her mind at once. She nearly got struck by a car. She couldn't let that happen. Her kids needed her.

But then that thought disappeared and the pure physicality of this man filled her senses.

She wanted to have sex. That's all she could think of.

With him.

Where did it come from? She had no idea. But all she could think about was how it would feel to have his body over hers. In hers. Everywhere.

Dear God, she needed to stop these thoughts. Right now.

"Mom!"

The sound of James' voice brought her back to earth. Her eyes were still on Marley's.

"You're pale," he said softly. "You sure you're okay?"

She nodded. "Just the shock."

"I got the plate number. I'll call it in later. Somebody needs to go talk to that kid. Before he ends up killing somebody."

"I'm fine, honestly. Thank you." She just needed to get home and take a cold shower.

He pushed himself off the car, letting the air rush between them. And before she could say anything else, she saw James arriving over his shoulder.

"Mom, we're allowed to go now," her eldest son told her.

"Great." She forced a smile onto her lips. "Jump in the front seat."

Marley gave James a nod and then took another step back.

"I'll drop your cooler and chairs off on my way home," Marley told her. "I'll leave them on the porch."

"My house isn't on your way home," she pointed out and it made him smile.

"One of these days you're gonna let me help without protest," he told her. "Or at least, I hope you will."

"Never gonna happen." Okay, she was feeling better now. "But thank you, I'd appreciate that."

"No problem."

The field was almost empty by the time Marley got back to the stage. Not that it was a stage anymore, half of it was already dismantled. Though they'd sent the juniors home, some of the fire volunteers had remained to help finish the break down, and of course Pres and Alex were still there, though Cassie had taken the kids home.

"Everything okay?" Tayto asked as Marley walked over to help him. He was looking red in the face as he carried the wooden planks from the dismantled stage to the van. At forty-eight, he was one of the older volunteers. What he lacked in physical fitness he more than made up for in experience.

"All good. Just making sure Paul's family got back to their car safely. Kate has her hands full with those kids." He wasn't sure why he mentioned Paul. Maybe because there was a little feeling of guilt pulling at him.

He was stupidly attracted to Paul's wife. And fuck, he didn't know what to do with that.

"She has her hands full, huh?" Tayto said, huffing as he

lifted another load of planks. Marley took the other end, helping him place them in the truck. "I saw one of the guys from the Maple Cross station checking her out."

"What?" Marley frowned.

"Don't worry. I told him she was off limits. What kind of sick fucker would go after Paul's widow?" Tayto shook his head. "He was one of ours, man. You don't do that to a brother."

Marley's stomach tightened. The memory of his body pressed against Kate's felt like a knife turning in his gut. She was so soft against him. It had messed with his brain. He'd liked it. Wanted more.

Wanted her. The one woman he couldn't have.

Fuck.

He squeezed his eyes shut, trying to push the memory of her body out of his mind. The smell of her shampoo, the way her big blue eyes always made him feel like he was about to get lost in the best of ways.

What kind of sick fucker would go after Paul's widow, anyway?

Not this one. He needed to get a grip. He'd promised to make sure she was okay, not to get a hard on whenever he saw her.

He owed that much to Paul.

CHAPTER *Ten*

AT FIRST KATE thought she must have missed Marley when he ran past her house on Monday and Tuesday. It had been lightly raining on both days, and Ethan had a project due at the end of the week that the whole family had worked on. He had to make a poster about the wildlife found in West Virginia. It had been spread out on the kitchen table every night as she, Ethan, and sometimes James, stuck pieces of information and pictures on it.

Maybe it was a good thing she hadn't seen Marley. Ever since his body had pressed against hers on Friday night, her head had felt a little messed up.

Because she couldn't be attracted to Marley Hartson. She just couldn't.

And yet on Wednesday night she sat out on the porch with a book and a glass of wine. James was studying and Ethan and Addy were in bed. She figured it would be a good time to try to make things right between her and Marley. She could maybe laugh and joke with him as he ran by.

But he didn't come. And for some reason she hated that.

By Thursday she knew he was avoiding them. And she didn't like it one bit. The kids were noticing, too. Addy had drawn a picture of him playing the drums and she wanted to give it to him.

So Kate sucked it up and messaged him.

Hi! Hope all is good with you. Haven't seen you for a few nights so I thought I'd message. Are you running past tonight? Addy has a drawing she made for you. – Kate.

She was at work when she got the reply. It was Stitch and Snitch day and she was getting the room ready when her phone vibrated in her pocket. She pulled it out, her brows knitting as she read the reply.

Probably not tonight. Give my thanks to Addy. I'll come over as soon as I can to grab it. – Marley.

It was stupid how disappointed she felt as she read the words. Like they'd formed a fist and punched her in the chest. Of course he didn't have to come over if he didn't want to. He was a free man, after all. He could do whatever he wanted.

Maybe he could sense she was getting attached to him.

Oh God, he probably saw her as some kind of millstone. Paul's poor wife. Nothing more.

He didn't want her. He felt sorry for her.

And the thought of that made her want to vomit.

She didn't need sympathy. She'd had more than her share of that. And yes, sometimes she still felt fragile. But she was trying so hard to rebuild her life. Determined to be the strong one, for her kids and for herself.

Finally, the room was all set up. The chairs were set in a

circle. There were only eight of them. She closed the door and checked her watch. Stitch and Snitch was due to start in half an hour. Before they arrived, she needed to go through the book orders for the month, so she sat down at the desk and opened up her library issued laptop.

"All ready for them?" Shana asked, leaning on the desk, a grin on her face. She'd popped in on her way to grab a coffee.

Kate nodded, making herself smile because the last thing she needed was the third degree from her best friend. She didn't want to talk about Marley with her. Or anybody, really.

And then she remembered their conversation from the other Sunday. About the dating app Shana had signed her up for.

"Can I ask you something?" she said to her friend, a decision forming in her mind. She needed to stop thinking about Marley Hartson. This had to be the way.

"Of course but I might not answer." Shana winked at her.

Kate took a deep breath. "You know that dating app?"

Shana sighed. "Okay, I'll delete it. But you're missing out."

Kate felt her heart start to thump against her chest. "You didn't delete it yet?"

"Don't hate me but no." Her friend looked sheepish. "I was hoping you'd change your mind."

Kate looked her in the eye. "I have. Because you're right. It's time to start getting out there."

"Seriously?" Shana's face lit up. "Oh my God, we're gonna have so much fun. You should see this guy who matched with you last night. Seriously good looking."

"You've been checking out the matches?" Kate asked, shaking her head. "Why don't you pay this much attention to your own love life?"

"Because yours is more enjoyable." Shana grinned. "And I'm officially inviting myself to dinner at yours tomorrow night. I'll show you how to download it onto your phone."

"Not in front of the kids."

Shana rolled her eyes. "Of course not. But maybe it's time to start dropping hints to them that you're thinking about dating again."

It already felt like too much. But Shana looked so excited she couldn't bring herself to say that.

She'd download the stupid app, and then she'd probably ignore it for a while.

"Come over at six tomorrow," she told her friend, resigning herself to her fate.

"Perfect." Shana's eyes danced with excitement. "I'll bring the alcohol."

The weather was so good on Friday that Kate decided to pull out the old barbecue from the garage. They hadn't used it in over a year and you could tell. It was a little rusty, more than a little dusty, and when she lifted the lid the inside was a whole lot greasy. It took almost an hour to clean it up, but the propane tank was still half full and the burners lit on the first press.

The physical exertion from scrubbing it felt good. She needed it. To work off the excess energy she'd been feeling more and more every day.

"Are we grilling tonight?" Ethan asked as he walked through the kitchen door to the yard. He looked excited. He had a weird fascination with fire. And then that made her think of James' party, and then of Marley bringing him home.

Ugh. She needed to stop thinking about him.

"Yes we are." She nodded.

"Can *you* grill?" Ethan asked her. "Didn't Dad used to do it?"

She swallowed hard. "Yes, he did, but now I'm doing it."

"Okay." Ethan shrugged. "Want some help?"

"Sure." She gave him a big smile. "First of all, we need to

do the prep. Make the burgers, cut up some onion. Make some salad to go with it."

He wrinkled his nose. "I meant with the grill."

"I know you did. But there's no grilling without food preparation." And she was trying to raise boys who knew that a cookout didn't start with lighting a fire. "Come on, I'll show you. It's fun, I promise."

And it *was* fun. They put on some music – Springsteen at his eighties finest – and Addy joined them, though she seemed to think food prep meant mostly eating the carrots that Kate was cutting up. Ethan washed the lettuce, and had a whale of a time spinning it around in the special bag to dry it, pretending he was about to throw a discus.

They were nearly ready to start the grill up when Shana knocked on the door. She was carrying some bottles of wine and cans of soda plus some sprinkled donuts she'd picked up from the local bakery, and Ethan and Addy threw themselves at her before she was even through the front door.

"Here, you take these," Shana said when they finally let her go, passing the donuts to Addy. "And these are heavier," Shana warned as Ethan took the cans of soda.

"Want me to take the wine too?" he asked Shana, a grin on his face.

"Nope. I'm keeping hold of these." She strode into the kitchen where Kate was washing her hands. "Abba, I approve."

"We had Springsteen on earlier. Decided to have a dance party while we prepped."

Shana grinned. "I approve of that, too." She grabbed two wine glasses from Kate's cupboard.

"None for me yet. I'll wait until after the grilling is done," Kate said, because you didn't marry a fireman and mess around when it came to barbecues.

"Ooh, we're having a cookout?"

"Yep."

"I should have brought ingredients for smores. Damn." Shana wrinkled her nose.

"Next time," Kate said firmly, aware that Ethan and Addy were getting more excited by the minute. "The donuts look perfect."

"Where's James?" Shana asked, as Kate started carrying the food out to the old table they'd set up on the back patio.

"Finishing his homework. He'll be down in a minute." Kate hunkered down to turn the propane back on. "Okay, everybody stand back."

"Can I turn it on?" Ethan asked.

"No. Just wait. I'll let you help me cook once the flames are ready."

To her amazement he didn't argue with her. Just nodded and watched her intently as she pressed the ignition and the burners came to life.

"Let's get an apron on you," she said to Ethan. "And some heat resistant gloves. And you have to promise to do exactly what I say when you're near the grill, understand?"

"Of course."

Shana and Addy started setting the table as Kate slowly showed Ethan how to slide each burger onto the long-handled turner, then slowly shake it so the patty set nicely on the rack over the hot flames. They did the first together, then he did the second on his own.

The third somehow slid between the grill rack and onto the burner.

"Oh shit." His eyes widened as he realized he'd said that out loud.

"Language," Kate murmured, though she knew she'd said worse herself. And in front of him, no doubt. "It's okay, we have extra. Let's get the rest on and I'll rescue that one later."

The sun was still beating warmth into the air when they sat down to eat. Ethan kept asking everybody how it tasted, reminding them that he'd cooked dinner.

"You know the penalty for losing a burger to the fire, right?" James asked, having eaten his own burger in about a minute flat. Kate pointed at his salad with a raised eye and he forked up some cucumber.

"There's a penalty?" Ethan asked, frowning. "Nobody told me that."

"You have to eat the charcoal patty," James told him. "No ketchup, no bun. Just burned cow."

Ethan blinked. "I don't have to do that, do I, Mom?"

"No you don't." She rolled her eyes at James. "And you did great. It tastes good."

James winked at him. "Just kidding. And yeah, you're a pretty cool cook."

Ethan glowed in the light of his brother's rare praise.

Kate took a sip of her wine and looked around the table.

Addy had made a person out of her cucumber, tomato, and carrot sticks and was eating them, limb by limb, giving a soft running commentary as she popped each vegetable into her mouth.

"Carrot legs are good, mmm." She swallowed. "Cucumber arms. So delicious."

Shana met Kate's eye, grinning.

James and Ethan were talking about what they could grill next week. They were stuck between more burgers – Ethan's choice – and kebabs – James' choice.

Kate let out a contented breath. Everybody was happy, they were full. They were here and they were safe.

And yes, there was somebody missing. But she was doing okay. They all were. Step by step they were building a new life.

A good life. She hoped he was proud of them.

"Come on, let's clear up the dishes," she said, when Addy had finished her tomato-head and James had eaten the half burger she didn't finish. "Then we can have donuts."

"Can we warm them up on the grill?" Ethan asked, a spark of hope in his voice.

"Not this time, honey. But I promise we'll do smores next time."

"Yes!" He pumped his fist into the air. "I'll be in charge of them, too."

"Alone at last," Shana said two hours later as Kate sat down next to her on the Adirondack chairs that faced the fields and the setting sun. As it slipped below the horizon, it was turning the cornfields into a golden vista.

"I poured you another glass." Shana passed Kate some wine. "I figured you'd need it."

"Because I just spent twenty minutes arguing with Ethan that he wasn't allowed to light the grill again?" Kate asked, smiling. He and Addy were finally in bed, though she'd agreed that Ethan could stay up to read for an hour. She hadn't told Addy that though, because her little girl would have thrown a fit.

Sometimes being the mom of three kids felt harder than being a diplomat for the United Nations. At least James had been easy. She'd agreed he could play on his Xbox for an hour, but not with his friends. He was still grounded – in name at least.

He hadn't put up much of a fight and she was glad.

"No, because we're about to choose your first date," Shana said, holding her phone up. "By the way, have you downloaded the app yet?"

"No. I haven't had a chance."

"Do it later. I'll send you the login details. In the meantime, what about this guy? He's thirty-eight. Works in a bank." Shana held her phone up. There was a photograph of a non-descript guy in a white shirt. He looked…nice, Kate guessed.

"Does he have kids?" she asked.

Shana blinked. "I don't know. Does it matter?"

"I'm not sure. But he has a moustache. I'm not sure I like moustaches. Who else is there?"

They went through all of Shana's choices. Ryan, who ran his own software business and had a three-year-old daughter. Sam who had two grown sons and was in his late forties, looking for somebody to 'make memories' with. And Luke who hadn't stated his job, but his photo was of him sitting in an expensive sports car which put Kate off completely.

"You couldn't fit Addy's car seat in the back."

Shana rolled her eyes. "That's not what you'd be doing in the backseat," she teased. "No car seats needed for that."

Kate wrinkled her nose. "I'm not having sex in the backseat of some stranger's car. Anyway, it's probably not even his car. Look at those plates, they're not West Virginia ones."

Shana laughed. "You've found an excuse for every single one of them. You need to give them a chance before you make up your mind."

"But there's no point in wasting their time or mine," Kate pointed out.

"What if they're great in bed?"

Kate's mouth felt dry. "That doesn't matter if you're not compatible."

"I thought you wanted something casual. If you're looking for Mr. Right instead of *Mr. Right Now* we might need to take a whole new approach," Shana said, sounding a little too certain for Kate's liking.

"Like what?" She was getting wary now. And yeah, maybe it still felt a little too soon. Her chest was tight, like somebody was pulling at her.

"I don't know. I'll think about it. But why not just choose

one of these for next week? Pop your cherry. Get it over with."

"You make it sound so romantic," Kate teased.

"It's more romantic than sitting at home on your own."

"I'm never on my own. I have three kids." And didn't she know it?

"Mom! Somebody's at the door!" James was leaning out of his window, his Xbox controller in his hands.

"What? Who is it?" she called back up, grateful that she and Shana had been talking in low voices. Not that James would have noticed. He was wearing headphones. The only reason he could hear the doorbell was because she'd put a ringer upstairs.

"No idea." His job done, James closed the window, presumably going back to whatever game he was playing.

"Stay here, I'll be right back," Kate told Shana.

"Oh, I'm not going anywhere until we've chosen a date for you," Shana promised.

Kate let out a breath. She'd worry about that fight later. The dishwasher had finished and was flashing as she walked through the kitchen and into the hallway, almost tripping over Ethan's shoes. She picked them up and put them in the closet, then opened the door, blinking when she saw Marley Hartson standing on her porch.

It had been a week since she'd seen him at the concert but the time had done nothing to temper her response to him. It was like it was inbuilt now, a reflex reaction to her eyes catching his.

"You're not in your running clothes," she said, because she couldn't think of any other words to say.

Or maybe she could, but they all sounded wrong. Where have you been? Have you been ignoring me?

"Can I come in?" he asked her. "I thought I'd stop by and pick up Addy's picture."

"Sure." She wasn't going to feel disappointed that Addy

was the reason he was here. It was sweet and kind and her daughter would be happy. That was enough. "It's in the kitchen."

She turned and walked down the hallway, hearing the click of the door as he closed it behind them both. God, she was pleased to see him, but she really didn't want him to see how much.

Because she'd made the decision to move on. That's what she and Shana had been doing for the last hour, after all.

When they got into the kitchen, Shana was already there, topping up their wine glasses. She looked from Kate to Marley.

"Hi." Shana's voice betrayed no surprise at seeing him. "Want a glass?" she asked, holding up the wine bottle.

He shook his head. "I'm driving."

"I brought soda, too." Shana grinned. "For the boring people."

"Yeah." Marley nodded. "That sounds good."

"Here's the picture," Kate said, passing him the white paper with Addy's drawing on the front.

Marley took it and stared at it, his throat bobbing as he swallowed. "It's great," he said.

He sounded genuine. Shana shot her an amused look.

"Addy will be happy you came to get it."

"Is she awake for me to say thank you?" he asked. His voice was as soft as wool.

Kate shook her head. "She's asleep. But I'll pass it on in the morning."

"Thanks." He took the can of soda Shana was holding out and popped the cap, taking a long drink. "She's a good artist."

"She'll be very pleased to hear that," Kate said dryly. "She ate her latest creation for dinner."

"Hannibal the painter," Marley said and Kate laughed.

Shana looked at him. "While you're here, can we get your

opinion on something?" Shana said. Kate shot her a confused look and Shana shrugged. "We need a man's opinion. Kate's thinking about dating again and we're trying to find the right guy."

Kate shot her a dirty look.

Thanks Shana, this was just *what she needed.*

"Come outside and sit with us." Shana shot Marley a wicked grin. "And tell me, if a guy has a sports car, what's the back seat for?"

CHAPTER
Eleven

"DAMN, MY PHONE IS DYING." Shana grimaced as Marley took the seat next to Kate's. She wouldn't look at him. And he couldn't look at her either.

He was angry. And he didn't have a right to be. He took a deep breath to get his annoyance under control.

Kate had every right to date. She'd been alone for two years after all.

And now he was regretting stopping here after leaving the station. He'd only come to pick up the damn picture, or at least that's what he was telling himself.

Because the alternative – that he'd come over because he couldn't keep away from her – felt unpalatable.

"You two stay here," Shana told them. "I'm just going in to get my charger and battery pack."

"You take a battery pack wherever you go?" Marley asked her.

Shana shrugged. "I'm a woman. The phone is my security. I always keep it charged up."

She hopped out of her chair and walked through the kitchen door. Marley turned to look at Kate. "So…"

Her cheeks were bright pink. "I'm sorry. I can't believe

Shana got you involved in this. I'm sure there's some place else you'd rather be on a Friday night than here, talking about dating apps."

Right now he'd rather be stabbing his eyes with knives. "Nope, it's good I'm here," he said gruffly. Mostly because if she was going on a date he wanted to know with who.

Because he was Paul's friend, that was all. He just needed to make sure she did this safely.

Nothing more, nothing less.

So why wasn't the annoyance disappearing?

Kate had her hair in a simple ponytail, revealing the sculpted features of her face. If she was wearing any makeup, he couldn't see it.

"I didn't download the app," Kate told him. "Shana did. I'm not even that interested. I don't want you to think I'm disrespecting Paul."

He kept his face expressionless. "Of course I don't."

"Or that I'm moving on too quickly."

"It's none of my business, Kate." It really wasn't. He just needed to get that through his thick skull. "And nobody would blame you for moving on. It's been two years."

Her eyes caught his. "So do you think I should go on a date?" she asked softly.

Fuck, no he didn't.

"I think you should do what's best for you."

She pulled her gaze from his, a frown playing at her lips. "I don't know. It's all so weird. And I don't know if it's a good idea to go on a date with a stranger."

Of course it wasn't. It was the first sensible thing she'd said. He opened his mouth to agree and then regretted the thought immediately.

"I'll tell you what," he said, the words coming out before he could stop them. "I'll come with and sit in the corner if you'd like. Wherever you go. Just as some support."

The backdoor opened and Shana walked back out,

carrying her phone that was now attached to her battery pack with an umbilical cord-like charging lead.

"Who's going to sit in the corner?" Shana asked.

"Marley. He says he'll be my bodyguard if I go on a date." She glanced at him and he shrugged. Because there was no way he was going to let her know that the thought of her dating another guy felt like some kind of painful purgatory.

She should be dating. She should be getting out there.

But with me.

He pushed that thought out of his head. Because he couldn't do that. Not to her, not to Paul.

What kind of sick fucker would go after Paul's widow, anyway?

Shana's eyes widened. "Oh no, that's not happening," she told Marley. "Look at you." She put her hand on his chest. "You're huge and gorgeous. You'd put any guy off. The date would be doomed before it started."

"Why would I put somebody off?" Though, yeah, the thought had occurred to him. "I'll just be the muscle in the corner in case of any problems."

"That," Shana said, jabbing her finger into his pectoral muscle. "Ow. But yeah, that's exactly what I mean. If you hang around they'll think you have some kind of claim on her. Look at you with those steel clad biceps. You'd send him running."

"Maybe that's a good thing," Kate muttered. For some reason she looked annoyed.

Shana lifted a brow. "No it isn't."

"What if I don't want to go on the date alone? The first one at least?" Kate asked her friend.

"Then I'll come too," Shana said, sighing. "I'm good at blending into the background. Unlike some."

He took that to mean him. Which was kind of laughable, considering he'd been blending into the background for the last two years when it came to Kate and her family.

"I need you to babysit," Kate pointed out.

And that's when a grin spread over Shana's lips. "That's okay, Marley can babysit. I'll sit in the corner wherever you go. Simple."

Kate caught his eye.

"Would you be willing to do that?" she asked him.

He blinked. Hell no. "Yeah, I guess." The words just came out. Because somebody needed to be there. And he wanted to make sure she got home safely. That's all it was. Not because it was killing him to think about her with somebody else.

She looked at him for a moment. Like she was trying to work him out. And then she pulled her gaze away.

"Okay then. I guess this is really happening."

"So let me get this straight." Pres smirked at him as the two of them sat on a wall at the construction site they were working on. "You're babysitting three kids on a Saturday night so that the woman you have the hots for can go on a date with another guy."

Marley lifted his bottle of water to his lips, swallowing half of it in one go. The weather was hot today. No clouds in the sky, the sun beating down relentlessly. He'd taken his shirt off an hour ago but he still felt overheated.

"I don't have the hots for her."

"Of course you fucking do." Pres shook his head. "What the hell are you thinking?"

"I'm thinking that a friend needs some help and I can provide it. It's not like watching the kids is gonna be hard. James is fifteen. The other two will be in bed. I'll just watch a movie and wait for her to come home."

Pres narrowed his eyes. Like Marley's, his pants were covered in dust. They were putting up the drywall today, and no matter how much you tried, you couldn't avoid getting dust covered yourself. "I'm not even gonna go into what an idiot statement that is. Because kids are not easy. You know that from watching me wrangle mine whenever we're together. But answer me this: what are you gonna do if she gets along with this guy?"

"What do you mean?" A rivulet of sweat was making its way down his brow. He reached up to wipe it away. They'd taken their hard hats off for the break, but as soon as they started work again they'd have to put them back on. He wasn't looking forward to that.

"I mean what if she likes this guy? What if she brings him home for coffee? You gonna be okay with that?"

"Kate won't bring him home for coffee on a first date. Her kids are there."

Pres shook his head. "You don't get it. She might not bring him home this time. But she will at some point. With some guy. For likely more than coffee, too. Are you ready for that?"

Marley frowned. "It's not up to me to be ready. It's on Kate." And yeah, he didn't like that thought. Not one bit. But fuck, what was he supposed to do? Tell her she couldn't date as if he was her father?

Frustration clouded Pres' eyes. "That's not what I'm asking and you know it. And you also know that I'm only saying to you the same things you said to me when I found it hard to move on."

"And I was right," Marley pointed out. He knew how hard his brother had found dating again after losing his first wife, Delilah's mom. Pres had fought against his attraction to Cassie every step of the way. Until he finally couldn't help himself.

And now the two of them were married with two more kids, and neither of them could be happier.

Not that Pres looked happy right now.

"Yes you were," Pres agreed. "So maybe you can also agree that I might be right about you and Kate."

"There is no *me* and Kate." Marley's throat felt scratchy.

Like he'd swallowed something too big and he couldn't cough it out. "There can't be. She was married to Paul. Nothing could ever happen between us. You know what it would be like. The gossip throughout town would kill her."

"And?" Pres gave him a pointed stare. Sometimes he liked to play the big brother, even though they were born only minutes apart.

"What do you mean 'And'?" Marley asked him. "There is no *and*. It's just a statement of truth. The woman deserves some peace after what she's been through."

"So you're refusing to tell her how you feel because you're afraid of a little gossip." Pres shook his head. "I thought better of you."

Marley frowned. "It's not about me, it's about her. And the fact she was married to my buddy."

"You're lying to yourself. Yes, this town likes gossip. But it also likes new things. The gossip moves along and we keep moving along. I know everybody gossiped about me and Cass when we first started dating. But I also know that we were yesterday's news within about a week. So don't use protecting Kate from gossip as some kind of shield. You won't put yourself out there because you're scared. It's as simple as that."

"I'm not scared," Marley scoffed. He climbed houses for a living. He fought fires. Yeah, he had a healthy respect for life, but he wasn't afraid of putting himself on the line when it counted.

"Yeah, you are. That's why you're going to babysit Kate's kids while she's out on a date. Because you'd rather lose her than have her reject you."

"Ah, fuck off with the pop psychology. I'm going to babysit because I'm a friend." Marley checked his watch. "It's time to get back to work."

Pres smirked. "Of course it is."

CHAPTER
Twelve

KATE CHECKED HER WATCH. Marley was due to arrive in five minutes. And then she'd go out to her car, drive to Maple Cross, and spend the evening with a man she'd never met before.

She took a deep breath. She'd spent most of the week thinking about canceling the date, because the thought of eating dinner with this Allen guy was making her stomach twist.

Sure, he seemed nice. After Shana had installed the app on Kate's phone, she'd actually managed to chat with him. He was a teacher, luckily not at any of her kids' schools. He taught math at a high school over near Charleston, but lived locally. Apparently, a lot of high school teachers preferred not to live near their schools, so they didn't bump into their students while they were trying to relax.

Truth be told, she hadn't liked it when he said that. It made her feel protective of James and also wonder how Allen would feel about her teenager. He hadn't asked much about her children, and she hadn't volunteered.

"That's a good thing. You'll have more to talk about on the date," Shana had reassured her.

But right now she wanted to take off the black sleeveless blouse and tight jeans she'd put on and climb into her pajamas and spend the evening watching movies with her kids instead.

"Can I try your lipstick on?" Addy asked. She was standing at Kate's bathroom counter, where her makeup was still strewn across the surface.

"Not now, honey. You just had a bath."

But it was too late. Addy was already smearing the pink goo across her lips. Well, around her lips at least. Kate tried not to laugh at the way her daughter looked like a clown.

"Come here," she said, grabbing a makeup remover wipe. "I promise I'll show you how to use it tomorrow, okay?"

Addy nodded as Kate wiped her face clean. "Can I stay up late tonight?" she then asked her mom.

"No. You have to go to bed when Marley says so."

"What about if I get nightmares?" Addy asked.

"You won't," Kate said, reassuringly. "And anyway, I won't be late. I'm just going out to dinner."

"With *a man*." Addy wrinkled her little nose. Kate knew the kids had been talking about it. She'd tried so hard to hit the right balance of being honest with them and making it *so not a big deal*. She wasn't sure she'd hit the mark, if she was being truly honest.

"With a friend." Okay, that was a bit of a lie. She didn't know Allen enough to call him a friend. But she also didn't want Addy thinking there was more to it. "That's it. And then I'll be home."

"Will you come see me when you get back?" Addy asked.

"You'll be asleep. But I'll check on you, I promise."

"If I get scared can I sleep in your bed?" Addy looked longingly into Kate's room at her queen size bed.

Kate let out a long breath. She was already working out how she could apologize to Marley if the kids misbehaved.

Maybe she shouldn't go. It was too soon. Not just for her but for them.

She'd barely been out of the house in the last two years without them. No wonder Addy was asking so many questions. Truth was, she was worried about Marley being able to handle the kids. Sure he had nephews and a niece, plus an extended family so big there were always kids around. But this was one-on-three.

And then there was the whole stupid thing of how attracted she was to him. *Oh Allen, please take my mind off him.*

"Okay," Kate said, deciding not to fight this one. "You can sleep in my bed but only for tonight."

Addy's grin was huge as she wrapped her arms around Kate's waist. "Thank you, Mommy. I love you."

"I love you too." She stroked her daughter's hair. When she looked up, James was standing in the doorway. "Go put the television on," she told Addy. "You can watch some cartoons before bedtime."

Addy didn't need asking twice. She was out of Kate's bedroom like a shot. Kate turned to her son, lifting her brow. "I get the feeling Marley's going to have his work cut out for him."

"I could have watched Ethan and Addy without him," James pointed out.

"I know you could." But she'd promised herself when she had Ethan – long before she'd lost Paul – that she wouldn't use their oldest son as a babysitter. It seemed even more important now. James deserved to have a childhood, not to be her crutch. "And I'd be grateful if you could help him with your brother and sister."

"Sure." James nodded. "So this guy…"

"Allen." It was strange how nervous she felt saying his name.

"Is he a good guy?"

It was funny, because this was the kind of conversation

she'd expected to have with her dad when she first started dating. But by then, her dad had passed and her mom hadn't shown any interest in her dating life.

It touched her heart just a little that James was sounding so protective.

"I don't know. I think so. But that's why you go out to dinner with somebody. To find out what they're like. It's not a big deal. I just want to know if he's worth talking to or not." She reached for his hand. "I promise you I'm not trying to replace Dad."

James' jaw tightened. Damn, she loved this kid. Watching him growing into a man was one of the biggest privileges of her life. Bigger now that she was the only parent that got to see it. He was learning to control his emotions. Deal with them. And yes, sometimes he failed – the party in the fields being the biggest example – but he was mostly winning.

"I know. Nobody can replace him."

She nodded. "If you'd rather I stay home, I will." And that was being honest, too.

"No, you go. It's fine. Just don't expect me to call him daddy."

She couldn't help it. She started laughing. And then – to her joy – James joined in. It was what she needed, maybe what they both needed. Because this was no big deal, it really wasn't.

"Mommy! Marley is here," Addy was leaning against the bedroom window, her nose pressed against the glass, her breath frosting against it.

"Come here," James said, pulling his sister into his arms. She squealed with joy. Any attention from her biggest brother was like a gift to her. He rubbed his nose against hers and she laughed.

"I'll go open the door," James said.

"Thank you." Kate smiled at him. "Tell him I'll be down in a few. Just as soon as I look presentable."

"You look great, Mom," James said. Then he glanced at her bare arms. "But maybe put on a jacket or something."

"Of course." Kate grinned at her protective son. "I wouldn't want to get cold in this eighty degree heat, would I?"

What the hell are you thinking? Pres' voice sounded so clear in his mind that Marley almost looked behind him to see if his brother was standing there on the stoop outside Kate's house.

But no, he was alone. It was just the memory of their conversation from earlier and maybe a little of his own thoughts, too.

He was a masochist. Plain and simple. That had to be it. Somewhere along the line he must have developed a need for pain.

"Marley!" Addy grinned as James opened the door.

"Hey kid." He forced a smile onto his face and ruffled her hair. His eyes caught James' and they both nodded like the man and almost-man they were.

"Come on in," James said. "Mom's almost ready."

"Cool." He steadied himself to see her. Because yes, she'd been on his mind almost constantly this week.

Ethan was in the living room, watching some cartoon that looked way too mature for him. The kind made for adults, not kids, but Marley wasn't about to start off on a bad note.

"Hey," he said, popping his head around the door, smiling at Kate's middle child.

"Hi."

Then he heard the footsteps on the stairs and it was like a billion bubbles were popping in his chest. He turned to see her, her hair glossy and wavy as it fell around her shoulders. She was wearing a pair of black jeans and a black silky sleeveless top, an ivory jacket in her hands. Little diamond earrings were fastened in her ears and she had a chunky silver bracelet on her wrist.

"Hi," she said softly.

He forced that smile again. "Hi."

Fuck, she was beautiful. He wanted to feel the smoothness of her top, the silkiness of her hair.

The warmth of her skin.

"You look good," he said, his voice thick.

Kate's smile was genuine. "I've promised James I'll wear the jacket."

"Good." Okay so that one escaped before he thought about it. But her smile didn't waver. "You heard from Shana?"

"She's already at the restaurant," Kate told him. "She's calling it a stakeout. Apparently, she's in all black like some kind of dating Ninja."

Of course she was. Damn, he liked Shana. "If anything happens, anything at all. Just call, okay?"

"Yeah, call us," James added. "We'll handle this guy if you need us to."

Kate looked from her son to Marley, her eyes crinkled with amusement. "It's dinner. The worst that can happen is that he's a messy eater." She lifted her hand to her hair, tucking a lock behind her ear. Her skin had a light tan to it, the way most people in town had at this time of year. No matter how much sunscreen you applied, it was never enough.

The underside of her arm, though, was pale. For a second he imagined how it would feel against his lips.

"Okay then." Kate looked like she was steeling herself to go into battle. "I'm going. Come here," she said to James, hugging him. Then she cuddled Addy against her. "Ethan, I'm leaving."

"See you later," he shouted back.

She shook her head and walked into the living room, then a moment later Ethan let out a squeal as she almost certainly squeezed him tight.

James and Addy wandered into the kitchen, so Marley was the only one left in the hallway when she came back out.

"Wish me luck," she murmured to him.

He crossed his fingers behind his back. "Good luck."

She didn't look in any hurry to leave. He liked that way too much. "Thank you for taking care of them," she told him. "If they cause any problems, let me know."

"They won't. It's just a few hours." And then she'd be back and he'd be able to breathe again.

She nodded, then hesitated for a second, before rolling onto her tiptoes and kissing his cheek. Her lips were soft, warm, and damn, he should have shaved before coming over. The sweet smell of her perfume invaded his senses. Made his stomach twist.

It was an automatic reaction to reach out and curl his palm around her hip. If you asked him, he'd maintain that stance until the day he died. But there was something about the feel of her body against his that caused desire to shoot through his torso and into his limbs.

A caveman-like need overtook his mind. His hold on her tightened. She pressed her palms against his chest, not to push him away, but to steady herself, and damn if he didn't flex his pectorals like a damn gorilla.

Her eyes went wide. And so close he could see the gold flecks in the green of her irises. Could see himself reflected back in the darkness of her pupils.

She opened her mouth to say something, then closed it again.

His fingers twitched with the need to slide them to her back, to feel the curve of her ass, the warmth of her thighs. For a moment he imagined hitching one of them around his waist, pushing her against the wall.

Carrying her up to bed.

Laughter came from the kitchen and Kate took a step back. She blinked like she'd just been stunned.

"Drive safely," he muttered. "And be careful."

Her chest hitched. "I just…"

"Go, Kate."

Because if she didn't go now, he wasn't sure he'd have the willpower to stop himself again.

She nodded and slid the jacket over her arms – good girl – before glancing his way one more time. There was a question in her eyes. One he didn't have the answer to.

"I'll be back soon," she said. It sounded like a promise.

He nodded. "Be safe."

CHAPTER
Thirteen

"OKAY," Marley said, clapping his hands together as he walked into the kitchen, because he needed something to take his mind off the woman who'd just walked out of the door. "Your mom is gone. Who wants to watch a movie?"

Addy had chocolate smeared all over her lips. It hadn't taken her long to dive into the snack cupboard as soon as Kate's attention was elsewhere. Marley bit down a smile.

"Can I go play on my Xbox?" James asked.

"Yes, but on your own. Your mom says you can't play with anybody else online," Marley told him. "Until you're not grounded."

"He does already," Addy whispered. "I heard him last night."

James shot his little sister a wounded look. "I was talking to myself."

"Is your name Ben?" she asked, putting her hands on her hips.

Marley bit down a smile, because these kids were killing him.

"I'm not gonna play with anybody else, I promise," James said to Marley. "Please?"

"Okay. But if I hear you talking..." He'd probably do nothing. But he was the babysitter here. He needed to assert some authority.

"I won't."

Ethan walked into the kitchen, his cartoon presumably over. "I'm hungry," he said. "Can I have a burger?"

"We just had dinner," Addy said. "You ate seconds."

"Yeah, well I'm hungry again." Ethan frowned. "I can cook us burgers on the grill. I know how to."

Marley blinked. "Ah, I don't think that's a good idea."

"You're not allowed to cook on the grill without Mommy. She told you that," Addy said in a singsong voice.

Marley loved the way that Addy was a little tattletale. He needed that.

"How about we make some popcorn?" he suggested instead, spotting the box in the pantry. "We could watch a movie."

"A scary one?" Ethan said hopefully. "One with lots of gore?"

"I don't like scary movies," Addy said, her lip wobbling. "I get nightmares."

"That's because you're a baby," Ethan told her.

"I'm not a baby," she shouted back at her brother. "Mommy told you not to call me that."

"Yeah, well Mom's not here, is she?" Ethan asked. "What are you gonna do, tell her? Snitch."

"Hey, hey," Marley took a step between them, noticing the redness in Addy's cheeks. "Let's calm down. Ethan, do you know how to work the microwave?"

"Of course I do. *I'm* not a baby." The kid looked almost wounded.

Marley tried not to sigh. "Okay, so you make the popcorn, and Addy can start looking for a movie for us to watch."

"How come she gets to pick the movie?" Ethan asked. There was a whining note in his tone.

"She doesn't. We all have to agree." Marley let out a breath. He felt exhausted already. "But we need to start somewhere."

"I don't want to watch any with princesses," Ethan warned.

"And I don't want to watch any of your stupid cartoons," Addy countered.

"At least my cartoons aren't for babies."

Okay, the baby thing was starting to grate on his nerves. Marley gave Ethan a pointed look. "Start the popcorn. Come on, Addy, let's go see what we can find."

She slipped her hand into his and nodded. "Okay." And it was weird, but that little gesture made his heart feel like it was too big for his chest. They walked to the living room and Addy grabbed the remote, jumping onto the sofa and turning on the television.

Then his phone vibrated. He pulled it from his pocket.

The Eagle Has Landed. – Shana.

There was a photo attached. He could see Kate sitting at a table, and the back of a guy's head. Kate looked nervous. She was holding a glass of water; her knuckles bleached. He zoomed in, but couldn't see anything of the guy apart from the bald spot on his head. Kate looked uncomfortable, though. He liked that way too much.

Thanks. – Marley

A moment later he sent another message.

• • •

Keep me posted on how it's going. – Marley

I intend to! – Shana

God, he hoped Kate didn't like this guy. He pushed that thought away and tried to concentrate on the kids.

"I've got an idea," he said to Addy. "You remember Delilah, my niece?"

Addy nodded. "She's super cool."

"She is. And her very favorite movie in the world is *Jumanji*."

"*Jumanji*? Isn't that scary?" Addy asked him.

"I think it might be a little. But it's also funny and entertaining, and I promise I won't let anything happen to you."

"Okay. But if I get scared, I'll need to stay up until Mommy gets home."

"I think I burned the popcorn," Ethan called out from the kitchen.

Marley let out a sigh. "Don't move," he told Addy. Fuck, babysitting was like herding cats. "No problem," he called to Ethan. "I'm a firefighter. I can deal with burned stuff."

Allen liked to talk, Kate realized. About himself mostly, but he was also very happy to weigh in on anything that required an opinion. Right now he was telling Kate about his vacation to Europe last year, which involved visiting France, Italy, Spain, and the UK. She was desperate to hear about the cities he'd visited, the museums he'd seen.

But he was too busy talking about the woman he'd gone with. His ex of ten years. And how she'd managed to ruin everything.

Was it time to go home yet?

She glanced over to see Shana watching her in the corner. Her friend lifted her thumb up and then down, trying to work out how the date was going.

Kate shrugged. She wasn't going to give a verdict yet. It was her first date in almost fifteen years, and her first date since losing Paul. She should at least give the guy a shot.

"So then she told me she'd found somebody else. We were standing at the bottom of the Eiffel Tower. And I was like, 'excuse me, we're in the most romantic city in the world, couldn't you at least wait until we're in Barcelona?'"

"She ended things with you in Paris?" Kate asked. Okay, maybe she felt a little sorry for the guy.

"Oh no, things were over before we even went. She didn't want to go, but I'd already paid for the flights and hotels. So I insisted."

He insisted? Kate took a mouthful of her water, really wishing it was wine.

"I pointed out how ungrateful it was that she was telling me about another man while she was on a vacation I paid for. And do you know what she said?" he asked. "No, you'll never guess. She actually told me that if I wanted to pay for somebody to be romantic with me I should have taken a hooker. Can you believe that?"

"No," Kate squeaked.

"And then I told her that at least a hooker would have put out during the trip. Rather than making me sleep on the floor, because all those expensive hotel rooms in Europe don't have two beds."

Kate checked her watch. It wasn't even eight-thirty yet. "Um, I just need to go make a phone call. Check that my kids are doing okay."

Allen blinked. "How many did you say you have again?"

"Three."

"Only one's a teenager, right?"

"Yes, that's right."

"Hmm. A handful, I bet."

"He's a good kid." She wasn't going to tell him about the teenage growing pains. She felt stupidly protective of him right now.

"You don't look old enough to have a fifteen-year-old." Allen said, looking at her. "How old are you again?"

Kate opened her mouth to tell him, but then shut it swiftly. Because it wasn't any of his business. She didn't like him, and she really wanted to go home. But she'd finish her dinner and leave.

"I'll be right back," she said, grabbing her clutch and walking outside. The air was cooling, finally, and it felt like a caress to her skin as she stepped into the inky dark night.

"Hey, everything okay?" Shana asked, following her out through the door. "Are you leaving already?"

"Did he see you follow me out?" Kate frowned. Not that she cared what he thought.

Okay, she did care. But not for *that* reason. But because she still had all that training from childhood inside her somewhere. *Don't make a fuss. Be a good girl. Men like it when you're nice.*

"No. But what happened?"

"It's fine," she told Shana. "I'm not leaving. I'm just going to call Marley to check on the kids."

"They're all good. I've been messaging him," Shana said.

Kate's stomach tightened. "You have? Why?" The thought of the two of them chatting without her made her feel weird.

It made her wish that Shana was the one on the date and she was the one messaging him.

"Just to keep him updated." Shana shrugged. "They're watching a movie."

"What movie?" Kate asked, wishing more than ever that she was home with them right now.

"I don't know. But you don't need to call them." She

tipped her head to the side. "So how's it going? What's Allen like?"

"He's… nice?"

"You don't sound so sure."

Kate took a long, calming breath. "I don't think it's going anywhere."

"Why not?" Shana sounded almost disappointed. "Is it the bald spot?"

"No." Kate shook her head. "I'm not worried about his hair." She didn't care about that at all. "He's just very, I don't know. He likes to talk."

"Isn't that good? Better than silence?"

"I guess. I would just like to get a word in sometime." She gave her friend a smile. "Listen, your work here is done. He's fine. He's not a serial killer. But he's also not my type. I'm going to finish dinner and head home." She hugged Shana. "Thank you for being here."

Shana tried to hide her disappointment. "You want me to leave?"

"Yes," Kate said firmly. It was painful enough sitting with that man. She didn't need her friend watching.

"So there's not going to be a wedding soon?" Shana pouted.

Kate laughed, because she knew her friend only wanted the best for her. "No. And there wouldn't be, anyway. I'm just dipping my toe in the water." And now she wanted to dry it off and go to bed. "I'll call you tomorrow, okay?"

Shana nodded. "I'll go pay my bill and go home, then. If you're sure…"

"I'm certain."

"I should have stayed at your place with Marley and the kids," Shana said, sounding wistful. "It would have been more fun."

There was that jealousy again. Kate shot her friend a grim smile and walked back into the restaurant to rejoin her date.

Because yeah, it wasn't going anywhere but she wasn't going to ghost him.

And she was definitely going to split the check.

The house was silent when she slid her key into the lock and pushed open the front door. Kate slid her shoes off and wriggled her toes, letting out a sigh at the relief at not wearing heels anymore.

Had Marley managed to get the kids to sleep without an argument?

Maybe he should come over every night and do the bedtime routine for her.

That thought sent a little thrill through her body that had no place being there. But she couldn't help but imagine him walking out of the kids' rooms and over to her, his lips brushing her own as he told her that the night was now theirs.

She needed to stop this train of thought. It was just a response to the date being so mediocre. Because that's what it was. Not bad enough to tell a story about. Not like Shana's terrible dating dramas. Just a little sad, a little boring. Not a single tingle in sight.

Pushing the living room door open, she noticed the television screen was the only light glowing. It was on the home screen, waiting for the next selection to be made. And then she looked over at the sofa and her heart did a little thud against her ribcage.

Because Addy and Ethan were there. Curled up on either side of Marley. And all three of them were fast asleep.

Addy's little head was nestled against Marley's chest. Her rosebud lips pursed as she softly exhaled, her cheek pressed against his dark t-shirt.

Ethan's head was against the sofa, but his side was

pressed into Marley. Like he was seeking warmth even in sleep.

As for Marley, he looked almost serene in his slumber. His eyes were closed, his jaw relaxed, his mouth slightly parted. His denim-clad legs were stretched out, whereas Addy and Ethan were curled up.

She could see the outline of his thigh muscles through the denim and it made her cheeks flush.

Addy let out a sigh so full of contentment it made Kate's chest tighten. When did her daughter last fall asleep against a man? James hated her trying to cuddle with him. She was used to Kate's embrace. Soft and warm.

But she looked so peaceful. So safe right now. It felt like a shame to wake her up, but Marley needed to get home. Kate tiptoed over to where her daughter was sleeping and touched her shoulder.

She'd take her up to bed first, then Ethan. If by some miracle Marley didn't wake between her trips, she'd deal with him last.

"Addy," she whispered. "It's time for bed."

"Mommy, I'm sleeping."

Kate's lips twitched because that was so Addy. "Come on, honey. Get up. We need to get you into bed."

Grumbling under her breath, Addy let Kate pull her to standing. And yeah, she was way too big for Kate to carry up the stairs. Maybe she should have called James for help, but then she wasn't sure what he would have thought at seeing his brother and sister all cozied up down here.

"Wait, what?" Marley's eyes opened. He immediately reached out with his fingers, as though grasping for something. "Where's my phone?"

She'd been a firefighter's wife for enough years to know exactly what he was thinking. "There's not an alert," she whispered to him. "I'm just taking Addy up to bed."

Marley was fully awake now. He sat up and gently moved

Ethan from him. "You're home," he said, his expression unreadable.

She smiled at the sleep-thickness of his voice. "Yeah. Let me get the kids to bed and then I can say goodbye to you."

"I can help." He glanced at Addy. "Want me to carry her up?"

"I want a carry," Addy nodded, looking suddenly awake. "Yes, please."

Marley stood and easily lifted her daughter into his arms. Addy melted against him. Kate reached for Ethan, shaking his arm. "Honey, it's bedtime."

"Mom?" he muttered, his eyelids fluttering.

"Yep?"

"We're watching a movie," Ethan muttered.

"It's over now." A smile played at her lips. His eyes were still closed.

"I didn't see the end."

"We can watch it again tomorrow," she promised.

She and Ethan followed Marley and Addy upstairs. They were both so tired they barely put up a fight as she helped them into their pjs and quickly brushed their teeth for them, like she used to when they were little.

Marley went back downstairs as she knocked on James' door.

"Come in."

He was sitting in bed, scrolling on his phone.

"Hey honey. Everything okay?" she asked, leaning on the doorjamb.

"Yeah, all good. Just going to sleep." He looked up at her. "How was your date?" he asked.

"It was…meh." She wrinkled her nose. And James gave her a sleepy smile.

"Maybe next time, hey?"

"Maybe," she said. "You should get some rest."

"Yeah. I only waited up to make sure you got home okay."

Then by some miracle he did what she suggested, putting his phone down and snuggling under the covers. She walked over to kiss his cheek.

"Night, sweetheart." She felt touched by his protectiveness.

"Night, Mom."

When she went back downstairs Marley was in the hallway. He had his shoes on.

"Want a coffee before you leave?" she asked him. "To keep you alert for your drive?"

He looked at her for a moment before nodding. "Sure. Sounds good."

It was warm in the kitchen. She opened up the back door to let the late evening breeze in, and grabbed two pods – a decaf one for her – and switched on the coffee machine.

Marley was leaning against the counter, his eyes on her. "So?"

"So what?" She turned to smile at him and their eyes connected. He'd been looking at her. The thought made her stomach feel fizzy, like she'd just swallowed a whole bottle of soda.

"So how was he?"

"My date?"

He lifted a brow. "Yeah."

She slid the first pod into the top of the machine. "He was… not suitable."

The machine started to hiss as the water heated up.

"Not suitable?" Marley repeated. "Not suitable for what?"

"Anything?"

He chuckled. There was a strange expression on his face.

"Is that funny?" she asked him, but she was still smiling.

"Yeah. Kinda. I was expecting more of a description. Like did he make you laugh?"

"No."

"Cry?"

It was her turn to chuckle. "No, definitely not. He was just different. We didn't have much in common. And he sounded like he doesn't like kids a whole lot."

"I thought you said he's a teacher?" Marley said, his brows knitting.

"He is. I guess he doesn't like dealing with them outside of school."

"So that's him out of the running, then." Marley definitely looked pleased.

"I didn't realize there was a race," she murmured, removing the first cup and sliding the second under the spout. She poured cream into Marley's cup and passed it to him, then turned back to the machine to grab her own coffee. This time when she turned back around, Marley was so close she bumped into him, her coffee swirling around her mug, almost spilling over the rim.

"Oh." He didn't move. The sheer size of him felt almost overwhelming. He was big. His body was hard. She was so aware of the smell of his cologne.

"There's a race," he said.

She looked up at him, her lips parted. What did he mean? There was a race for what? *Her*? She wasn't exactly a prize. She was getting up the gumption to remind him of that when he put his mug down on the counter beside her, then took hers out of her hands and placed it next to his.

Her heart was slamming against her ribcage as he leaned in even closer, sandwiching her body between his and the counter. But she didn't feel caged in. Weirdly, she felt as free as a bird. Like she was soaring.

He reached out to cup her face. His touch was tender. Almost reverent. Her heart was racing. And slamming. Was it even tethered to the rest of her body?

"Who's in the race?" she whispered.

A half-smile pulled at the corner of his mouth. She was

mesmerized by it. Couldn't help but reach out to touch the way his lips curled.

Marley let out a rumble of a groan. Deep in his chest. It made her thighs clench. And then he was leaning forward, his mouth capturing hers, his hands sliding down to her sides to steady her.

It wasn't a gentle kiss. It was hungry. Wolfish. Like he hadn't eaten in months. She wrapped her arms around him, marveling at his warmth, at the thick ridges of his muscles. Her fingers curled around the fabric of his t-shirt as his mouth moved against hers.

She parted her lips, ignoring the warning in her head that she shouldn't be doing this. His tongue slid against hers and she shuddered, pulses of electricity shooting through her nerve endings. She wasn't sure how long this could last. She was already getting breathless. He must be too.

But she didn't want it to end. Didn't want him to stop kissing her. Didn't want these tingles all over her body to stop.

She moved her hands up, sliding her fingers into his hair and Marley let out another rumbling groan. Another wave of pleasure pulsed through her. This big, dominant man was kissing her like she really was the prize.

Like he'd won the race she hadn't even known was taking place.

When they parted his eyes were dark. Darker than she'd ever seen them. His gaze was directly on her, like he was trying to work her out.

"Fuck it." He leaned back in, kissing her again. And damn if she wasn't the one to let out a moan this time. His fingers slid down her side, reaching her hips. And then he lifted her until her ass was on the kitchen counter and his body fit perfectly between her thighs.

He was already hard. She could feel the thick ridge of him pressing against her. It felt so good that she let out another groan. He was kissing her harder now, one hand on her chin, angling her head, the other gently kneading her side, his fingers so powerful it made her ache for him.

Kate's hands were on his back. She could feel the powerful knots of his muscles, the warmth of his taut skin. And when he pulled away this time, she refused to let go of him.

"The kids," he said. "What if they come down?"

And damn if that didn't make her want him even more.

"Let's go outside." Her voice was sure. And yeah, there'd be bugs, but she'd worry about that tomorrow.

All she wanted in the moment was to feel this man's body against hers.

He didn't need telling twice. Before she could slide down from her position on the counter he was lifting her again, holding her tight against him. She clung to his neck and wrapped her thighs around his waist as he turned and carried her easily out of the back door.

She wasn't going to overthink this. Not now, anyway. Maybe tomorrow, when there was daylight and shame and Shana to talk to. Right now she just wanted to kiss him. So she did, as he carried her outside.

This man was way too good to feel any regret.

CHAPTER Fourteen

MARLEY FOUND an old Adirondack chair and sat down on it, lifting Kate's body until she was straddling his thighs. There was a full moon out tonight – he'd been wary about that when he'd offered to babysit. Full moons always meant call outs and he'd expressly told the other volunteers he wasn't available tonight.

He'd still kept his phone on, though, and the alert app open. But nothing came through. Maybe for once the town was behaving.

Which was more than he could say for himself. But he didn't want to think about that right now. All he wanted to think about was this woman. The way her skin looked almost porcelain in the cool light of the moon. The way she was looking at him like he was the only man in the world right now.

Not suitable.

He liked her description of her date way too fucking much.

Because laying here together their bodies just fit. They did. Her inner thighs clamped around his like she was trying to squeeze the hell out of him. Her hips were undulating softly as he slid his fingers through her perfect, glossy hair. Their mouths worshipping and teasing like neither of them ever wanted it to stop.

He knew he didn't.

And that's how it went for the next hour. They'd part for breath and then they'd kiss again, like they couldn't help themselves. He started off being reverent – or as reverent as he could be when he was devouring the woman he wanted. But then she'd slid her hands beneath his t-shirt and he'd felt the full fucking power of her touch, and it had sent him a little crazy.

Enough to do the same to her. To feel the soft silkiness of her skin. To trace his calloused fingers over her stomach, along her back, then up to her breasts.

Her nipples were hard beneath her bra. And yes, he pinched them, because how could he not? The action made her gasp into his mouth so he did it again.

He couldn't remember the last time he made out, fully clothed, for an hour. It was like he was back in high school. Kate moved in his arms, sliding her body until she was prone against his, her breasts touching his chest, her mouth still kissing him like she never wanted to stop.

And then she touched him *there.*

It was like a thousand fireworks exploding in his brain. Her palm cupped his hardness through his jeans, then her fingers wrapped around him through the denim, moving up and down.

He was a breath away from coming in his pants like a sixteen-year-old kid.

He kissed her lips, her jaw, her neck. "Kate."

"Huh?" Her gaze was hazy.

"I need you to stop touching me," he told her, his voice rough with need.

For a second he could see the hurt in her eyes. "Because

I'm about ten seconds away from coming," he added truthfully.

"Oh." Her voice was soft, but she moved her hand.

And for a moment he wished he hadn't said anything. Regret mingled with relief.

"I'm sorry," he told her. "It's been a while."

This time she smiled. It was a little wobbly but it was there. And he realized she was on a cliff's edge of emotions. He wanted to wrap his arms around her and keep her away from the danger. "That's kind of sexy," she whispered.

He went to sit up and she did, too, moving so she was sitting on his lap.

It was so exquisitely painful having her there it was messing with his brain.

He reached out to stroke her hair. Kate let out a long breath. "Well…"

The corner of his lip quirked. "Well, I guess I didn't see that coming."

"Literally."

He grinned. Damn, he liked this woman. "Let me take you out on a date," he said, brushing her neck with his lips.

"I just got back from one."

"With the wrong guy," he pointed out.

"And whose fault was that? You're the one who offered to babysit." She tipped her head to the side, giving him more access to her neck. He trailed his mouth along it. "Why did you?" she asked.

"Why did I what?" he murmured against her skin.

She let out a contented sigh. "Why did you let me go on a date with another man? If you wanted me?"

He kissed her lips again. Damn she tasted sweet. "Because I needed to know you're ready."

"What if I'd clicked with him?" she asked.

"Then I would've said my piece. Let you choose between

us." He'd been thinking about it ever since his conversation with Pres. He'd needed to know for sure that she was ready. That it wasn't just him. She'd had so much shit in her life over the past few years. He wasn't about to press her if she wasn't ready.

She cupped his jaw with her hands, her gaze intent as she leaned in to kiss him again. "You said it was a race. I'm not a prize."

"Yes you are."

She shook her head, looking earnest. "I'm not. You said you needed to know that I'm ready. I don't know if I'm ready. I have three kids, a job, a house that always has something falling apart in it. I still cry myself to sleep sometimes. I'm not exactly the kind of woman men fight wars for." She took a deep breath. "And kissing you was hot as hell. But I'm not a prize there either. I haven't had sex for years. And if I'm being truly honest, I'm absolutely petrified about that."

There was a vulnerability to her voice that made him want to protect her from the world. "I'm talking about a date," he told her, kissing her again. Mostly because he couldn't bear not to. "That's it. You and me. Some food. A little wine. See where things go."

Her eyes caught his. And yeah, he knew where he wanted things to go. But he also knew she was new to this. He didn't want to make a mistake. To scare her away.

They'd take this at her pace, no matter how glacial it was. He wasn't going to mess things up now.

"Where would we go?" she asked him.

"Not to the restaurant you just came from." And yeah, there was a bit of petulance in his voice. Not directed at her though. At him.

Because he might be mild-mannered but it didn't mean he liked the thought of her dating another man.

"If we go anywhere around here people will talk."

"We can go to another town. Or you can come to my place. Whatever you feel most comfortable with."

"Do you cook?" she asked him, tipping her head to the side.

"Of course I cook. Do I look like I'm starving?"

She grinned, running her hands up his arms, squeezing the muscles there. "No."

"Then yes. I can cook. I'll cook for you if you want. Any time."

She was smiling now. And fuck if that didn't make him want her more. She leaned in closer, so her lips were feathering against his. "A date sounds good. It's a yes. But right now I need you to kiss me again."

The library was quiet on Monday morning. Which was annoying because it meant Kate was alone with her thoughts and they were chaotic. They had been since her date.

Or more specifically, since after the date. The hours spent laying on the Adirondack in the nighttime air had taken a toll on her mind and body. She couldn't stop thinking about the way he'd felt – so thick and strong beneath her. Or the way he'd kissed her, like she was the sweetest piece of fruit that he was addicted to.

When she'd gotten up the next morning her lips were swollen like they'd been stung. She had to make up some stupid story for the kids that she'd eaten some shellfish she was mildly allergic to.

That hadn't explained the redness on her face as a result of stubble burn from Marley's kisses, but at least she'd been able to hide that with a judicious application of makeup.

But now the door to the library was opening and there he was, walking into the foyer, wearing a pair of old, faded jeans and a navy fire department t-shirt.

As soon as he saw her standing behind the counter his lips curled into a smile that she felt deep inside her body. He strode toward her with an easy gait, as though he hadn't spent hours a few nights ago plundering her mouth with his.

"Hi." Marley leaned on the counter. His arms were tan from all the outdoor working he did. The tiny hairs on his skin were bleached by the sun. She could see the tautness of his tendons beneath his skin.

"Hi." She felt breathless. Like a teenager talking to a crush. "Aren't you supposed to be at work?"

"Waiting on a delivery at the site." He reached out to slide his hand into hers. "I've come into town to grab lunch for everybody ."

"What are you planning to feed them?" she asked him, inclining her head at the shelves. "Books?"

Marley grinned. The little lines at the corners of his eyes did something to her. "Nope. I already put the order in at the diner, so I decided to come visit my favorite librarian while I wait. Plus, you owe me an answer."

Because she hadn't confirmed their date. "I can't get a babysitter," she told him. And yeah, she felt disappointed by that. Shana had a date herself on Friday and was busy on Saturday. "Maybe the next weekend?"

"That's too long." His blue eyes met hers. And of course her gaze dipped to his lips again. Remembering how they made her feel.

How hot they got on that chair together.

"I'll bring dinner over for you on Friday night," he said firmly.

"You'll have to bring dinner for five of us. The kids will be there."

"I know. I'll bring pizza. We can watch a movie."

"And then what? We make out on the couch next to them?" She shook her head, trying to imagine her kids' reactions to that. Addy would probably fall asleep. Ethan would try to ignore them. James would be apoplectic.

No, that wasn't going to work.

"I have some self-control," Marley said mildly. "I'm just bringing food over to spend time with you. As a friend. That's all."

"Is that what you are?" she asked him. "A friend?"

He nodded his head at the office door behind her. "Anybody in there?"

"No." She only used the office when there was somebody else working the counter. Otherwise, it stayed stubbornly empty.

"Good." Without saying another word, he walked around the counter and took her hand in one of his, using the other to push open the office door.

"What are we doing?" she asked him, a smile playing on her lips as he closed the door firmly behind them. Truth be told, just having her hand in his was making her feel a little giddy. He was so warm, so strong.

He still hadn't said anything. Letting go of her hand, he cupped her face with his palm. Then he leaned in, his lips so warm and soft against hers that it made her thighs contract with need.

He wasn't desperate this time. It was sweet and tender. She felt like she was about to swoon.

"Does that feel like a kiss from a friend?" he asked her when he pulled away, his voice thick.

"No," she breathed. And dammit, she wanted him to kiss her again. If she wasn't at work she'd have wanted more. So much more.

She just wasn't sure the Hartson's Creek Memorial Library was ready for that kind of fire.

"Right answer." There was a smirk playing on his lips. "What time shall I come over on Friday?"

Kate let out a long breath. "I'm not sure it's a good idea. The kids… they're not always on their best behavior at the end of the week."

"Nor am I." He winked at her. "And I'm not coming over

to see them on their best behavior. I'm coming over to see them and you. As you are. And that's how I want you to be."

"You're coming over to see the kids?" she asked, because was this man for real? He'd seen Addy throw a fit. He'd seen Ethan get upset over a t-shirt. Damn, he'd even brought James home drunk from a party.

She loved her kids, she really did. But they weren't always the best company.

He leaned down to kiss her jaw. "Kate, your kids are part of the package. I like them. I enjoy their company." He kissed her throat and it sent a shiver down her spine. "I like their mom even more."

Somebody hit the bell on the front counter, the sharp trill making her jump. "I have to go," she told him, reluctance pulling at her chest.

"Then go." He nodded at the door.

"Can you..."

"I won't let them see me. In fact, I'm just gonna climb out of that window," he said, nodding at the glass on the far side of the wall. "Nobody will ever know I was here, I promise."

The bell rang again. Whoever was looking for assistance was getting tetchy. "What are you, fifteen?"

"Nope. I'm a firefighter. I'll see you on Friday, Princess."

"Princess?" She shook her head. Nobody had ever called her that.

"Whatever that woman who threw her hair out of the window was."

"Rapunzel."

"She's a princess, right?"

Kate blinked. Was she? She couldn't remember. Addy loved the movie, though.

And then the bell rang for a third time, and she had to go.

CHAPTER *Fifteen*

"MOMMY, YOU LOOK PRETTY," Addy whispered as Kate poured her a glass of juice on Friday evening. "Are you going on another date tonight?"

"No, I told you, I'm staying home with you tonight."

"But Marley is coming over, isn't he?"

Kate let out a breath. "Yes, he is."

"To babysit us like last time?" Addy took the glass and sipped at the juice. Her face was bright red from running around outside with Ethan. He was still out there, currently climbing on the swing set rather than swinging on it.

"No, he's coming over for dinner," Kate said. "I told you. He's bringing pizza." She got a feeling he was trying to curry favor with her kids. And she liked that – way too much.

"Does he know I don't like pepperoni?" Addy asked.

"Yes. He's bringing a plain cheese for you."

"And then we can watch a movie with him?"

"Of course."

Addy tipped her head to the side. Her brows were scrunched up like she was confused. "But what will you do?" she asked. "While we're being babysat by Marley?"

Kate opened her mouth to explain – *again* – that he was

coming over as a friend, not a babysitter. But maybe she was taking the wrong direction.

"Marley's babysitting me, too," she told Addy.

"Oh, okay." Addy didn't look at all perturbed. "So you get to eat pizza, too?"

Kate tried not to smile. "Yep. All of us will."

"Even James?"

"What about me?" James walked into the kitchen. He had one earbud in. "What am I supposed to be doing?"

"Marley's coming over to babysit us," Addy told him. "He's bringing pizza." She had an orange moustache from her juice. Kate grabbed a tissue and dabbed at her face.

"I didn't know you were going out again," James said, looking at his mom. "I thought you were staying home."

"I am." Kate shook her head. Why was nothing ever easy? She was already on edge at the thought of Marley coming over. Seeing them all in their natural, messy habitat.

"Then why is Marley coming over?"

"Because I invited him for dinner." Okay, so technically he'd invited himself. But James didn't need to know that. "To say thanks for last week."

"He's bringing a special cheese pizza for me," Addy whispered.

"Why is he bringing pizza? He's never come over for dinner." James caught her eye. "Does he want to talk about me? About the party? Am I in more trouble?"

Oh, so that's why he was edgy. "No, honey. Nothing like that. He says you're doing really well. I just thought after having Shana over the other week, we'd have Marley over this week. Like dinner with friends on a Friday."

"Who can we have next week?" Addy asked, her eyes wide. "Oh, can we have Mr. Burrows from next door?"

"Mr. Burrows moved into a home." James rolled his eyes. "Before we left the old house, remember?"

He'd been their neighbor when they lived closer to the

town center. He'd doted on all the kids, buying them Christmas and Easter chocolates, and telling them long stories about the things he got up to when he was a kid.

"Whose home?" Addy asked, looking confused. "Why does that stop him from coming over?"

Kate caught James's eye. He shrugged. "It doesn't matter. He's just old and he likes eating at his own home."

There was a rap at the door. Three short knocks that sent her heart into a tailspin. Before Kate could even try to get it under control, Addy was running to the door. By the time Kate made it into the hallway Marley was half inside, Addy jumping up and down in front of him until he picked her up.

As he held her daughter in his arms, his gaze met hers.

She opened her mouth to tell him to come the rest of the way in when the back door opened and Ethan started shouting for her.

"Mom! I cut my hand. There's blood everywhere."

He sounded a little too excited for an injured child. Kate shot Marley an apologetic glance and ran back into the kitchen.

Ethan was holding his hand out. Sure enough, there was a jagged cut on the meaty part of his palm beneath his thumb. It wasn't exactly pouring with blood, thank the lord. Her stomach turned, because despite being a mom of three, she'd always hated dealing with blood.

Still, she was nothing if not prepared. She swallowed a mouthful of air and grabbed the first aid kit from the cupboard, washed her hands, then guided Ethan to a seat.

"Want me to help?" Marley asked her through the ringing in her ears.

She took Ethan's hand in hers, trying to keep them both steady. "It's okay, I've got it."

"Mom hates blood," Ethan said, sounding happy about that.

"I don't hate it, I just…" She grabbed an antiseptic wipe

from the packet and started to clean the wound. Her stomach only twisted a little. She blew out a breath. "I just don't particularly like it."

"I love it," Ethan said. "It's so cool. Did you know the president's car has spare blood for him in the trunk in case he needs it?"

Okay, now she was feeling woozy. "No, I didn't, sweetheart." Thank god it was a shallow cut. Her hand was starting to shake as she reached for the Band-Aids.

And then a warmer, stronger hand took hers. "Let me do this," Marley said. "I'm qualified, I promise."

"Qualified in what?" Ethan asked. "Are you a medic?"

"No he isn't, dufus. He's not an EMT." James shook his head. "But all the volunteers are first aid trained."

"How about you?" Ethan asked him.

"Not yet." James sounded a little annoyed at that. "But I will be."

Marley grabbed a chair and put it on the other side of Ethan, turning him around in his own chair like her son weighed nothing. Ethan grinned at the sudden spin, and didn't protest a bit as Marley took his hand and finished cleaning him up.

"James, get your mom a glass of water," Marley told him. He looked over at her, frowning when he saw how pale she was. "Take some deep breaths. Let me finish up here, and I'll help you."

"I'm not going to faint," she told him. She was just a little lightheaded.

And then she felt it. The swirl. Her head felt like she was spinning, even though she was sitting down. Nausea rumbled through her stomach as she tried to fight it but then…

"Kate? You okay?"

She opened her mouth to reply but there was nothing. Nothing at all, as her eyes closed and everything in the world disappeared.

"What's happened to my mommy?" Addy wailed as Kate slumped forward on her chair, her head hitting the table with a thump. "Why did she just close her eyes? Is she dead?"

"She's not dead. She just fainted." James glanced at Marley. "What do we do?"

"You take over here." Marley passed Ethan's hand to James and rushed over to Kate. "He just needs a Band-Aid and he's good."

Addy was softly sobbing next to Kate, where she was slumped face down on the table.

"Your mom's fine," he reassured her. "Fainting happens to a lot of people. Let's just give her some space, okay?"

"When will she wake up? What if she doesn't?" Addy's words were peppered with sobs. Her chest was hitching as she spoke.

"She will."

He leaned in close. She was breathing. At least he wasn't lying to her kids. Her lips were parted. Soft.

Focus, man.

There was a pulse undulating in her neck. He debated asking James to help him move her to the floor, but he figured he'd try waking her first.

"Kate?" He kept his voice low because he didn't want to alarm her kids. But there was no response.

This time he shook her arm. "Kate." His voice was louder, commanding.

And by some stroke of luck from the Gods, her eyelids started to flutter.

"There, you're done," James told Ethan. "Now stop being an idiot and making Mom faint."

"I didn't make her faint." Ethan looked mutinous.

"Yes, you did. You told her about the president and then she just went boom."

Kate's eyes fully opened. She still looked as pale as a marble statue. Marley helped her sit up, then ran his fingers over her face to check for any injuries from hitting her face on the table. There were none.

"You fainted. You were out for a minute, tops," he told her quietly. "Everything's okay."

"Mommy. Are you sick?" Addy asked.

Kate ran the tip of her tongue over her lips, still looking woozy. "No sweetie, I'm fine."

"When did you last eat?" Marley asked.

Her brows pinched. She still looked dazed. "I'm not sure. Breakfast, maybe?"

Marley restrained himself from rolling his eyes. No wonder she was so dizzy. "James, do you have any juice?"

"She can have mine!" Addy said excitedly. She ran to get a glass. It was covered in greasy fingerprints, but yes, there was juice there.

He took it from her and gently put it to Kate's lips. She was still quiet. Still confused. "Drink," he said softly. "We need to get some sugar into you."

"How could you forget to eat?" James asked, looking appalled. "I get hangry if I don't eat every two hours."

"I was busy at work." Kate took a breath. Her eyes were focused now. "Sorry. I didn't mean to scare you."

"I thought you were dead," Addy told her, her bottom lip wobbling. "And that we'd have to go live with Grandma." She climbed onto Kate's lap, putting her arms around her mom's neck. "And she always makes me finish my dinner. Even when it's carrots."

James coughed out a laugh.

"It's fine. I'm fine." Kate cupped her face. "I just fainted, that's all. It happens to some people."

"Why?" Addy asked.

Kate's eyes met his. And fuck if he didn't want to kiss her. Surrounded by her kids in this kitchen.

He wanted to be the man who could kiss this woman anywhere. Not just in her office, hidden away.

"Your mom didn't eat enough today," Marley told her. "She probably has low blood sugar. Couple that with the blood and excitement, it made her blood pressure drop."

"What's blood pressure?" Addy asked. The hint of a smile pulled at Kate's lips. As though she was curious to see if Marley could answer a six-year-old's incessant questions without blinking.

"It's the speed your blood pumps around your body," he told Addy. "Your mom's just got a little slow there. The juice will help."

"*My* juice," Addy said proudly. "It's like medicine."

He gave her a grin. "Yeah it is." God, he loved that kid.

"Hey!" Ethan said. "Why's nobody looking at me or asking how I'm doing? I'm the one with an injury here."

This time, Kate was smiling at him. *Welcome to the madhouse,* her eyes were telling his.

Yeah, well, he was pretty psyched to be here.

CHAPTER
Sixteen

AFTER THEY'D ANNIHILATED the pizza, Ethan insisted they make smores.

"You promised," he told Kate. "You said we could do it the next time we had a Friday night dinner."

"What about your hand?" she asked him. "Doesn't it hurt too much to cook?"

"Of course it doesn't. I'm not a baby." He looked at her beseechingly. "Please?"

"Okay," Kate agreed. "But first I want you and Addy to put your pajamas on. It's almost bedtime."

So James had pulled the gas grill out and set it up, looking to Marley for confirmation that he'd done it right, while Kate had gotten the two younger kids cleaned up and in their pajamas.

Now all five of them were sitting outside, their graham crackers and marshmallows and chocolate squares wrapped in foil and sitting on the top of the grill while they waited for them to melt. Kate had put on some music in the kitchen and it was spilling out into the yard. Some old, mellow rock album that made the air around them feel soft and warm.

"I put some wine in the refrigerator earlier," she said to

Marley as they sat on two chairs facing the grill. James was standing over the cooking smores, Ethan next to him, with a pair of tongs in his hands, waiting for the right moment to take the packets off the rack. Addy was on the swing set.

"I have to drive home," he told her. "Remember?"

"You could walk." She shrugged. "Or run."

The corner of his lip lifted. "My car's outside. What would everybody say if it was there overnight?"

She tipped her head to the side, her jaw jutting out. "Let them talk."

"You're just high from the carbs," he said. "You'd hate that."

"Honestly, I don't care. Have a drink with me."

The smile he gave her made every cell in her body start to vibrate.

"Okay then." He stood. "I'll get us both a glass."

After the kids finished their smores, and Kate and Marley had finished half the bottle, James went upstairs to shower. Kate agreed with Addy and Ethan that they could watch a cartoon on their tablets in bed for half an hour if they promised to brush their teeth extra well.

An hour later, all three of them were asleep. She'd been in to check on each one. Addy was curled up like a ball, Ethan's arms were slung out over his head like he was doing some kind of cheer, and James had nodded off with his headphones still on his ears. She managed to gently pull them off, and then plugged his phone into the charger so he'd have some juice in the morning, all without waking him.

It had been a long week. Kate hoped they'd all sleep in late tomorrow.

"Everything okay?" Marley asked as she walked into the kitchen. He was loading the dishwasher. The man knew how to foreplay.

"Everything is perfect. By some miracle they're all asleep."

Her lip curled as she stepped toward him. And there they were, those flutters again.

She was getting used to them whenever he was around.

He closed the dishwasher and reached for her, his palm curling around her hip, his other hand cupping her face. And then his mouth was on hers, like he'd been aching for this all night.

She knew she had.

Kate tipped her head up, feeling the soft, sure pressure of his lips. The gentle slide of his tongue. The way his body felt so hard against hers. In every way. She curled her arms around his neck, pushing herself against him.

This man was undoing her in every way. Her thighs clenched with need for him.

When he pulled back his eyes were hazy. "Outside?" he rasped.

She nodded. "Outside."

This time he grabbed her hand, pulling her through the kitchen door into the cool evening air.

But instead of taking her to their favorite Adirondack chair, he turned her until her back was against the wall. As though he couldn't wait any longer to touch her. To kiss her.

To make her feel like her world was shifting.

Her heart was pounding as he slid his hand down her side, his fingers dipping beneath her t-shirt. "This okay?"

"Yes," she breathed. She craved his touch. And when his hand slid up her stomach, to her bra-clad breasts, she let out a little cry into his mouth.

He rolled her nipple between his thumb and forefinger, forcing a low groan from her lips. She had to steady herself against him, her hand on his waist. The thick ridge of him was pressed against her stomach. She arched against it, wanting to know just how needy he was for her.

Oh yeah, he was super needy. She liked that too much.

His lips slid to her jaw, then her neck. Then he

suddenly dropped to his knees in front of her, both hands on her hips. His face pressed against her t-shirt-covered stomach.

"I just need to kiss your skin," he told her, his voice thick. "Just for a minute."

"Yes please." She stroked his hair. It was so soft against her palm. He nudged the fabric up, his mouth hot against her belly. She wondered if he could see her silvery stretch marks in the moonlight. If he could feel the indentation of them against his mouth.

Maybe she should care. Be worried about that. But it was difficult to think properly about anything when this man was on his knees for her. Worshipping her.

He kissed her hip, her stomach, her belly button. Then he pushed her t-shirt higher up, kissing his way to her ribcage before sliding his lips along the edge of her bra. Every touch of his mouth felt like fire. She scraped her fingernails against his scalp, whispering his name.

And then he closed his mouth around her nipple, through the lace of her bra, and her knees started to buckle.

Pulses of pleasure were making her thighs tight and her body slick. He sucked at her nipple again, his teeth scraping against her. "So fucking beautiful," he muttered.

Despite the cooling night air, her face was heated, her body on fire. He slid his hand down, cupping her, his mouth still hovering where she needed him the most.

"Are you wet?"

"What do you think?" she said, grinning.

He looked up, his eyes catching hers. She jolted at the connection. What was happening here?

"Let me make you come."

"Here?" Her heart hammered against her chest.

He nodded. "Right here. Right now. Let me make you feel good. Please."

"With my clothes on?"

"I wasn't about to strip you naked in your backyard." He lifted a brow. "*Yet*."

"Okay," she breathed. Every cell in her body danced with delight at her answer. And he gave her the sweetest, sexiest grin she was sure she'd ever seen. He stood, his mouth capturing hers again. God, she could never get tired of kissing this man. Feeling his big, hard body against hers was fast becoming her favorite thing.

His fingers flicked open the button of her jeans, then he slid down the zipper, all while still kissing her. *This man has game.* The thought crossed her mind and then she forgot about it all together because his fingers were *there.*

He groaned into her mouth when he felt the slickness of her. The swell at the apex of her thighs. He touched her lightly, murmuring her name against her lips.

"You're perfect," he told her. "Every part of you. Better than I ever imagined."

"You've imagined me?" Her voice was tight. He'd found a rhythm now. One that was making her feel so achy she wasn't sure she'd be the same again.

"All the time."

"What do you do when you imagine me?" she whispered. He slid a finger inside her and it made her eyes roll to the back of her head. His thumb was still circling, his finger sliding.

He pushed a second one in and she gasped against his mouth.

"I touch myself until I come so hard I can't breathe," he told her.

She imagined him doing just that. With those talented fingers wrapped around his cock, his lips parted as he pumped himself until he reached his peak.

The picture in her mind was enough to start a chain reaction in her body. His mouth was on hers, his fingers inside her, his thumb circling and circling until she thought she couldn't take anymore. And then she felt it, the hot pleasure, starting to uncoil in her belly, sparks flying through her nervous system, down to her toes, up to her brain.

"Marley..."

He must have felt her tightening around him. "I've got you. You're so damn beautiful, Kate. Let me see you come."

Her chest hitched, her toes curled. Her body wanted to bend in two but he wouldn't let her. He kept her upright with his mouth, his fingers plundering her body until she wasn't sure she could take any more.

"I'm so close," she whispered.

He pressed his mouth harder against hers, swallowing her cries as she started to convulse around him, her hands holding onto his shoulders for dear life. He curled his fingers, hitting her at a spot she didn't even know she had, prolonging the pleasure as she came apart with his touch.

And when she finally caught her breath, his eyes were staring into hers. He slowly pulled his hand out of her panties and lifted them to his mouth.

And slid them inside.

Oh.

"You taste like heaven," he told her. "Next time it'll be my mouth between your thighs."

"What about you?" she asked, so aware of his hardness pressing against her.

"What about me?"

"Don't you need to..." She slid her hand down between them, cupping him.

He let out a grunt of pleasure at her touch.

"No, not now." He shook his head. "The first time I come with you is going to be inside you."

Her cheeks pinked up at his words. God, she wanted that. So much.

"I'm sorry that I can't take you inside and... well. Sorry that my life is so complicated."

"It's not complicated," he told her. "It's real. And you don't know how much I like that." He kissed her brow and it felt almost more intimate than her lips. "Thank you for letting me have this."

"I can't believe you have to walk home now."

His mouth curled into a smile. "The walk of shame."

"It makes a change having the guy do it."

He cupped her face with his warm palm. "Don't you get it yet? I'd do anything for you. Walking a couple of miles isn't even a blip on the radar."

CHAPTER Seventeen

"MOM!" Ethan's voice cut through her slumber.

No, no, no. Kate didn't want to wake up. Didn't want to leave the dream she was having about Marley. But the shouting continued so she reluctantly opened her eyes, groaning when she saw it was only seven in the morning.

"What is it?" she croaked.

"I don't know. Grandma's here."

His words were like a cold bucket of water being dumped all over her face. "Grandma?" she said back. "She can't be here. She's in Des Moines."

"Nope." Ethan shook his head, running out of the room to watch what was going on outside. "She and Grandpa are climbing out of a taxi," he shouted from the landing.

Kate sat up quickly, the movement making her dizzy. What were her parents doing here? Her mom and stepdad never gave any notice they were coming. "Are they at the door yet?" she yelled at him. "Let them in and tell them I'll be down in five minutes."

"Okay!" Ethan shouted back.

It took her three minutes to pull on her clothes from

yesterday, frantically yanking her fingers through her hair, and run down the stairs.

And sure enough, her mom and stepdad were there in the kitchen. Ethan was talking a mile a minute about something he did in class yesterday.

She'd padded down on bare feet so they couldn't hear her coming. It gave Kate a moment to try to compose herself. Her mom looked her usual glamorous self. Full make up, hair perfectly coiffed despite the early hour. Her designer clothes cut to fit her slender body.

Carlton – her stepdad – was the one who saw her first. "Kate," he said, giving her a big smile. "It's so lovely to see you. Sorry for arriving so early."

She took a deep breath. "What a lovely surprise. How did you get here so early?"

"We were at a thing in DC," her mom told her, fluttering her hand like it was a usual thing, just dropping in on her daughter after. "A fundraiser for Carlton's alma mater. Thought we'd come see you all before we head home."

Washington DC wasn't exactly 'dropping in' distance. "Did you take a taxi the whole way?" she asked them.

"No, silly. We took a helicopter." Her mom said it like it was a normal occurrence.

"You came in a helicopter?" Ethan asked. "That's so cool."

"It messed with my hair," her mom complained. Then she looked at Kate. "Have you been sick? You look pale."

"She fainted last night," Ethan blurted out before Kate could say anything.

A look of concern washed over her mom's face. "What caused it? Have you seen the doctor?"

"She just forgot to eat. That's what Marley said. I cut my hand and it was bleeding and then she knocked out." Ethan held out his bandaged hand. "Look."

"Marley? Do I know her?"

Of course that's what her mom would latch onto. "Why

don't you go get dressed?" Kate said to Ethan. "Wake up Addy and James. Tell them Grandma and Grandpa are here." She looked at Carlton. "Would you like some coffee?"

"I'd kill for it." He gave her a big smile.

"Or am I getting confused with the girl at the library?" her mom continued, as though nobody else had spoken. "Sharon, is it?"

"Shana," Kate murmured, shooing Ethan out of the room. She grabbed the water carafe to fill up the coffee machine. "We only have cereal for breakfast if you're hungry."

"No thank you." Her mom smoothed her skirt. "I'm watching my weight."

"You got any of those Fruit Loops?" Carlton asked.

"In the cupboard next to the sink."

"You know they're bad for you," her mom chided. "You should be watching your weight, too."

Carlton's eyes met Kate's. He rolled them and she smiled.

She liked him, she really did. He was good for her mom.

"So who's Marley then?" her mom asked. She really wasn't letting this go.

"Marley was Dad's friend," James said, walking into the kitchen in his pajamas. "Hi Grandma." He kissed her cheek. "Hi Grandpa."

"Marley's a he?" her mom asked, turning to look at Kate.

"Yes."

"Does he come around here a lot?" she asked.

Dear God, once this woman got an idea in her head she never let it go. Kate could feel her head start to pound.

"He just helps out sometimes. All the firefighters do." Kate slid a pod into the coffee machine. "Did you know James has joined the junior firefighters?"

"You have?" Carlton asked, smiling. "That's great."

"It should be good for his college transcript," Kate added, knowing what a hypocrite she was. But seriously, she needed to move her mom's attention away from Marley.

"If I go," James said.

"Of course you'll go," Carlton said, his spoon of Fruit Loops stopping mid-air. "College days were the happiest days of my life." He looked over at Kate. "If you're worried about the cost…"

"We're not," Kate said quickly. "James has a college fund."

Her stepdad swallowed down a mouthful of cereal. "Come over here," he said to James, patting the empty chair to his right. "Tell me all about the junior firefighters."

Kate passed the first coffee to her mom. Black, no sugar, of course. "Are you sure you don't want something to eat?" she asked her.

"No." Her mom gave her a smile. "I'll eat at lunch. We'll take you out."

"Can we go to the diner?" Ethan asked, running back in.

Her mom wrinkled her nose. "I don't think so, sweetheart. I prefer somewhere with tablecloths."

"How long are they staying?" Shana asked later when Kate called, sounding somewhere between amused and appalled. Kate's mom was taking a nap in the guest room. Carlton and the boys were watching a movie. Addy was playing with LEGOs in the kitchen, so Kate had taken the opportunity to call her friend to vent.

She was already pulling her hair out. Her mom had made at least ten comments about that same hair needing a cut and Kate's skin needing better moisturizer, because 'nobody likes crepey necks'. Not to mention her pointed remarks about how the house needed a man in it to do all the odd jobs. She hadn't asked about Marley again, but it was only a matter of time before she circled back to that conversation.

Her mom was a bloodhound. She could smell a single man from a fifty-mile distance.

"Apparently they're staying until next weekend," Kate said, her voice thin.

"For the whole week? Sheesh, you're gonna need a vacation after that."

"I know." As soon as she'd seen the suitcases in the hallway she'd known this wasn't just a quick stop. According to her mom, Carlton had some business in Charleston later in the week, so they'd decided to make Hartson's Creek their base. Of course Ethan and Addy had been delighted that their grandparents were staying.

James had looked a little more resigned.

"That's not the worst of it," Kate told her friend. "The worst part was that Marley's truck was still outside when they arrived."

"What? Why? Was he there? Oh, my God did you two…" Shana sounded like she was a second away from combusting. "Why wasn't this the first topic of conversation? Parents, schmarents. I need the Marley gossip."

"It's not as exciting as you're thinking." Okay, that wasn't strictly true. But she knew Shana's mind. A truck staying over meant a man staying over. "He had a glass of wine and walked home. Said he'd pick it up this morning."

"So what happened when he did?"

"I messaged him and asked him to sneak it away." And she felt terrible about that. She really did. She owed him an explanation. Sure, she could have introduced him to her mom and he'd see it for himself, but she didn't want to scare him away.

Not more than she already had.

"Why would you tell him to sneak around outside?" Shana asked. "Are you sure you two aren't doing it?"

"We're not doing *that*, no." She took a deep breath. "We might have been kissing a lot, though."

"What kind of kissing?" Shana sounded excited.

"The kind that involves lips."

That made her friend laugh. "Stop this. Come on, I need more."

"There is no more. That's it," Kate told her.

"Damn, that's a shame. Oh, by the way, did I tell you about the guy who messaged me last week?"

"Was this the one you went on a date with last night?"

"Oh god no, a different one. This was a guy from Winterville. Where we went last summer."

"I remember."

"Well, apparently he's a huge Christmas fan. So much so that he likes to dress his little Saint Nick up in a red robe and send pictures."

"His *little Saint Nick*?" Kate repeated. "Is that what I think it is?"

"Oh yeah. Had a little red hat with a white cotton ball too."

"STOP!" Kate was giggling now. Was this what the world was coming to? Dick pics dressed as Santa.

"That's not all," Shana continued. "He started asking me about my Mary Christmas. I've never blocked a guy quicker in my life. How am I going to binge watch Hallmark Christmas movies without thinking of him now? So I need the details, lady. Give me all of them. Unless he likes to dress his pecker up…"

"Eww. He doesn't."

"So you've seen his pecker! Gotcha." Shana sounded ecstatic. "It's big, isn't it? Oh my god, no Little Saint Nick there."

"If you mention Little Saint Nick again I'm hanging up," Kate warned. "And no, I haven't seen it."

"Have you felt it?"

"Possibly." Her cheeks pinked at the memory of him pushing against her. How damn thick he felt. She let out a soft breath.

"Yass! I need to know everything now. I promise not to

interrupt. The last thing I knew he was babysitting while you were dating another guy. What happened?"

The truth was, Kate did need to talk to somebody about this. Keeping it buried was making her feel panicky. She quickly filled her friend in, and by some minor miracle, Shana managed not to interrupt until Kate finished talking.

Then, of course, she exploded.

"Dude! Oh my God. You're kissing. You're making him hard. And he loads the dishwasher. You need to get a ring on it and fast."

"Don't." Kate shook her head. "You sound like my mom again."

"Does she know about Marley?"

"No. But she's found every bit of chipped paint and dented dry wall in the house. She's making a honey-do-list for any man that comes in shouting distance. So I'd prefer she doesn't know about him, thank you very much."

"I bet he'd do it. And if you asked him nicely, he'd probably take his shirt off for you to watch while he did."

Kate let out a low breath, the memory of his chest against her fingers making her body heat up. Damn, he was hard everywhere. All those ripples and dips. She wriggled her fingers.

"Mommy! I think I swallowed a LEGO head!" Addy shouted from the kitchen.

Kate winced because her kids were a walking ER visit right now. "I've got to go."

"Okay, but we need to meet for coffee. Soon."

"I'll see you at church tomorrow. And at the diner after."

"I meant alone. Where people aren't listening." Shana was almost certainly rolling her eyes right now.

"It's a deal. Now I really have to go. I may need to do the Heimlich maneuver on my kid."

"So," Marley's mom said, as he lay on his back on her cool kitchen floor, his hands tightening up the U bend under the sink. "I heard you spent the night at Kate Connelly's last night."

He lifted his head and bashed it on the underside of the cabinet. "Shit." He winced. So that's why she'd called him over to check the pipe for her earring, which she swore must have fallen off when she was washing the dishes.

And with his dad away for the weekend it had come down to him to sort it out.

"I didn't spend the night anywhere but my own bed," he grunted, touching his brow. "Not that it's anybody's business."

"But your truck was at her house all night."

Jesus Christ. Why hadn't he moved to a larger city when he had the chance? He got to his knees, wiping his hands on the towel his mom passed to him. "Are you sure you lost that earring here?"

She gave him a smile. "It might have been in the bathroom sink."

He shook his head. "I'm not unscrewing that U bend too. I'll buy you another damn earring."

"Or it may be in my jewelry box. I probably should have looked there first." Her smile was wider now, and damn if he wasn't smiling too. His mom was terrible at lying. She didn't have a devious bone in her body.

Or at least he hadn't thought she did. Until now.

"There's nothing going on," he told her, because he needed to nip the rumors in the bud before they started. For Kate's sake. "She's a friend. I like her kids. That's it."

His mom caught his eye. Thank God he was a better liar than she was. "Oh. I just wondered…"

"You don't need to wonder. If there's any news I want you to know about my love life, I'll tell you." He lifted a brow. "When I'm ready."

"I've seen how you look at her."

He tipped his head to the side. "How do I look at her?"

"Like you used to look at Ariel when you were a little kid and insisted on watching it every night."

"I never watched *The Little Mermaid*. That was Pres."

"It was?" She frowned. "Well, you two are identical. So it's the same expression, anyway."

Marley started to laugh. "Mom, I don't look at Kate like that. Yes, I like her. She's a good woman who's been dealt a really shitty hand."

"And Paul was your friend."

His chest felt tight. "Yes, he was."

"I guess that means you're watching over her for him."

He took a deep breath. He didn't want to think about that. He couldn't. His need for Kate overrode any misgivings he had about her being his friend's widow.

His mom walked over to the refrigerator. "Want a beer?"

"I'm on call. I'll take a coffee, though."

She nodded and busied herself grabbing a bag of beans and pouring them into the grinder. She made her coffee fresh. He liked that about her. He liked a lot about his mom. She was a kind woman. She loved her family fiercely.

Just as she switched the machine on to brew, his phone vibrated in his pocket. He'd sent Kate a message as he was getting in his truck to drive to his mom's place.

How's the plumbing going? BTW, thank you for moving the truck like a stealth ninja. Today has NOT turned out how I planned at all. – Kate

His mom still had her back to him. He frowned, because he didn't like that she was having a less than stellar day.

. . .

What's up? Need me to come over and bash some heads together? – Marley

A moment later she replied.

Just the usual mayhem. My parents arrived unannounced. Addy thought she'd swallowed a LEGO head. Turned out it was in her glass of juice. I have NO IDEA why she had the thing in her mouth. She's six, not six months. Anyway, I just wanted to say I'm sorry. I'm not ghosting you on purpose. I miss you. – Kate

Fuck, that sent a little dart of pleasure through him. She missed him. Well, he missed the fuck out of her.

I need to see you again. – Marley.

There it was. Laying it on the line. Last night felt… interrupted. The unfinished business between them was piling up.

I need to see you too. But my parents are staying here for a week. I have no idea when I'll get some alone time. – Kate

Well, damn.

• • •

Can you sneak out? I'll take you to the bar and we can underage drink. – Marley

Haha. We'll have to make a date for when they leave. – Kate

Can I at least call you tonight? What time do you go to bed? – Marley

Eleven, usually. – Kate.

I'll call after that. Wear something pretty. – Marley

Why? What are you planning to do to me? – Kate

Wait and see. – Marley

"There you go," his mom said, holding out the cup. "Who were you messaging with?"

"Just Pres." He slid his phone into his back pocket and took the coffee from her. "Thanks."

"No problem." His mom was smiling at him. "By the way, Pres dropped his phone in the driveway this morning. Cassie messaged me to say it was shattered."

Busted. But he didn't care.

Because he was still smiling like a damn loon.

CHAPTER *Eighteen*

IT WAS A QUARTER AFTER ELEVEN. Kate knew because she'd been checking her phone every two minutes. She'd sent Marley a message at 11:01pm to tell him that everybody was asleep. And then, yeah, she'd sent him a photo of her silky pajamas. Short and revealing.

Because this man made her come, then walked away without making any demands. She felt he deserved a treat.

But he still hadn't called and now she was worried she'd gone too far. What if he thought she was being too forward?

The man made you come on his fingers. A photo of you in your pajamas isn't forward. It's practically Victorian.

But then the wail of a siren cut through the nighttime silence. It was so familiar yet the high-pitched sound still made her wince. She got out of bed and opened the curtains to look outside.

She could see the flashing lights in the distance, on the main road out of town. And she knew exactly why he hadn't called. She watched as it disappeared around the corner, and then two minutes later another engine followed.

Was he on the first? The second? What kind of call was it?

Her chest felt almost too tight to breathe. She'd been the

wife of a firefighter for way too long not to know about the dangers he'd face as soon as they arrived at the call out. Her stomach twisted at the thought of him getting hurt.

Or worse.

"Mom?" Ethan's voice called out.

"Yes, honey?" She grabbed her robe and wrapped it around her, padding on her bare feet out into the hallway. When she pushed open his door, Ethan was sitting up in bed. He was wearing one of Paul's FDHC t-shirts Marley had given them.

"Was that a fire engine?"

"I think so." She gave him a soft smile. "Go back to sleep. They've gone past now."

"Is there a fire?" he asked, his eyes wide.

"I don't know. If there is, it isn't nearby. I can't see any flames or smoke." She walked over and stroked his hair. He felt so warm and soft. Sometimes it was hard to believe he was already eight. "Try to get to sleep. We have church in the morning."

"James doesn't have to go to church," he muttered.

"Because James goes to junior firefighters."

"Can I join junior firefighters?" Ethan asked, a hopeful look in his eyes.

The thought of it forced the breath from her lungs. It was bad enough that James had insisted on joining. The thought of Ethan wanting to be part of that world was too much.

What if Addy wanted to join when she was older?

"You're too young. Now go back to sleep." She leaned down to kiss his cheek. "Love you."

"Love you too." He turned on his side and closed his eyes.

If she never heard the wail of a fire engine again it would be too soon.

Because now she had somebody else to worry about, and she wasn't sure her heart could take it.

The buzz of her phone woke her up a couple of hours later. Not that she was in deep sleep. Her mind had been too fitful for that. She reached out for it, frowning when she saw it was almost two am.

No good news ever came at this hour of the night.

It took three tries to unlock her screen. Mostly because she was frowning and for some reason the facial recognition didn't like that. But when she did, she saw she had a message.

Open your window. – Marley

She ran the tip of her tongue over her dry lips. According to the time stamp it had been sent a minute ago. And then her heart started racing as the memories of the sirens from earlier in the night filled her mind. Was he okay?

She practically sprinted to the window.

As soon as she pulled the curtains she could see him standing on the porch below. She opened the window and leaned out.

"What are you doing?" she whispered.

"Hoping you'd be awake." He gave her the most delicious smile. Before she could say anything else, he launched himself at the wall of the house, his hands grasping onto the drainpipe as he climbed up it like some kind of monkey, his movements so sure it took her breath away. In less than thirty seconds he'd reached her window, his fingers curling around the sill, his feet firmly planted on the brackets of the pipe.

"Can I come in?" He didn't even sound breathless.

She stepped back, trying so hard not to watch as his thick

thighs scissored over the opening of the window, his running shoes landing with a thud on her carpet.

And then, as though he was some kind of polite visitor dropping in for dinner, he took his shoes off and lined them up neatly on the floor.

Her mouth dropped open. "Did you really just climb up to my window like some kind of Romeo on acid?"

"Romeo never climbed up to the balcony," Marley pointed out. "He just stayed on the ground like an idiot." He strode up to her, brushing the hair from her face, then kissed her softly. "Hi."

"Hi." She felt herself go stupidly weak at the knees. "Do you know I'm thirty-five years old and nobody's ever climbed through my bedroom window before?"

He grinned and touched his brow with the tip of his fingers. "Happy to be your first, ma'am."

"I heard the sirens earlier." She looked him over almost subconsciously, checking for injuries.

"I figured you did. And I might be a little cocky, but I assumed you might want to know I'm okay."

"I do." She nodded quickly. "What kind of call out was it?"

"Barn fire. Twenty minutes away."

"Anybody hurt?" she asked.

"No." He shook his head. "Had to save some little calves but that was it."

And now she was picturing him carrying baby cows out of a blazing barn. "I was worried," she admitted to him. "I didn't like hearing the sirens."

He cupped her face with his palm. "I know. And I'm sorry. It must bring back bad memories." Their eyes caught.

"Not really." She shook her head. "I was just… I like to know you're safe."

He took her hands in his. Pressed them against his face.

Then moved them down to his chest, his side, his hips. "I'm okay," he promised. "No broken bones, no bruises. Just a burned out barn and some homeless baby cows. That's all that happened."

This time. She didn't say it, but it was always there. She didn't know any relative of a first responder who didn't think that way.

"Have *you* ever climbed into a girl's room?" she asked him, suddenly curious and wanting to change the subject. She was so aware of how big he felt standing in front of her. She'd designed the room around her own tastes. It was dainty. Pretty. Flowers and soft carpets and more scatter cushions than most men could bear to see.

His lip quirked. "Nope. It's my first time, too. Be gentle with me."

"It's like we're both going through our teen years together. If it helps, my parents are here to make it even more authentic."

He laughed. "We'd better be quiet then."

Her mouth dropped open. "We're not doing *that.*" Though being in his arms was making her body heat up.

"I know." He winked. "I told you before. The first time isn't going to be rushed. But teenagers make out, right?"

"Right."

He brushed his lips against hers. "I very much want to make out with you, Kate."

Oh.

"By the way, I like this." He ran his finger over her silky pajama top. It was camisole style, in black. "And these." He cupped her behind, his palm against the matching shorts.

"I put them on for our video call."

His eyes were dark as they caught hers. "I'd be annoyed I missed it, but seeing you in the flesh is so much better." He kissed her throat.

Her nipples hardened against the silky fabric. All this man

had to do was press his mouth against her skin and she felt like she was about to combust.

"Come to bed," she told him, sliding her hands into his.

"I thought we weren't doing that."

"I prefer to make out horizontally." She smiled because damn, she liked this man. Liked having him around.

Even if they had to be sneaky.

She glanced at his clothes. "Take off your jeans."

"Kate…"

"I just want you to be comfortable." And she didn't want the denim between them. If they were going to be making out – and she really wanted them to – he could at least be half undressed. Like her.

"It's only fair," he conceded, glancing at her bare legs. Then he was unfastening the top button of his jeans and sliding them down. She swallowed hard as she took in the hard ridge of him pressing against his black shorts. Next came his t-shirt. He pulled it over his head and threw it to the side, and she couldn't help but take a long, delightful look at the ridge of muscles that led to the waistband of his shorts.

Taking his hand in hers, she brought him over to her bed, pulling back the covers. Lying down on the mattress, she pulled him on top of her. Needing to feel his weight, his strength.

His thighs pressed against the outside of hers.

Before she could tell him how good he felt, he slid his hand down her side, pushing his fingers up beneath the silky camisole. His lips were soft as he started kissing her. Undemanding. Almost lazy.

It still set her on fire, though. She could feel herself getting slick between her legs.

"Do you know how much I've thought about you today?" he asked her. Then he lifted her camisole up, over her head, and moved his mouth down at an aggravatingly slow pace.

Kissing her shoulder, the dip in her throat where it met her chest, then the tops of her needy breasts.

"I thought we were making out with clothes on," she said, the words fizzling out on her tongue as he captured her breast in his mouth.

It felt different than yesterday. Maybe because yesterday she'd been standing up, her back against a wall. Today they were in bed, horizontal. With his hard body pressed against hers. He was taking his time, his tongue swirling against her nipple, his teeth scraping so softly it made her back arch.

Then he moved to her other breast. Teasing her over again. She tangled her fingers in his soft hair, scraping her nails against his scalp.

"Have I told you how much I like it when you do that?" he asked her, looking up.

"No."

"I do. I'm going to need you to do that the first time I'm inside you.

The first time. The thought of it made her shiver.

Truth was, she needed him inside her *now*. She was so slick and swollen. It felt like he was the only one who could soothe the ache that seemed to engulf her. She wrapped her legs around his waist and rolled her hips against him. Needing the connection, the friction.

Everything.

"Fuck." He tried to pull his hips away, but she tightened her thighs around him. "Kate, I'm not going to last long if you keep doing that."

"I know." She smiled at him. "You made me feel so good yesterday. Let me do that for you." She slid her hand between their bodies, feeling the thickness of him. He groaned again when she circled her fingers around him.

"Where do you want to be?" she whispered. "In my hands, my mouth? Between my legs?" She dragged her fingers up him, then down again, loving the way he looked, almost dazed as their gazes connected.

"Between your legs," he rasped. "I want you to come with me."

"Then it will be two one."

"I'm not counting." He tipped her face up, his mouth harder against hers now. The gentleness was gone. She could feel the pull of his need as his tongue plundered her mouth.

She hooked her legs around him, lost in his mouth, in his kiss. In the teasingly perfect rhythm of his hips as his body moved against hers.

There were two layers between them. His shorts and hers. And it was too much. She needed more.

She started to tug his shorts down his hips.

"What are you doing?"

"Don't you want to feel the silk against you?" she asked innocently.

"Christ, you're killing me here, woman."

And she was loving it. Loving the way he looked like his sanity was hanging on by a thread as they kissed and moved and ground against each other. Like teenagers, but without the angst. Just the knowledge that they were two adults who really, *really* liked each other.

Could it actually be that easy? She pushed the thought away because he was kissing her breasts again, dragging his tongue against her in a way that made every part of her body clench with pleasure. Her breath was starting to hitch, her heart rate speeding out of control.

He made her feel so good. So wanted. She was getting addicted to him.

He helped her get his shorts off, and she was so aware that he was naked against her. He rocked his hips and groaned.

"Fuck, you feel so good. You're so wet." He kissed her again and she smiled against his mouth.

"I know. That's how you make me. I've been thinking about you all day, too."

That made him groan harder. She slid her hands down his back, feeling the tightness of his ass as he flexed against her.

Then she dug her fingers into his warm flesh.

"Do that again and I'm coming in two seconds," he told her.

"Is that a threat or a promise?"

He groaned. She wasn't sure whether it was because he felt so good or because she was teasing him. Maybe both.

It made her heart feel tight.

"Are you close?" he asked her, his voice urgent.

"So close." And she didn't want it to end. This warm, delightful pull. The way he knew exactly how to grind himself against her until her body was coiled like the tightest of springs.

"Kiss me," she whispered. "Kiss me while I come."

This time he was soft. His warm lips brushed against hers, his movements slowing but somehow getting deeper. She was clenching for him, desperate to feel him inside her.

"Marley?"

"Baby."

"Please let me feel you."

"What?" There was that dazed look again.

"Just for a minute. Skin on skin."

His lips parted as he looked at her. Like a man who couldn't refuse her anything, he pulled away from her, his fingers warm as they tugged at the silky waistband of her shorts.

"Are you sure?"

"Yes."

"Protection?"

"Covered." She ran her tongue over her lip. "Bad periods. I have an IUD."

He blew out a mouthful of air. Like he was trying to regain some control. "I'm clean. Had a physical two months ago."

"No sex since?"

He rolled his eyes. "Only with myself."

She giggled. *Don't let me fall in love with you.*

Where did that thought come from? She wasn't sure, but it made her heart hurt again, and she didn't want to feel that. She wanted him. There.

And a moment later, he was back between her thighs, kissing her softly again, his thick hardness sliding against the neediest part of her. It was all she could do not to hitch her hips and have him slide inside her.

She wanted to. So much.

But then he shifted his body and it was like he'd flipped the pleasure switch deep inside her. The swollen head of him was *right there*. Her eyes widened, her mouth slack, and her whole body started to convulse.

"I need you inside me," she whispered. "I need…"

His mouth swallowed her words as he trailed his fingers down, sliding them between her legs and inside her right as her orgasm hit. She tipped her head back, her breath stilted as her legs tightened around his hips. He curled his fingers, finding the spot she never knew she had, intensifying her orgasm until she wasn't sure she remembered her own name.

He did, though. He was groaning it as he suddenly pulled away, his free hand clasped around himself, as he started to come in thick ribbons, the essence of him coating her stomach.

And if she thought he was glorious naked, he was even more impressive in the throes of pleasure. His jaw was tight, almost mean. His chest glistened in the half-light of her bedside lamp, his stomach muscles tight as he emptied himself onto her.

"Fuck," he rasped again, slowly pulling his fingers out of her. And yes, he licked them again, before almost collapsing on top of her, his forearms the only barrier between her and suffocation-by-Marley.

"I thought we said we were just going to make out," he said, kissing her tenderly. She couldn't stop smiling.

She never wanted to.

"Yeah, well apparently we're adults," she murmured against his lips. "And our bodies want what our bodies want."

"My body wants you," he told her softly. "All the time."

CHAPTER Nineteen

KATE WAS LAYING in his arms, her head resting on his chest. She wasn't asleep yet, but he could feel the rhythm of her breaths getting steady.

"I should go," he murmured, stroking her silky hair. She had her pajamas back on. He'd insisted, after he'd found a washcloth in her ensuite to clean her up. Mostly because apparently his body still wanted every part of her, even though he'd just dry humped himself against her to heaven.

And yeah, he liked stroking her back with the silk over her skin. It felt good.

"Stay for a little while," she said against his chest. He could feel the warmth of her breath. "You feel too good."

"So do you."

More than good. She was perfect. And yeah, coming on her stomach wasn't how he'd planned their first time. But somehow it had felt better. More real.

He wasn't sure he could feel closer to her if he'd been inside her.

"Where's your car?" she asked him, her finger drawing a lazy circle on his chest.

"Left it at home."

"You walked over?"

He kissed the top of her head. "I mostly ran. I didn't want to leave my truck outside your house two nights in a row."

"Why not?" She lifted her head to look at him.

"People noticed last night. My mom called me over to ask about it."

"Seriously?" Her voice lifted.

"It's okay," he said, kissing her head again. "I put her off the scent."

"You did? That easily?"

He cupped her face, tilting it so their mouths met. "Yeah. She asked. I told her there was nothing going on. It was fine."

"I wish my mom was that easy to put off."

"Does she suspect there's something going on between us?" He didn't feel bad about that. Not really.

Kate shook her head. "I don't think so. Not yet. But she did seem interested that a guy was here for dinner."

"A guy who made you come."

She rolled her eyes at him, but there was no disguising the smile on her face. "Shut up."

"Just saying. She wouldn't be wrong."

"She only wants me to find somebody because she thinks the house is falling apart."

His brows pulled together. "What's falling apart? Want me to take a look at it?"

"No. That's not why you're here. And anyway, don't you think her suspicions might become founded if you start fixing the plumbing in the kitchen in your underwear and nothing else?"

"I wasn't suggesting I do it now," he told her. "But I'm a construction worker. I know my way around a house. And plumbing."

She lifted her head to kiss his rough jaw. "Thank you, but no."

"One of these days you're gonna let me help you."

"You already help me. Way too much."

She had no idea what too much was. Truth was, he wanted to do everything for her. Keep her and the kids safe.

There was a creak on the floorboard outside the room and he froze. Then a door opened and the sound of heavy feet padded along.

"James," Kate whispered. "He drank way too much soda last night. I'm guessing it just caught up with him."

"Will he come in here?"

She shook her head. "No. He's probably only half awake. He'll head straight back to sleep."

"I'll go as soon as he does," he promised, kissing the top of her hair.

"No, stay."

Marley blinked. That was the last thing he expected her to say. And yet it made his chest feel tighter than a vise grip.

"Until morning?" he asked. "Because we're gonna have some explaining to do if your kids see me."

She ran her tongue over her bottom lip. "Until the sun rises. Let me sleep in your arms."

Fuck, he liked the way she needed him. Made him feel about ten feet tall. The fact was, he'd do anything for this woman. Sleep, stay awake, fight a fucking dragon.

Lie to the people he loved.

"Okay. Set your alarm."

She grabbed her phone and pressed on the screen before putting it back on the table next to the bed. "Five," she told him. "I'm sorry."

He'd take what he could. And he knew this was all she had to give right now.

"Come here," he said softly, wrapping his arms around her. Within minutes, they were both asleep.

"Your mom has one of her headaches," Carlton said to Kate as he walked into the kitchen the next morning. Her stepfather was wearing a pair of tailored jeans and a crisp checked shirt which was tucked neatly into his waistband. His belt was tight across his slim hips. "I told her to stay in bed. I'm pretty sure she'll be out of commission for the day." He looked apologetic.

Kate flashed him a smile. She had a headache herself, but she was doing her best to ignore it. It was self-inflicted, anyway. They'd only gotten a couple of hours' sleep before her phone had woken them up, and Marley had gotten dressed and climbed out of the damn window again, even though she'd begged him to tiptoe down the stairs and out of the front door.

He'd messaged her about thirty minutes later when he finally made it home.

And then, of course, she hadn't been able to get back to sleep. Instead, she'd laid staring at the ceiling, her mind full of thoughts that felt like insects buzzing inside her skull.

She shouldn't have asked him to stay and sleep with her. In a strange way it felt more intimate than anything else they'd done last night. Maybe it was the fact she'd slept better in those two hours than she had in months, years even. A deep, almost drugged kind of rest that made her whole body relax against him.

It felt too good. Too right. And as soon as he was gone a blanket of guilt came down over her.

He had been Paul's friend for years before he died. It felt like a betrayal being in his arms. And okay, technically the bed wasn't the one she'd shared with Paul, but it was the one she shared with his memory every night.

His photograph was in a frame on her dresser, after all.

That's when the tears had started flowing. Because she didn't know what she was doing. The relief of Marley being okay after hearing the sirens had overwhelmed her. The need to connect with him was like her need to inhale.

She felt safer in his arms than she had in a long, long time, which was completely stupid.

Because her heart was at more risk than ever.

"You okay, Kate?"

Carlton's voice brought her out of her thoughts. She attempted a smile. "I'm fine. Does Mom need some painkillers?"

"No. I just gave her two." He grabbed two mugs from the cupboard and started up the coffee machine. And this was why she loved her stepfather. He might be rich, but he was a regular caffeine addict, just like her. "So I was thinking I might go watch James at his training today. At the fire station."

"Oh. You don't want to come to church with us?" It was a Sunday morning, after all.

He gave a little chuckle. "Not really. And James said a lot of the other trainees have their parents come watch. I know I'm not his parent but…"

"You're his grandparent," she said firmly.

"I know." He gave her a warm smile. She could still remember the day she introduced Paul and James to her mom and Carlton. James had been a toddler then. As intrepid as he was now. He'd climbed straight into Carlton's lap and her stepfather had pretty much fallen in love with him.

Her mom, however, had been more reticent.

"It's a lot to take on another woman's child," she'd told Kate. "You're young. Too young. Are you sure you know what you're doing?"

"He's also my child," Kate had said firmly. Because she'd fallen in love with James as much as she'd fallen for Paul. "I'm adopting him after the wedding." And she had. He was her son. Had been since the day they'd walked out of the courthouse.

Sometimes he felt like more than that. Because he'd found her when she needed him the most.

"How come the trainees get to skip church, anyway? Doesn't the pastor have something to say about that?" Carlton asked her.

Kate smiled. "His house caught fire about fifteen years ago. He won't hear a word against the department after that. He says that as long as they are pure in their hearts he believes God knows they need to train on Sundays."

Paul and Reverend Maitland had had a good relationship. God, why was she thinking about the past so much?

"Morning," Ethan said, walking into the kitchen. "Hey Grandpa."

Carlton ruffled his hair. "Hey kiddo."

"Can I sit next to you at church?" he asked. Carlton's eyes met Kate's.

"Ah, I was planning to go watch James at his junior firefighter training," Carlton told him.

Ethan pouted. "That's not fair." He looked at Kate. "Can I go with Grandpa to watch him too?"

Carlton gave her an 'I don't mind' kind of shrug.

Truth be told, she didn't have the energy to fight with him this morning. "Okay. If you promise to be good for Grandpa you can go with him."

"Where's Ethan going with Grandpa?" Addy asked, walking in. Her sweet face was still creased from where she'd slept on her pillow, and her hair was sticking to her cheeks. Kate brushed it away, kissing the top of her daughter's head.

"We're going to watch James at the fire station." Ethan said it firmly, like he was still worried Kate would change her mind.

"I want to go with them," Addy said. "Mommy, can I go?"

"I…"

"It's fine by me." Carlton passed her a coffee. She took it gratefully.

"And you'll come too, Mommy, right?" Addy asked.

"Come where?" James said. He was wearing a pair of sweatpants and his fire department t-shirt. His hair was a mess.

"Bend your head," Kate told him, raking her fingers in an attempt to tame his curls. "You should have showered."

"I'm showering after training," James said patiently. "Why would I do it before?"

Teen logic was strong. She had no answer for that.

"We're coming to watch you at the fire station," Addy said excitedly. "All of us."

A half smile pulled at James's lips. "All of you?"

"Me, Ethan, Grandpa, Grandma, and Mommy," Addy chanted.

"Not Grandma. She's staying in bed," Kate said hurriedly.

"But the rest of you are?" James asked, his lips curling.

Kate let out a breath. "Yes," she said firmly. "As long as that's okay with you."

His warm eyes met hers. His cheeks were flushed, as though he was secretly pleased but way too cool to show much emotion.

"Yeah, that's okay with me." He shrugged. "As long as we still get to go to the diner afterward."

Of course it was never going to be as easy as just walking back into the fire station after all this time. She hadn't anticipated the number of hugs she'd get, or the murmurs about how much they still missed Paul.

And she hadn't realized they'd put his photograph up on the wall of the training yard, along with a plaque that made her chest ache.

Paul Connelly. Father, husband, firefighter. Fallen in the line of duty.

There were flowers beneath it. Looking at the photo made her eyes start to tear up.

"Mommy, that's my daddy," Addy said, pulling at her hand. "Look, he's in his uniform."

"That's right, honey." She nodded, finding it hard to breathe.

"James never said they had Dad's photo here," Ethan said, looking around. "Hey, is this where he…"

Kate's eyes met Carlton's. They both knew what Ethan was going to ask. And she wasn't prepared to answer it, not here.

Because yes, her husband had died right where they were standing. Collapsed to the ground.

She felt sick thinking about it.

"Come on, kids, let's find somewhere to sit," Carlton boomed, in an attempt to get their attention away from the memorial. There were some benches on the far end of the gray concrete yard. Carlton walked them over there, while she stood staring at the photograph.

A tear slowly rolled down her face.

How would he feel if he knew what she'd been doing with Marley? She never, ever in her life imagined she'd have to find love again. She thought she and Paul would be together until they were old.

She never thought she'd have to do this alone.

Lifting a hand to wipe away the tear, she jumped as the door to the main station opened. Marley walked out, his brows dipping when he saw her.

And then he saw what she was looking at.

"Kate." His voice was thick.

She couldn't catch her breath. Her chest felt tight. "What are you doing here? Aren't you doing the warm up?"

"I had some paperwork to finish up. Tayto's leading the run, then I'll do the training." He glanced at the photograph of Paul. "You okay?"

She nodded. "Yes. I didn't realize you had this..." She could barely speak. The guilt was killing her.

"You were invited to the unveiling ceremony." His gaze didn't waver from hers.

Kate had been invited to a lot of things. And she'd been a mess back then. She could barely remember the first year after he died.

"Marley!" Addy came running over to where they were standing, stopping in front of him and holding her arms up. He swung her up, and she started to giggle.

"Hey kiddo. You okay?"

"We've come to watch James train," Addy said to Marley. "Can I stay with you and watch? Ethan and my grandpa are talking about baseball. It's boring."

"Marley is leading the training," Kate told her. "You can sit with me."

"But I want to stay with Marley." Addy pouted.

He put her down gently on the ground. "I'll tell you what, you can be my assistant. But you have to wear a uniform and do exactly what I tell you to."

"Do I get to wear a hat?" she asked excitedly.

"You sure do." He nodded, his voice serious.

"Yes." Addy bumped her fist into the air, delighted at that.

"Are you sure you're okay with this?" Kate asked him. "I know you're busy."

"It's all good." He looked solemnly at Addy. "I could use some help. Maybe they'll listen to you more than they listen to me."

"I'll be super loud," Addy promised.

Kate leaned down to brush Addy's hair out of her face. "Be good and do everything Marley tells you," she instructed her. "If she gets in the way, bring her over to me."

"It'll be fine, Kate." Marley took Addy's hand. And her heart did a little dance at the size difference between them. Addy skipped along as he walked her over to the equipment shed, and Kate turned to walk back to where Ethan and Carlton were sitting.

"Sorry," Carlton said as she reached them. "Addy ran over before I could stop her."

Kate took a seat next to him. "She's helping with the training."

"She's not helping," Ethan said. "I bet she just wanted to hang around Marley. She's such a baby."

"Don't let her hear you calling her that," Kate said. She couldn't deal with their arguments today.

It was only two minutes before the volunteers and junior firefighters arrived, led by a sweating Tayto who jogged them into the center of the training yard. A few other onlookers had joined Kate, Addy, and Carlton on the benches, watching as the volunteers got into formation.

James grinned over at her and she realized just how tall he was getting. He was a good few inches taller than any of the other juniors. And he looked so much like his dad it made her heart hurt. She waved back.

"Your mom said you didn't want him joining the juniors," Carlton murmured as they were put into teams.

Kate sighed. "I still don't, really. Paul's dream was always for him to go to college."

"He can do both, can't he?" Carlton asked.

She swallowed. "He can. But I'm scared he's going to sign up to be a firefighter straight out of high school."

Their eyes met. Carlton pressed his lips together. "Would that be so bad?"

Yes, it would.

One of the men she loved had his photograph on the wall. She couldn't bear for there to be two of them.

James' team walked over to the tower and Addy ran over to him, hugging his legs. He ruffled her hair then peeled her off them, before Marley lifted her up onto his shoulders so she could be at face height with them all.

"Who's that guy?" Carlton asked, watching as Addy giggled at being up so high.

"Marley Hartson," Kate said softly. Addy had an oversize helmet on, and every time she moved her head it looked like it might fall off.

"One of Paul's friends?"

"Yes." She couldn't even look at her stepfather. Because then he might figure it out. That she was falling for the man Paul called a friend.

That she was betraying her late husband in more than one way. And her heart felt like it was cracking.

Addy started tickling Marley's face. He lifted her easily off his shoulders and started swinging her around to the front, growling at her in a way that made her laugh even more.

"He seems good with her," Carlton said.

"He's good with me, too," Ethan told him. "He babysits for us sometimes. When mom goes out on dates."

"You go on dates?" Carlton asked. And though there was no judgement in his voice, she felt it anyway.

"I went on one. That's it."

"And then Marley came over the other night and we made smores," Ethan said. "Do you like smores, Grandpa?"

"I love them." He was still looking at Kate like he was trying to work it all out.

"We should make some tonight," Ethan said, excitement pulling at his voice. "I'm great at them. Mom lets me use the grill." He looked at her.

"I don't know. You have school tomorrow."

"Please, Mom?"

Addy was shouting at the trainees. She was still in Marley's arms, resting easily on his side as she called up at the juniors on the first deck of the tower. He turned to whisper something to her and she nodded happily.

Then he turned his head to look over at Kate.

There was an intensity to his stare that made every part of

her feel tight. As she watched him hold her daughter in his arms.

When she inhaled this time, it felt like there was a cheese grater in her chest.

"Mommy, look at me," Addy shouted. "I'm a firefighter."

All the surrounding people laughed. And Kate tried so hard to as well. She at least forced a smile onto her face.

But then she looked over at the far side of the yard. Where Paul's photograph was watching them all.

I'm sorry. Please forgive me.

Because right now, she couldn't forgive herself.

CHAPTER Twenty

"SO, what is this adorable photograph all about?" his mom asked, turning her phone so that Marley and his brothers – and their dad – could see it.

It was later that day and his mom had insisted he come over for a late lunch. When he'd arrived – after taking a shower post training – Pres and his wife Cassie were already there, along with their three children. Hendrix was there, too. Their youngest brother was five years younger than Pres and Marley and had moved back home for the summer. He was currently working on their uncle and aunt's farm.

"What is it?" Pres asked, leaning in. Then he lifted a brow. "Oh, you're fucked," he told Marley, a huge grin pulling at his lips.

Marley took a look at his mom's phone screen. It was a picture of him holding Addy. Addy was leaning back, one hand holding the oversized helmet he'd given her, the other resting on his chest. She was laughing uproariously, her eyes on his face as he grinned back at her.

"She came to watch her brother's training. She wanted to help me." He shrugged.

"And was her mom there, too?" his own mom asked.

"Yeah, was Kate there?" Pres asked, looking amused.

"Kate Connelly?" Cassie asked. "Oh, she's lovely."

Christ, they were ganging up on him now. "James' family was there, yeah."

And to be honest, he was still a little confused by the whole thing. Maybe it was the way he'd caught Kate crying when she saw Paul's photograph on the outside wall.

It had felt like a kick to the gut. Which was wrong, he knew that. She was entitled to feel sad about her dead husband, for god's sake.

But seeing her standing there. Where it happened. In the place he'd seen his friend fall to the ground and die within minutes. While he desperately tried to save him. As he cried over his body.

It had felt like his heart was being squeezed by an iron fist.

Thank God for Addy. He was pretty much in love with that kid. The same way he felt about all of Kate's kids.

The same way he felt about their mom.

"You should invite them over next Sunday," his mom said. "I'd love to cook dinner for them. They're such lovely kids."

He looked at Pres for help. But his twin was just grinning at him.

"I'm busy next week," Marley said.

"Doing what?" Hendrix asked. "Watching paint dry?"

"It's more interesting than watching you," Marley said.

Hendrix lifted a brow. Then he launched himself at his brother, knocking him off the chair.

His brother liked to play fight. Probably because it was the first time in his life that Hendrix was the same size as Pres and Marley. And all those hours on the farm were making him strong, so it was hard to fight him off.

Growing up, they had every advantage over him and they weren't afraid to use it.

But now he had surprise on his side. And for a moment

Marley lay beneath him, wounded, while his mom shouted out admonishments and Pres just laughed loudly.

"Fuck's sake," Marley muttered. Because he wasn't in the mood for this. He tried to push Hendrix off him, but damn, the kid was like a ten ton weight.

"Get off me, you ass," Marley grunted.

"Not until you admit you and Kate Connelly are a thing," Hendrix taunted.

"I'm not admitting jack to you." Marley grabbed his brother by his upper arms, then lifted his legs in an attempt to throw him off, but Hendrix pushed down on him, laughing.

"Admit it, then I'll let you go," Hendrix panted.

"Fuck you," Marley growled.

"Let him go," their dad said firmly. "What are you all, five?"

"I'm just trying to teach him not to tell lies, Dad," Hendrix called out, barely breathless. "Like you taught me."

"I didn't teach you by fighting," their dad muttered.

With a low grunt, Marley managed to dislodge his brother, twisting his body around so Hendrix's back was against the floor and Marley was above him, his knees on his thighs, his hands holding down his arms.

Hendrix started to laugh. "Fuck, you're pissed at me. I'm sorry."

Marley let him go, slowly moving off him.

"It's okay. Ignore me. I'm just tired," he muttered. He let Hendrix get up, and the two of them walked back to the patio table where the rest of the family were sitting, as though they weren't grown men who'd just rolled around fighting in the grass.

His mom lifted a brow. "Are you three going to still be fighting when you're drawing your pensions?" she asked them.

"I didn't do anything," Pres pointed out. "I'm your good boy, Mommy."

Everybody started laughing. And Hendrix slapped his back. Marley punched his arm in return, because that's how they showed love.

Hey, how's it going? I just finished at the station and am heading over to my parent's for lunch. I miss you. And your kisses. – Marley

His message had arrived two hours ago. And she hadn't answered it. She'd made every excuse to herself. She was busy with the kids. She needed to be alone when she replied. She'd do it tonight.

But the truth was, she was scared. She felt guilty and sick.

The second message arrived twenty minutes ago.

Did you get back okay from the station? I'm a bit worried about you. – Marley

And now her phone was ringing. His name was on the screen. "Aren't you gonna get that?" Carlton asked, looking up from his newspaper.

Her chest felt so tight. "Yes," she breathed. "I think I'll take it upstairs."

"Sure. I'm gonna head out to play with the kids."

Addy and Ethan were in the yard. James was in his room. Kate tiptoed to her own and slid her finger across the screen.

"Hello?" she said softly.

"Hey."

The sound of his voice made her feel a little weak. "Hi."

"You okay? I sent you a couple of messages."

"I…" She had no idea what to say. And then she heard somebody shouting, echoing through the line.

"Are you with your family?" she asked him.

"Yeah. Just got jumped by my brother, the asshole."

"Do they know you're talking to me?" Her voice lifted. The thought of them knowing, of them judging…

"No." His voice was low. "But would it be a problem if they did?"

She let out a long breath. "Yes, it would."

He didn't reply for a moment. And she was trying to think of something to say to fill in the gap. To explain that she couldn't think straight. That she hadn't been able to since she saw Paul's photograph on the wall of the fire house.

That every part of her hurt right now.

"Why?" he asked. "Are you ashamed of me?"

His question felt so pointed it was a knife to her heart. "No," she whispered. "I'm ashamed of me."

That was the truth of it. A tear rolled down her cheek.

She could hear Marley's sharp intake of breath. "Well at least you're honest," he said.

"I'm sorry. I just…" She tried to get her breathing under control. "Seeing Paul's photograph. It made me upset. Like it was a sign."

"A sign?"

"Maybe we're taking this too fast," she told him. "Maybe we shouldn't have done what we did last night."

"You regret it?" There was hurt in his voice. And she hated it.

She hated herself more.

"I don't know." There were more tears. She wiped them away angrily. "I'm sorry. I'm a mess."

"Let me come over." His voice was gentle. "We can talk."

"No!" The thought of it made her panic. "You can't come over. Not during the daytime."

There was a pause again. Then he cleared his throat.

"Kate, I hate hearing you so upset. Let me help you."

But he couldn't. She felt like she was spiraling. She looked at her bed, remembering what they did in it last night. How he made her feel so good in his arms. How he took care of her.

She didn't deserve it. She didn't deserve him.

"I have to go," she told him, because she couldn't let him hear her break down.

"Don't go. Not like this. Kate…"

But she hung up. And turned her phone off, right as the sobs started wracking her body.

She'd messed everything up. She felt so torn.

She let herself cry for five long minutes, then went back downstairs because she was a mom, and she had responsibilities.

"Everything okay?" her mom asked as Kate walked into the kitchen. She was finally up, sitting at the kitchen table, sipping some water. And she actually did look ill. Her face was pale and free of cosmetics, her hair swept back.

Kate opened her mouth to say everything was fine, the way she always did.

But instead a sob escaped her lips. Because no, everything wasn't fine. It hadn't been fine for years. She'd tried so hard, tried to be strong.

And moments ago she'd messed things up with the one man who'd made her feel alive again.

Kate's mom stood up and wrapped her arms around her. "Oh honey, you poor thing. Carlton told me you'd been upset at the fire station." She stroked Kate's head, like she used to when she was little.

Her mom smelled of her childhood. Like daisies. God, it made her feel worse.

"Carlton told me about Paul's photograph."

Kate sobbed again. Because seeing his photograph on the fire station wall felt like an ending. He'd never change. He'd always be that man smiling out from the wall. And she was moving on. Or at least she'd thought she was last night.

And now? She just felt sick.

"Did you feel guilty about Dad?" Kate whispered. "When you married Carlton?"

Her mom stroked Kate's hair. "Of course I did. But I knew he would have wanted me to move on. I was young, like you. But I wasn't brave like you are."

"I'm not brave."

"Yes, you are," her mom said softly. "You have three kids. You have a job. You were already in college when I lost your dad. I didn't have to be strong for anybody. I just wallowed."

"I've been wallowing, too."

"No." Her mom's voice was sure. "I've been watching you. I've never seen anybody as strong as you are. You've been there for the kids, been there for everybody. Except yourself." She cupped Kate's wet cheeks with her hands. "Is this about the date you went on?"

"Carlton told you about that?"

Her mom nodded.

"It's not about the date," Kate told her. "That was no good."

"But you tried. And I'm so proud of you."

"You shouldn't be," Kate said honestly. "I'm an idiot. I'm weak. I should be able to do this alone without crying. I just need to be strong."

"You think strength is about doing everything alone?" her mom asked, frowning. "That's not strength. That's trauma. And it's understandable, honey. You've been through so much. Losing Daddy. Losing Paul..."

And now she felt like she was losing Marley before they'd even begun. No, not losing him, pushing him away. Which was so much worse. Because she was the one shutting the door on him.

"I think I've found somebody," she told her mom. "But I'm messing it all up."

"You have?" Her mom's face softened. "That's wonderful."

"That I've messed it up?" Kate frowned.

"No, that you're opening yourself up again. That's all I want for you. To know that there's a future out there. Happiness. And new beginnings don't have to mean you didn't like the old life. That you don't yearn for it sometimes. It means you're alive. And honey, you need to live."

Kate looked at her phone again. Messaging wasn't working. She wasn't sure talking with her voice low on the phone would either.

"Mom, can you and Carlton look after the kids for a while?" she asked her. "I need to go talk to somebody."

"Him?"

She nodded. "Marley." There, she'd said his name out loud. If only that could erase everything that had just happened on the phone.

"Oh!" Her mom beamed. "Of course. You go and do what you need to. Take your time. Hell, don't come home all night if you don't want to."

"I'll be home in a couple of hours. It's just talking."

"Shame." Her mom smiled at her. "Sometimes actions speak louder than words."

CHAPTER
Twenty-One

I'M AT YOUR HOUSE. *Can we talk? – Kate.*

Marley stared down at the message on his phone. After his shitshow of a conversation with her, he'd helped his mom clean up the kitchen. Cassie and Delilah were playing with the boys in the backyard, and Pres and his dad were watching the ball game, along with Hendrix. He'd just sat down to join them when Kate's message appeared on his phone.

I'm still at my mom's. Is everything okay? – Marley.

I just need to see you. I can come there if you'd like? – Kate.

He took a deep breath. Either she wanted to apologize or say goodbye. Either way, they needed to be alone.

• • •

Wait there. I'm on my way. – Marley.

"I gotta go," he said, standing up. "I'll see you guys later."

"You got a call out?" Pres asked. His brows knitted together. He knew that his twin worried about him when he was out on an emergency.

"No, just need to pick something up." He hugged his brothers and his dad. Then walked over to his mom who was getting some drinks for the kids outside. "Mom, I'll see you later. Thanks for the late lunch."

"You're leaving so soon?" She frowned.

"Yeah. But I'll call you later. Love you."

"I love you too," she told him. "And I'd love you more if you and your brothers would stop fighting."

"Never gonna happen," Hendrix shouted.

His mom's nose wrinkled.

After he waved goodbye to Cassie and the kids, he headed over to his car. He'd driven today because he *was* actually on call. As one of the single guys in the department, he liked to make sure he covered Sundays.

It was only a few minutes before he pulled up outside his house. It was just beyond the town square, on the road next to the fire station. And yeah, he'd chosen it for the proximity. He liked being the first to respond. He took his job seriously.

But his home had never looked this good before. Because Kate was sitting on the front stairs, her elbows resting on her knees, her chin propped in her palms. Not doing anything to hide the fact she was sitting outside his house.

"Hi," he said softly, holding his hand out to help her up. "You could have waited in your car."

"I don't think I could have." She stood, her hand in his. He didn't want to pull it away so he used his left hand to slide his key in the door, so aware of this woman as he pushed it open and they walked inside.

"Want a drink?" he asked her.

"No thank you." She looked around the hallway. When he'd first moved in he'd put photographs of his family on the wall in a burst of energy. "There are so many of you," she said softly, looking at each photograph in turn.

"When your kids have kids, there'll be a lot of you, too," he pointed out.

"There will, won't there?" She took a deep breath. "Can we sit down?" she asked. "I just don't think I can do this in the hallway."

So it was an ending then. Okay.

Actually, no, it wasn't okay but he'd survive. It wouldn't kill him.

He just wanted to punch something. Anything. Get rid of the pain in his chest.

She followed him to the back of his house, to the upholstered seats overlooking his backyard. It was small compared to hers. Full of flowers though, thanks to his mom who came to garden every week.

"This is beautiful," Kate said. "Look at those roses."

"My mom has a thing for them." He waited as she sat down on one of the chairs, trying to keep his breath even.

But damn, he needed this pain to be done with. "If you're ending this, can we do it fast? I'm not one for long drawn out emotions."

"You think I'm ending things?" She frowned.

"After our conversation earlier? I'm pretty sure you are."

She reached for his hand again. "I'm not ending things. I'm saying sorry. I've been so scared I've been pushing you away without even realizing it. And this morning..." she trailed off. "I felt so guilty I couldn't breathe."

"Guilty?" He frowned. "About what?"

"About Paul. I'd just spend the night in another man's arms. I wasn't expecting to see his picture on the wall a few hours later. I felt so bad, Marley. Like I was being judged. It is nothing to do with you, it has to do with me."

The softness of her voice cut him to the core.

"You have his picture on your dresser," he pointed out. "Seeing his photo on the wall shouldn't be that much of a shock."

"You saw that, huh?"

"I did."

Her eyes met his. "I guess I'm used to that one. The one in his uniform, where he…" She looked at him. "Is that where he…?"

"Yes." His voice was tight. He hated thinking about it. Hated it even more when he was sitting next to the woman he desired.

"I was blindsided. And I didn't react well. And I'm sorry you bore the brunt of that."

Marley shook his head. "I don't care about seeing that. I want to see your emotions, Kate. I want to be a part of them. I miss him, too. So much I don't know what to do with the anger I feel sometimes. I get the guilt. I get the sadness. I just want you to share them with me, not push me away."

"You want me to talk about Paul?" she asked, her brows reflecting her confusion.

"I want you to talk to me about anything you're feeling. I want you to be honest with me. To be real. I want you, Kate. All of you. In case you hadn't realized that already."

"Climbing into my bedroom gave me a little hint," she said, a smile playing at her lips.

Christ, she was so beautiful it hurt. Memories of last night rushed through him. Of their bodies together. Of laying spent on her bed, the soft cadence of her breathing as she fell asleep. Of never wanting that feeling to end, because the cold light of day always felt like a bucket of frigid water.

He didn't want the water. He wanted the happiness. He wanted to make her smile, not cry.

"I know this is hard for you. One of the hardest things you've had to do." He took her hand in his. "You've been so fucking brave, Kate. Can you be brave a little longer? Let me show you how much I want this."

Her eyes met his. "It's not just me," she told him. "I come in a pack. There are the kids. One teenager who has emotions so big he doesn't know how to deal with them, so he throws them at the nearest adult on a regular basis. An eight-year-old who has taken to sleeping in his dad's t-shirt every night because he's afraid he's going to forget him. And a little girl who can't even remember her dad, so she's looking for somebody to fill that hole. And I'm afraid they'll get attached to you, and then you'll walk away."

"I'm not walking away," he told her, his voice rough.

"You don't know that." She ran her tongue along her bottom lip. "That's the thing. None of us know what will happen in the future."

He took her face in his hands. "Kate, I will do everything that I possibly can to make sure that doesn't happen. I love your kids. I will never hurt them. I promise you that."

"What if we break up?"

Not gonna happen. But he knew that wasn't what she needed to hear. And he was so very aware that to break up they needed to be together.

Were they together?

"I would protect their hearts like they were my own kids."

A watery smile pulled at her lips.

"And I'll protect your heart, too. I know it's battered and bruised. Let me try to help you mend it."

A tear rolled down her face. He wiped it away with his thumb.

"I don't want to tell them yet," she said. "Not until we're sure."

"Until *you're* sure." He smiled, brushing his lips against hers. "And that's okay. I'll take what you're able to give. And

I'll do whatever it takes to prove to you that I'm staying around. I'm here. I want you, all of you. I'll be your friend to them, their buddy. Whatever. But to you, I want to be your boyfriend."

"Boyfriend?" She was smiling wider now.

"Lover. Significant other. Whatever you want to call it."

"I like boyfriend. It works perfectly with you climbing into my bedroom window and making out every night."

"I'm not sure I can do that every night," he said, leaning in to kiss her again. God, she felt good in his arms. Warmth flooded through him. "But I do have one request."

She touched his face, her gaze steady on his. "Name it," she said. "It's yours."

"I want to take you out on that date. This week. Your parents can babysit."

Kate grinned. "You've got it all worked out, haven't you?"

"Yep." He brushed his lips against hers. "I have."

"Okay, I need you to send me a picture of you in your dress," Shana said a few days later, her voice echoing through the speaker of Kate's phone as Kate drove to Marley's house to start their date.

As Marley suggested, her parents were babysitting. And although they knew the reason why she was going out she'd told the kids she was seeing Shana. Who, of course, loved being part of the conspiracy.

"I'm driving," Kate said, shaking her head. "You can use your imagination."

"In my imagination it's a fuck me dress," Shana said. "And Marley's going to drop at your feet like a drooling fool."

"Yeah, that's exactly it," Kate said, shaking her head as she turned the corner onto Marley's road.

Carlton and her mom were planning on taking the kids out for dinner and had been getting ready to leave when she had. Addy and Ethan were too busy talking about whether turkey or beef made the best burgers to even notice her.

Her mom had though, taking in Kate's cream dress, her shiny hair, and her high heels. "Oh, you look lovely." She hugged Kate tight. "Have a wonderful time, darling."

"By the way, do we need to have the safe sex talk?" her friend asked as Kate parked in Marley's driveway.

"Shut up." Kate smiled. "Who said we're having sex?"

"You're wearing a fuck me dress. I'd say sex is guaranteed." Kate switched off the engine. "At least tell me you shaved."

"Of course." Kate rolled her eyes.

"Down there."

Kate blinked. "It's… tidy." And that was all the information she intended on telling her friend. Because yes, she made sure she was ready for Marley to see her naked, if that happened. And yes, she panicked as she stared at herself naked in the bathroom mirror and saw the silvery stretch marks from having two kids and the little pooch at the bottom of her stomach that she tucked into her jeans because no matter how much she worked out it never went away.

"Anyway, he's seen me naked," Kate pointed out, grabbing her purse from the backseat. "I've got to go now. Wish me luck."

"Good luck, and don't forget I need all the juicy details later."

"Goodbye, Shana," she said firmly.

"All of them!" Shana shouted out as Kate disconnected and walked up the steps to Marley's front door.

He opened it before she could even knock. And her heart did a little loop-the-loop. The man she was so used to seeing in sweats or jeans, or thick working pants, had dressed up for her.

He was wearing a white shirt, unbuttoned at the neck. And dark gray pants that clung to his hips. As soon as she stepped inside she could smell the spiced notes of his cologne.

He took one look at her and grimaced. "Fuck," he muttered, taking her hand and spinning her around, before marching her back down the stairs onto his broad driveway.

"Is something wrong?" she asked, frowning. "Do I look awful?"

"No." His voice was thick. "You look beautiful. Gorgeous. I just need to have you wait outside while I grab my keys, because if you step inside my house we won't be leaving until morning."

Oh. She looked down at her dress. Yes, she'd chosen it specifically. It was sleeveless and made of lace, the neck a low v that revealed a hint of her cleavage. It was cut short, flaring out right above the knee, revealing her smooth legs, because yes, thank you, Shana, she *had* shaved.

It took him a minute to grab his keys and wallet and lock up the house. Then he turned to look at her. Damn, this man was handsome. He filled his shirt out perfectly. The sleeves were rolled up because despite the fact it was the evening, it was still balmy outside.

"I can't tell you how good you look," he told her. "Seriously, you blow my mind."

"You don't look so bad yourself." She smiled at him. "I would have been happy staying in your house, by the way."

"Don't say that. I promised you a date. And I intend to keep my promise."

He took her hand and led her past her own car to his truck, opening the passenger door for her. There was a little flutter in her chest. This felt so real and yet so right.

"Where are we going?" she asked as he climbed into the driver's seat and started the engine.

"It's a secret." He flashed a smile at her. "We have one stop to make on the way."

At first she thought he was driving her to Maple Cross. But he took a right off the road out of Hartson's Creek, driving deep into the country. The sun was an orange ball in the sky as they drove through the cornfields, covering them with a bronze hue. Marley took another left, down a one-track lane, his truck lifting and falling with the divots of mud.

He pulled into a small makeshift parking lot and Kate recognized the place right away. Creek Edge Restaurant was one of the best eating establishments in the state. Famous for only serving local produce and being hard to find.

"Stay here," he said. "I'll be back in five."

"Aren't we eating here?"

He shook his head. "Nope. We're taking some food to go."

She vaguely remembered the restaurant was owned by Marley's uncle and aunt, along with the farm it was attached to. Just as he promised, he was back within a couple of minutes, putting a big cooler of food in the flatbed of the truck before climbing back into the cab beside her.

"We have one more little drive then we're done," he promised her.

"I don't mind. I like being in here with you." He had this sure, unrushed way of driving that made her feel safe. And watching his arms tense up as he slowly turned the wheel to reverse out of the lot was a bonus.

The man was gorgeous. As they made it back to the country road, he took her hand, put it on his thigh, pressing his own palm over the top. She liked that too much. Liked the way his thigh muscles felt beneath her touch. Liked the way they could do this without anybody watching or talking about them.

She wanted to do so much more to him. But that would have to wait.

It took another five minutes before he pulled off the road

again. This time she recognized it right away. "We're going to the movies?" she asked.

The Chaplin Drive-In Movie Theater was owned by another of Marley's uncles and his wife. It was a huge part of summer life in Hartson's Creek. They ran seasons of old films, along with some of the seasonal blockbusters.

It wasn't until he drove over the grass toward a space in the center that she realized something was strange.

"Where is everybody?" she asked him. Theirs was the only vehicle in the whole field.

"I rented it out." He gave her a half smile. "Family privileges."

"Seriously?" Her eyes widened still.

"Yep." He parked, grabbed his phone, and tapped out a message. A moment later, the huge screen at the front of the parking lot flickered to life. Marley climbed out of the truck and walked over to her side, helping her down, because this dress might be pretty, and these shoes might make her legs look good, but they weren't made for climbing in and out of trucks.

"I brought a blanket," he told her. "But we can go sit at a picnic table if you prefer.

"A blanket is perfect." She took her shoes off, because grass and heels weren't a great combination. Marley put the blanket on the ground, then grabbed the food, setting it out between them as the movie started on the huge screen.

"Oh my God," she said, smiling. "Is this what I think it is?"

"*High Society*, yeah." He'd asked for it specifically. Luckily, his uncle and aunt had a huge library of movies.

"How did you know it's my favorite?"

He opened the first dish. "I remember you talking about this movie once. You used to watch it with your dad."

"When did I say that?" She couldn't get over the fact that he remembered it.

"I don't know. A few years ago maybe. At some firefighter cookout I think."

The movie opened with an overhead shot of some expensive homes on the New England coast. There were speakers set up so they could hear the sound of Louis Armstrong singing about Rhode Island and how he was going to sing in his pal Dexter's jazz festival.

"Have you seen it before?" she asked him.

"Yeah. After you said it was your favorite." His eyes met hers. "I figured you had good taste."

He passed her a glass of wine and a tiny tart with tomatoes on it. "Try it," he said. "Those tomatoes grow in the greenhouse at my uncle's place."

"Was he in the restaurant when you picked up the food?"

He gave her a grin. "Yep. Him, my aunt, and my cousins. I had to forcibly restrain them from coming out to say hi to you."

"I wouldn't have minded."

He shrugged. "Maybe I do. I've just managed to persuade you out in public with me. I don't want my family putting you off."

"Your family is lovely."

He gave her a heated look. "Not as lovely as you."

God, he knew how to make her feel good. In every way. And he'd chosen the exact kind of date she'd wanted. No pressure, just a movie, some good food, and some even better company.

It was hard to remember why she'd been fighting this for so long.

CHAPTER *Twenty-Two*

"THAT WAS SO GOOD," Kate groaned, touching her stomach. "But I shouldn't have eaten that last piece of brownie."

She still had some crumbs on her lips. He reached out to wipe them away, and her breath quickened.

He wanted to pull her under him right now. The only thing stopping him was the fact that at least two members of his family were here, running the movie for them. Even though he'd parked so nobody could see them, he still had some self-restraint.

Not much, though. Not when this woman had dressed just for him. She was leaning against him, her hair tumbling down over her smooth shoulders, her bare legs stretched out in front of her, as she watched Grace Kelly get drunk and start to flirt with Frank Sinatra.

He slid his arm around her. "You warm enough?" he asked. "I brought another blanket."

"I'm good. You have enough heat for the whole town."

Yeah, he'd always been hot-blooded. It mostly came from never being able to sit still. He could now though. Having her against him, her soft body molded into his, felt like a little piece of heaven. He didn't want it to end.

"What did you tell the kids you were doing tonight?" he asked.

"I just said I was going out with Shana." She turned to look at him. "Not because I'm trying to hide anything. I just…" She smiled softly at him. "Their hearts are tender, I guess."

"You don't need to be afraid of me. My intentions are real." There, he'd said it. "I know we need to get them used to us slowly. I'll go as slow as you want. But I'm not going anywhere." He just wanted her happy, always.

Her lips parted but she said nothing. Just stared at him like he was some kind of eighth wonder.

"What do you see in me?" she whispered. "Most guys would see a single mom with three kids and run."

"The guys on your dating app didn't."

"I deleted that as soon as I could." She rolled her eyes at him, smiling. Because he knew this.

"Good." He reached out to trace her jaw with his calloused fingers. He'd never get used to how smooth her skin felt. It made his body feel tight. Needy. "And what I see in you is a prize. Your kids aren't a burden. They're part of you. And I want all of it." He shook his head. "Don't you see? I've been waiting for you to be ready. You don't have to worry about me."

Her chest hitched. "What about when Addy and Ethan are teenagers? Screaming around the house? Will you feel the same, then?"

"Do you feel the same about James?"

"Yes," she said without hesitation. "But he's mine."

"And I'd like them all to be mine, in time." He kissed her jaw. "And I'm not trying to erase Paul. They'll always be his. But maybe they can be mine, too." He needed that like he needed her. Not just because he wanted to protect them, though that was always important. But because he loved spending time with them. The same way he loved being with her.

"Are you still talking about the kids?" she whispered, her voice full of emotion.

"Partly." But they both knew he was talking about her, too. "I'm serious about this. About us."

He knew she was finding it hard to move on. And he'd wait for as long as she needed.

"And I like to think that Paul would be okay with this." He'd been thinking about it a lot. "I never would have touched you if I didn't believe that."

"He would." She nodded. "He had the most generous heart."

"And so do you. And your kids." He wiped away the tear that escaped her eye. "I know it's been hard on you. So damn hard, Kate. Being alone. Trying to rebuild your life. Taking care of three kids. But you don't have to do it on your own. Let me in. Let me be a part of it. Part of you. Let me look after you."

She didn't reply. But then she didn't need to, because her mouth was on his, kissing him so softly it made every part of him ache. It was a yes without words, an opening. He curled his hand around the back of her neck, kissing her back.

Every part of him felt like he was on fire. In the best of ways. Like she was burning away the old him, revealing new skin, new everything. She groaned against his lips and it felt like they were leaving everything behind.

The future looked good. It was his and hers to take.

And then his phone started beeping.

Kate's eyes widened because she knew that alert sound as well as he did. Every wife of a firefighter knew it. Even those who hadn't heard it for a couple of years.

"I'm not on call tonight," he told her, firmly swiping the alert app shut and throwing his phone back on the blanket.

And yeah, it had almost killed him not to read what the alert was about. But she was important. More than important.

He needed to show her that.

"Don't you want to know what's happening?" she asked him.

She knew him too well.

"It doesn't matter."

Her eyes met his. "Of course it does. I know you better than that." She picked his phone up and held it out to him. "You can look. If it's bad…"

If it's bad he'd need to go. Because the service always came first. "Kate…"

"Just look. It's okay. If somebody's in trouble…" She rolled her bottom lip between her teeth. "It's okay," she said again. "Please look."

So he did. Pulling the app back up, he quickly skimmed the words on the alert. Then he looked at her, a soft smile on his lips. "It's a request for backup from the Maple Cross volunteers. They're taking the lead. It's fine."

The sound of a siren cut through the night air. And yes, he could feel the call of it. The way any of the volunteers did when they weren't available. The guilt, the need to take care of the team never truly went away.

But this woman… she was more than any of it. He needed to show her.

"I would never expect you to ignore a call out," she told him. "Not ever. I need you to know that. Yes, I find it hard at times. I'm afraid that you might get hurt. But I know it would hurt you more not to be part of the department."

"You're afraid that I might get hurt?" he asked, half smiling again.

"Is that funny?"

"No. It's sweet." He liked that way too much.

"You're not the only one who's falling, you know," she whispered.

And damn it, he had to kiss her again. Their mouths moved slowly together as Bing Crosby started singing again. Her hand was on his chest, moving down. Every part of him felt like he was on fire.

"You know the best thing about having a favorite movie?" Kate asked him, her mouth sliding down to his jaw.

"What?" His voice was as tight as the rest of his body. She was falling for him. He ached for her. Why did he think it was a good idea to take her to his family's drive-in movie theater?

"I know the ending." She pulled away from him, smiling. "Now take me to your house. Before I start humping your leg like a puppy."

He wasn't as much of a steady driver on the way home. Maybe because she had her hand on his thigh, near the top of it, her fingers kneading his hard leg muscles as he drove along the empty country road. He hadn't bothered to put on any music, and she was glad about that.

She liked the silence. The tension. Because tonight she was going to give everything to this man.

Being wanted by him was all she wanted right now. And yes, there was still that nervous feeling popping and firing in her lower belly.

They drove past her road, and she couldn't help but look down it, to the house on the end. A fleeting glance, that was all, because her mind was on other things.

On this man and the way he could kiss. The way he made her feel so good.

When he pulled into his driveway she yanked her door open before he could walk around to help her down. She'd put her shoes back on, so it was with tentative feet that she tried to climb out of the cab of his truck.

"You took my job," he murmured, taking her hand and helping her down the rest of the way.

"Call your union," she told him dryly.

He grinned. "Haven't got time for that."

She wasn't sure which of them was more eager to get inside his house. She managed to only stumble once in her hurry to get up the steps to his front door, and he scooped her up again, one arm around her, the other holding his keys, opening the door and pulling her inside before he closed the world out.

He pulled his shoes off and she went to do the same.

Marley shook his head. "Keep them on. For me."

Oh, he liked them. She could tell that from the way his gaze slowly rose up from her shoes, her legs, to the deep vee of her dress. She liked that way too much.

"Did I tell you how gorgeous you look?" he asked.

"You did. But you can do it again." She was smiling now, because she felt so at ease it wasn't funny. Yes, there was that delicious lick of anticipation too, but she wasn't afraid. Not of him.

He'd proved more than once that he knew how to take care of her. That her comfort was his goal. She wanted this. She wanted him.

More than she'd wanted anything in a long, long time.

And he'd made it quite clear he was hers for the taking.

This man had given her so much. Not just the way he took care of her – though that was more than enough. It was the way he understood her. Took things at her pace.

And when she'd wavered earlier in the week, he'd accepted that. Given her the space she needed to realize that this was what she wanted.

She reached behind herself to pull down the zipper of her dress. Marley swallowed hard, his eyes dark as the lace bodice fell to her waist. There was a look of wonderment on his face as he took in the lacy ivory bra she'd bought especially for him. And the way her creamy breasts spilled over the demi cup. It was completely impractical yet so perfect for tonight.

He let out a long, low breath.

"I have matching panties on," she whispered.

"Fuck," he groaned.

"That's what I'm hoping for." She kissed him again, wrapping her arms around his neck, pressing her aching breasts against the hard planes of his chest. He was hard already. She loved the way she could feel him pressed against her stomach.

She had plans for this man. He'd given and given. It was time for him to take. And she was the willing donor, that was for sure. There was nothing she wanted more than to see this man lose control. To see him finally relax. To stop taking care of everybody else and think of himself for once.

She let her dress fall to the floor in his hallway. His eyes widened. Darkened. As he took in her ivory lace thong, and the stupid high heels she was still wearing.

"Do you know how much I want you right now?" she asked him.

"Tell me."

Oh, he was making her work for it. Good. She wanted to. "I want to feel you in my mouth so badly. It's all I've thought about all day. I want to taste you."

She wanted to worship him, let him feel the way he made her feel.

"You don't have to."

"I know that." Her gaze didn't waver from his. "But I want to."

Before he could say anything else, she dropped to her knees and pulled at his zipper. Her hand curled around him, through the cotton fabric of his shorts. Feeling the thickness, the heat.

"You look amazing," he told her. "Your body is so damn beautiful."

She adored this man. Because she knew he meant her breasts by the way he was staring at them.

"I bought this lingerie for you," she told him. "It's all for you."

"Then let me kiss you."

"Not until I've kissed you." She pulled him out of his shorts, her breath hitching at the sight of his thickness. He reached down to touch her breasts, his fingers tracing the swell of them, then dipping inside the lace.

Was it possible to come from giving somebody a blow job? Or before you've even wrapped your lips around them? She wasn't sure, but damn, she was already close.

Taking a long, slow lick of him, she let out a groan. He did, too. His fingers moved into her hair as she wrapped her lips around his tip, sucking at him, then slowly hollowing her cheeks to pull him into the warm velvet of her mouth.

"Christ," he muttered.

She moved her mouth along his length, savoring the hard heat of this man.

"Look at me," he said hoarsely.

And she did. There was something in his gaze that made her want to give him everything. Not just wonder, but pure need, too. She curled her tongue around him, sucking him in again, finding a rhythm that made his breath speed and his fingers curl into her hair.

He needed this. She did, too. Needed to feel the pure maleness of him. To connect with him on a level she hadn't realized how much she missed. She felt feminine at his feet. But not weak, not at all.

There was a power to the way he was whispering her name. A strength to the way she could make this man's body respond to her.

"Kate, you need to stop," he grunted, trying to stay the movement of her head with his palm.

But she didn't want to. She wanted his pleasure. There would be later orgasms. They had all night. She needed to taste him. To show him just how much he meant to her.

She looked up at him through her thick lashes, and he let out a strangled groan.

"Do you know how beautiful you look with me in your mouth?" he rasped.

Yeah, she did, because she could see it reflected back in his gaze. Yes, there was lust. And wonderment too. But more than anything there was emotion. So much of it. She could see it in every sweep of his lashes. His fingers were threaded through her hair as she hollowed her cheeks again, pulling him in so deep she had to hold her breath.

Before she could protest, he was pulling out of her mouth, her lips feeling empty as his hardness slammed back against his stomach. He pulled his shorts back up and lifted her, his mouth hungry and demanding as he pulled her legs around his hips and turned to walk to the stairs.

"I'm not coming in your mouth," he told her. "Yet."

She grinned at the qualifier. Because she was going to taste this man, that was for certain. But tonight – or this part of it – was his. She'd already decided that. If he wanted to carry her up the stairs in her bra and panties, he could have at it. She kicked her shoes off, afraid she might impale him with the stiletto heels, and they clattered down the steps, as she tightened her thighs around him.

Kate had her arms around his neck as he strode up the stairs, his shoulder muscles twisting and knotting as he carried her with him. His room was the first on the right, and he kicked the door open and practically threw her on the bed.

"Stay there," he told her, as she reached for him. "I need to look at you for a moment."

Their eyes met and she could feel his adoration down to

her toes. And she did as she was told, because she could sense he needed this.

"Do you know how much I've imagined this. You in my bed?" There was a hoarseness to his voice that sent a shiver down her spine.

"You don't have to imagine anymore," she whispered, unfastening her bra and throwing it to the side. She couldn't think of anywhere else she wanted to be right now more than on this man's perfectly made bed, her body open to him.

She felt like she was falling and had no idea if there was a soft landing.

A slow smile pulled at his lips. "Show me the rest of you."

She hooked her thumbs into the waistband of her panties and shimmied them down her hips. She'd never felt more beautiful, more wanted, as he let out a low groan of appreciation.

She looked up at him expectantly. "Are you going to undress too, or are you just going to stand there?" she teased.

"I just need to stay here for another minute." His eyes were raking her body. "I just…" He shook his head. "I never thought…"

That she would be in his bed... "And yet here I am," she murmured. "And there's nowhere else I'd rather be."

He unfastened the buttons of his shirt, shucking the cotton off his shoulders to reveal his perfectly sculpted body. Her thighs clenched at the sight of him in the pale light of the bedside lamp. He reached down to take off his already-open pants, sliding them over his thickly muscled thighs, before kicking them to the side until he was just in his shorts, the plush tip of him escaping from his waistband.

With his eyes on hers, he slid them off, too. They were naked. Alone in his house. It felt like a gift she'd never thought she'd receive.

"Please…" she reached for him, because she couldn't bear

not to touch him for one more moment. He strode toward her, dropping to his knees and opening her legs.

"Marley," she whispered.

"Yes?" His gaze flickered to hers once more. His eyes were dark. Full of need.

"I don't want to come in your mouth either. I need you inside me."

His chest hitched. "I need you to come first."

And there he was. The man who always gave before he got.

"Feel how wet I am for you," she murmured, taking his hand in hers. She slid it to where she needed him the most.

Marley's throat rumbled. "Damn. I haven't even touched you yet."

"Your body has that effect on me."

He grinned again. And yeah, she was still falling. Afraid and exhilarated and oh so full of desire. He climbed over her, cupping her face and brushing his lips against hers. "I need to tell you, this is probably not going to be pretty. It's been a while."

"Ditto." She kissed him back, her tongue slowly sliding against his. Her fingers feathered down his back, her nails softly scraping his spine, his ass. He hitched his hips against her until he was *there.*

The tip of him was right where she needed him. She thought she might cry if she didn't have him inside her soon.

"Please…"

"I'm trying to remember the last ten winners of the Stanley Cup," he murmured.

"Why?"

"Because if I don't think about something else I'm gonna come. And I'm not coming until you do."

"Get inside me," she said, smiling against his mouth because this man was going to kill her in the sweetest of ways.

And then he was there, opening her up, filling her to the hilt. And it made every part of her ache in the best way. He let out a low groan and she felt it deep inside her belly.

"Kate..."

"You can come as soon as you want," she told him. "I just need you. That's all."

And of course that's all it took for him to start moving. Because she needed him and he liked that too much.

Truth was, she did too. She liked the way he kissed her like she was some kind of goddess sent just for him. The way he looked at her as his cock swelled inside her. The way he murmured her name as her breath quickened and her body tightened with rising pleasure.

"Better than I ever imagined," he told her, brushing his lips against hers. "So much better."

And the thought of him imagining making love to her, when he was alone in his bed, was enough to tip her over the edge. Her muscles tightened around him, pleasure radiating through her stomach, her thighs, the tips of her toes. She called out his name, clinging onto him as he gently rolled his hips through her orgasm.

And then he stilled inside her. "Kate, fuck..." His breath caught as he started to spill inside her, his mouth falling open against hers as she held him, their bodies a slippery mess as he slowly came down.

They stayed there for a moment, him braced above Kate, as she lay beneath him, her body so relaxed she wasn't sure she could move if she tried.

He cupped her face and kissed her softly, his eyes catching hers.

"I'm in love with you," he told her. "And I don't need you to say it back. In fact, I don't want you to. I just need you to know that."

CHAPTER
Twenty-Three

"I'M IN LOVE WITH YOU."

His words echoed around Kate's head as the usual weekend mayhem exploded in her house. After their first time having sex, she and Marley had laid together in his bed, talking and laughing, and then she'd tried to get her way to taste him, but he'd insisted on her riding him, and damn if the memory wasn't making her blush as she mainlined coffee, ready to face the day.

She had to work this morning. Addy and Ethan usually came with her when she worked on Saturdays, but her mom and Carlton had offered to babysit.

Her mom walked into the kitchen right as Kate was pouring another cup – because it felt like a two-coffee morning.

"How was last night?" her mom asked, an expectant smile on her lips.

"It was fun."

"You didn't get home until three."

Damn, she thought her days of explaining herself to her mom were over. "Mom…"

"It's okay. I'm glad you had a good time. By the way, we met Marley's mom at the diner."

"You did?" Kate asked, surprised. Her mom wasn't the diner type of person. Nor was Carlton. They were usually fine dining all the way.

"Mmhmm. She invited us to their place for lunch tomorrow."

Kate blinked. "I thought you were leaving this afternoon." After she got back from work. That had been the plan. Carlton had meetings back home on Monday. And as much as she'd actually enjoyed their visit, she was looking forward to things in the house getting back to normal.

And maybe having a chance to think about last night.

I'm in love with you.

The words made her heart pound against her chest.

"Well, we decided to leave after lunch on Sunday instead." Her mom beamed at her. "Maddie is lovely. Did you know Marley's dad is Gray Hartson? The singer?"

"Yeah." Kate nodded. "I know."

Of course her mom would be impressed by that. She loved famous people. Especially rich ones. And she loved going out. Being invited to Marley's parents' house for lunch would definitely mean them leaving later.

Before she could reply, Kate's phone buzzed.

How are you feeling this morning? Because my bed feels empty. Wish you were here. – Marley xx

She smiled, despite knowing her mom was watching.

Pretty satisfied, actually, thanks to you. A little tired, though. Thank you for taking such good care of me. – Kate xx

If 'taking care of you' is a euphemism for sex, then the pleasure was all mine. – Marley xx

Before she could respond to that one, another message from him flashed up.

By the way, my mom says she met your mom. And that

you're all invited to lunch tomorrow. Did your mom tell you? – Marley xx

She grinned, because from the sounds of it, he was as happy about the situation as she was.

Yes. It feels a little like a medieval set up, doesn't it? Like they're negotiating our betrothal. Do you think my stepfather will pay a dowry? – Kate xx

He wouldn't have to pay me, Kate. I'm yours for free. – Marley xx

---

"Isn't he wonderful with the kids?" her mom asked as Kate stood with her and Carlton in Marley's parents' backyard the next day.

Not that 'backyard' was the proper description for it. The sprawling ranch house that his parents had built almost thirty years ago stood on a big expanse of land. It wasn't the only building on the estate, either. There was a separate guest house which was originally built for Maddie's mom, but after she died the boys had used it. Currently it was Marley's brother, Hendrix's, base when he was home. Which he was for now.

The huge grass lawn was filled with people holding glasses and chatting. Most were members of the Hartson family, but there were some friends there, too.

And Kate and her family. At least her stepfather was always at ease in a crowd. Carlton had started up a conversation with Marley's dad and uncles about the baseball season. James was helping Pres carry out chairs and tables from the garage.

And Marley was running a game of softball over on the far side of the lawn, Addy hanging onto him as he threw a ball toward Ethan, who was swinging the bat.

"Yeah, he's great with kids," Kate agreed.

Marley looked over and caught her eye, smiling softly. And her heart did a little leap.

She smiled back at him, and then Addy started tugging at his hand, talking nonstop.

"Mom!" James ran over to her. She reached out to hug him because she hadn't seen him since he'd headed off to Junior Firefighters that morning. Marley had brought him back here to shower and help set things up.

"Guess what?" James said, his eyes shining.

"What?" She smiled at how happy he looked. Even if she had to lift her head up to catch his eye now, he was still her baby in so many ways.

"One of the kids has dropped out of camp. There's a space for me to go."

"What camp?" she asked, confused.

"Junior firefighter camp. At Jackson's Mill. I wasn't picked originally since I am still new, but Nathan had to pull out and there's an open space. I heard Marley and Tayto talking about it. They're gonna ask you if I can go." His eyes were full of excitement. "I can, can't I?"

"That's lovely." Her mom beamed at James. "What a great opportunity."

"I told Grandpa," James said. "He thinks it'll be great for my college applications."

Kate took a deep breath. "You're already signed up for science camp." All three of the kids went to camp in the summer. Not every day, but enough that she could cover her shifts at the library.

"I know, but that's after this one. I can do both." His smile was bursting. And her heart hurt. Because she knew it would be good for him. Not just for his college applications, but because he loved being part of the firefighting community. He always had, since he was a tiny child.

"I'll need to see if I can afford it," she said softly, not wanting her mom to overhear, because she knew that

Carlton would offer to pay if he knew money was a problem.

"It's already paid for. The station raised all that money at the concert, remember? I just need to show up. Please, Mom?"

She hugged him again, mostly because she needed that closeness with her oldest child. He felt solid in her arms. Her almost-man child.

Kate took a deep breath. "Let me talk to Marley. But if the offer is really there you can go." Her chest still felt tight at the thought of it.

His smile was huge. "Thanks, Mom. I love you so much."

"I love you too."

And sometimes love meant letting go. Even if it hurt her to the core.

"He wasn't supposed to overhear that," Marley said to Kate later. "I was going to talk to you first. I don't want him putting any pressure on you." His fingers brushed against hers, because he was trying to be discreet, since they were not alone.

But to his surprise she slid her fingers between his and squeezed his hand tight. They were standing on the side of his parents' house. It was getting later in the day. All the kids were in the den watching a movie, and some of the older guests had gone home. Kate's parents had left about an hour earlier, but not before her mom and Carlton had cornered him.

"Thank you," her mom had said, hugging him. "For taking such good care of my daughter."

Carlton had shook his hand and said he hoped to see him again.

Marley hoped he would, too.

His parents and uncles and aunts were sitting around a

small fire. Some of his older cousins were there, as well. He was tired and part of him wanted the night to be over, but then Kate would go home and he wouldn't be with her.

Funny how much more relaxed he felt when she was around. Like he could breathe easy again.

"I told him it was okay," Kate said, still holding his hand. "As long as the offer is real."

"It's real. Nathan broke his arm."

"At the station?" she asked, sounding alarmed.

"No, playing football with his brothers. Did an amazing tackle but then ended up with his arm twisted the wrong way beneath his body."

"Ouch." Kate grimaced. "Poor kid."

"And lucky James." He was pretty happy that her son was the first reserve for the place. Not just because he loved the kid – and he did. But because he knew James would step up to it. Sure, he'd had his moments this year, but overall he was a great kid. And he'd thrive at camp.

The camp was run by the fire service at their state academy within the university, and had a mixture of class based learning and practical training taught by professionals. Marley had taught there himself a few times, but not this year.

"I was thinking," Marley said, his thumb brushing against her wrist. "Maybe we could drive James to camp together." He gave her a half smile. "Stay the night there and come home the next day."

"The two of us?"

"Yeah. We can find a hotel somewhere. Break up the drive."

She smiled at the way he was looking at her. His gaze was pointed. Needy. "It's only a couple of hours away," she pointed out.

"Yeah, but a very tiring drive." He lifted a brow.

"Addy and Ethan will have to come with."

"I thought about that. I know Pres and Cassie would love to have them stay over."

"They already have three kids. I'd feel terrible dumping two of mine on them." Kate shook her head, the smile still lingering because the thought of spending the night with Marley, just the two of them, with no need to worry about kids, was kind of enticing. Yes, it was great when he'd climbed into her room, and when she'd gone back to his after their date.

But being away, just the two of them, if only for a night, felt like something they needed.

"I'll ask Shana," Kate said. "She'll jump at the chance."

"You sure?"

He wasn't just asking about Shana babysitting. She could tell that. He was asking if she was ready for them to be alone together.

For people to know they were together. Because James wasn't stupid. If they drove him together he'd know there was something more than friendship there.

"Yeah, I'm sure." She ran her tongue along her bottom lip, lifting her gaze to his. "I trust you," she whispered. "To take care of my kids' hearts. And mine."

And damn if that didn't feel like he'd just won the lottery.

"Good. Because I'm not going to let you down."

CHAPTER
Twenty-Four

"MARLEY? YOU HAVE A DELIVERY."

He was at the back of the construction site when he heard his name being called. His face was red with exertion and covered in dust. The house was nearly complete, thank god, because summer was heading toward its peak. Whenever they could, they took a needed break in July and August. Not just because it was hot from dawn until dusk, but because a lot of their crew had kids and Pres liked to give time off during the school vacation.

Marley wiped his face with the back of his hand and walked around the building. He wasn't expecting any deliveries today. And then he saw a girl looking completely out of place in the mess of the construction site, holding a huge bouquet of red roses.

He blinked. "You okay?" he asked her.

"Are you Marley Hartson?" she frowned.

"Yeah. But I'm not expecting a delivery."

"These have your name on them. And this is the right address." She lifted a card from the bunch of flowers.

Marley Hartson. The construction site next to 1223 Warrington Road.

"Here you go," the girl said, pushing the flowers toward him. "I have a lot of other deliveries to do."

Before he could say anything else, she was rushing away, right through the wire gate that Pres was holding open, a huge grin on his face as he looked at his twin.

It had been two weeks since his first real date with Kate. A lot longer than that since he'd started falling for her.

Pres was still grinning as he walked over. "How come you get flowers? Nobody's ever sent me roses before."

"That's between you and your wife," Marley said. He pulled the little envelope open and took the card out.

Thank you for loving me. – Kate xx

Pres leaned over Marley's shoulder, reading the card before Marley could slide it back into the envelope.

"Fuck. That's pretty sweet." Pres tipped his head to the side. "You told her you love her?"

Marley sighed. "Do we have to talk about this? Can't I just go back to building my wall?"

"Nope. I need all the juicy details. Cassie's gonna want to know."

"Cassie doesn't need to know anything." Marley slid the envelope into his back pocket, because he was planning on keeping the card, his other hand still holding the bouquet of roses.

"Of course she does. And anyway, that was code for me needing to know but not wanting to show it." Pres grinned. "So it's serious between the two of you?"

"For me it is."

"And for her?"

"It's more complicated. She has the kids to think about." Truth was, she planned to talk to the younger two next week.

School ended today and tomorrow he and Kate were driving up to Jackson's Mill to take James to camp. She'd already spoken with him and explained that she and Marley were dating.

Though dating didn't seem a strong enough word for it in his opinion.

Whatever, words didn't matter. Their relationship did. And they were progressing. And he'd take it at whatever pace she wanted.

"She loves you though, right?"

She hadn't actually said the words. He got the feeling they were difficult for her. "She cares, yeah." And that was all Pres was getting. He didn't need anymore.

"Good. Because you're a catch, man."

"Says the guy who looks just like me."

Pres laughed. "Just saying it how I see it. And I like Kate. She's good for you."

"She is?" Marley's brows knit. "What do you mean?"

"I mean you seem calmer. Less... I don't know, busy I guess."

"I'm not busy because you're making me talk to you," Marley muttered.

"You're happy though?" Pres continued. "At least tell me that."

Yeah, he was happy. Though again, that word didn't seem strong enough. He wished he was as well read as Kate. She'd know the right words to use. Ecstatic, maybe. Blissful.

He was in love with her and she cared for him and he'd take that.

"I'm happy."

"Good. Now go put those flowers in some water before they shrivel up." Pres grinned.

It was impossible not to smile back. Because the sun was shining, the flowers smelled sweet, and the woman he was stupidly in love with had sent them to him.

Yeah, he was happy. And tomorrow, when they got to spend the night together, they'd be even happier.

Because just like his woman, life was sweet.

"Why can't Marley babysit us?" Ethan said, frowning as James carried his suitcase downstairs.

"Because you're stuck with me," Shana said dryly, ruffling Ethan's hair. She didn't look at all upset that she was second choice in Ethan's mind, which Kate was thankful for. She already felt jittery leaving her younger son and Addy with Shana overnight.

"And you're going to be good for Aunt Shana, right?" Kate said, lifting an eyebrow at Ethan.

"Yes…" It was drawn out, like he was trying to decide whether to tell the truth or a lie.

"It's fine. I've got this." Shana winked at her. "I brought my rope with me. If he doesn't behave I'm gonna tie him to his bed."

"You can't do that." Ethan frowned. "It's against the law."

"Watch me, kiddo."

"I'm gonna carry this outside," James said, lifting his luggage. Then he glanced at Kate's overnight bag. "Want me to take that, too?"

"Yes, please."

She hugged Ethan tight. "I meant what I said about being good," she whispered in his ear. Then she called for Addy, who ran out of the living room. A high voice was blasting out from the television – one of the many cartoons she was addicted to.

"Bye, sweetie. Have a good night. And do what Aunt Shana tells you."

"I will." Addy looked over at James. "Are you going to die when you're at fire camp?" Her voice was light, like she was asking him if the sun was going to shine while he was away.

For a second, none of them said anything.

"Ah, no, wasn't planning on it," James said, his brow dipping.

"Isn't that what firefighters do?" Addy asked. "They die, right?"

"Hoo boy," Shana murmured. "This one's yours, Kate."

Yeah it was. And she had about a minute before Marley was supposed to pick them up. "Not all firefighters die, honey," she said to Addy. From the corner of her eye she could see James carrying their bags out of the door.

She couldn't blame him. Who wanted to hear this discussion?

"But Daddy did."

"Yes." Kate hunkered down to look her right in the eye. "But he didn't die because he was a firefighter. He died because he had a brain injury, remember?"

"An aunty," Addy said, nodding.

"Aneurism," Kate said softly.

"Does James have an aneurism?" Addy asked. She was playing with Kate's hair now.

"No, honey. None of us do."

"So none of you will die, right?"

Kate glanced up, her eyes meeting Shana's.

"Everybody dies eventually, honey. But none of us are planning to do it anytime soon."

Addy nodded solemnly. "Okay. Can I go watch my cartoons now?"

"Sure." Kate hugged her one last time, before Addy ran back into the living room, closely followed by Ethan. It was less than a second later that she heard the television change over, and Addy let out a howl.

"Oh God," Kate squeezed her eyes shut. "You can pull out of this if you want to. I wouldn't blame you."

"And miss out on this domestic bliss?" Shana asked her, grinning. "No way. Now get out of here. Have a good time. And I want all the gory details when you get back."

James was sitting on the front step when Kate walked out, pulling the door closed behind her. She sat down next to him, marveling again at how tall he was. He'd gone up a size this year in clothes, and he was still growing. She felt tiny sitting next to him.

"Did you remember your toothbrush?" she asked him.

He rolled his eyes. "Of course. Did you remember yours?"

She bumped his arm with her shoulder. "Yes."

"I'm okay about you and Marley, you know?"

She let out a long breath. She'd talked to him a few nights ago, when she'd told him that she and Marley would be driving him to camp, before asking him not to tell Addy and Ethan until she thought they were ready.

He'd nodded and she'd asked if he had any questions and he'd just shook his head.

"You know it doesn't change anything, right?" she said to him. "You and Ethan will always be my number one guys."

A smile pulled at his lips. "I'm kinda glad, to be honest. If I do go to college it'll be easier to leave knowing you'll have somebody to take care of you."

His words made her heart do a little twist. "I can take care of myself," she reminded him.

"Yeah, I know that. But it's better if you don't need to. Just like me. I know I'm growing up and leaving home, but it's always easier knowing you're here." His eyes met hers. "I'm so glad you're my mom."

Now she was going to cry. "It's the biggest privilege of my life," she told him. "I'm so proud of you."

She pulled him close, hugging his oversize body to hers. Her head fit perfectly in his shoulder.

"Uh, Mom?"

"Yes?"

"Marley's here. We need to go."

She looked up, and sure enough his truck was pulling into the driveway. James pulled out of her grasp and she wiped away the stray tear that had spilled over with the tip of her finger.

"Your dad would be proud of you, too," she told him.

James nodded, his gaze catching hers. "He'd be proud of you, too, Mom," he said softly. "For everything that you are."

And wasn't that just a way to start her crying all over again?

"Hey, Hartson, I didn't know you were teaching this year."

Marley turned to see one of the firefighters he knew from DC walking toward him. Craig was in full gear, his helmet in his hands. They'd arrived on campus twenty minutes ago, and he'd dropped Kate and James off at the induction center before parking his truck. He'd been walking over to join them when he'd heard his name being called.

"I'm not." He shook Craig's hand. "Paul's kid is here. I drove him up with his mom." He inclined his head toward the registration desk where James and Kate were filling out some forms. James was lifting a lanyard around his neck and taking the yellow camp t-shirt that every junior firefighter was given to wear during their stay.

It had taken them just over two hours to get here. Kate had been pretty quiet, and he could feel the tension radiating from her as he pulled into the tree-lined campus at West Virginia University, heading toward the large extension campus where the WV Fire Academy was based.

"That's Paul's kid?" Craig said, lifting his brow. "Jesus, he looks like his dad." Then somebody called out his name and Craig gave Marley a nod. "You picking him up, too?"

"Next weekend, yeah."

"Nice to see you're looking after him," Craig said, giving him a nod. "You're good people. I'll see you next weekend, bro."

Kate was trying to hug James, but he wasn't having any of it. Marley bit down a smile as her son lowered his head to kiss his mom's cheek, then stepped away, into the mass of fourteen to seventeen-year-olds waiting to be taken to their dorms.

She turned to look for Marley, her eyes finally catching his. He gave her a smile and walked over to her, because he knew how much she hated this.

He could remember his own mom crying every time she dropped him and Pres off at camp when they were kids. And then at college, too. Their dad, on the other hand, would just press a twenty-dollar bill in each of their hands and gruffly tell them to be good.

"You ready to head out?" he asked her, sliding his arm around her shoulders.

"Nowhere close." She let out a long breath. "Tell me they'll look after him."

His expression softened. "They will. Like he's their own. He's gonna have a blast, I promise you. Now let's go before he sees you cry."

She let him take her hand and lead her to his truck. And she looked back only five times. "You know what you need?" he asked her after they'd both climbed into the cab.

"What?" She tipped her head to the side, a smile finally playing at her lips.

And fuck, he'd do anything to keep that smile there. It made everything inside him feel alive.

"Ice cream."

"I really thought you were gonna say sex." Her smile widened. And now he was grinning too.

"I was," he admitted. "But it felt like it was too soon."

"Too soon for sex, or too soon to talk about it?" she asked him.

"Is it ever too soon for sex?" he asked, his brows lifting.

Her eyes dipped to his mouth and back up again. And he felt that pull in his stomach. The one he always got when she was close.

"No, I don't think it is," she told him. "But now I want ice cream."

"Ice cream then sex. Got it."

"And possibly ice cream after as well." She pulled her lip between her teeth. "Just in case I need cheering up again."

"You won't need cheering up after I'm finished with you," he told her gruffly.

"We'll see," she teased. "Now, are you gonna get me that ice cream or what?"

CHAPTER
Twenty-Five

KATE GASPED as Marley scooped an ice cold dollop of ice cream onto her nipple. A moment later she felt the warmth of his lips wrapping around her, his tongue swirling, scooping up the ice cream, his mouth sucking at her peak until her back was arching against the bed.

She was so pleased he'd booked a cabin in the middle of nowhere, because she couldn't keep her voice down. Not when he was doing this to her. And of course it had been his idea to bring the pint of ice cream back here with them.

"Vanilla." He'd smirked, looking at the box. "Let's try to prove it wrong."

He pulled her legs open, his mouth kissing his way down her body. Then he dropped a mound of ice cream right there, and the shock made her eyes widen. "Holy hell!"

"I was hoping it was heavenly." His eyes were hooded as he looked at her from between her thighs. He looked drunk.

Inebriated by her.

She could understand that. Because she felt the same way.

He'd been so sweet all afternoon. Distracting her with ice cream. Then putting on a playlist with all her favorite songs – she still needed to ask him how he knew them all – as they drove to the cabin. And when they'd walked inside there were flowers and chocolates on the bed, along with a bottle of champagne.

And the ice cream they'd picked up, of course.

He dipped his head back between her thighs, and her head dropped back because the intensity of his tongue against the ice cream was too much. Her chest was heaving, her body felt like it was caught in one of those electric cages.

"Where did you learn how to do this?" she asked him, her breath ragged.

"Ice cream school."

She started to laugh, but the mirth dissolved from her lips as he pulled her clit between his lips, sucking hard as he slid two fingers inside her. Dear God, the man was schooled well. He'd reduced her into a puddle of need within minutes of them walking into the cabin.

"I need you inside me," she whispered, pulling at his hair.

"Just one more minute."

"No, now."

She tugged insistently and he climbed over her, his warm lips capturing hers. She could taste vanilla and *her*.

For some reason it made every muscle inside her clench.

He slid his tip against her, teasing her. She let out a groan.

"Please, Marley."

"That's what I like to hear. A little begging." He grinned.

"Shut up and get inside me."

He kissed her again. "Your wish is my command."

And then he was there. Just where she needed him, filling her up, making her feel whole. Everything about this was so good. The way he angled himself against her, the thickness of him inside her body. The way he kissed her soft then hard, his breath warm against her lips.

She could feel the pleasure starting to rise.

"I need to tell you something," she whispered.

He blinked, his eyes focusing on her. "What?"

"I love you," she whispered. "So much." She kissed him softly, her hands on his muscled ass, encouraging his movements. Needing the friction. "I love feeling you inside me. I love the way you take care of me." She moved her lips to his jaw, his throat, the dip where it met his chest. "I don't ever want you to stop."

"I won't ever stop," he told her, sliding his hand beneath her, angling her body until every stroke felt like he was setting her on fire. His mouth caught hers again, his kisses needy, demanding. His movements were getting faster, more erratic as he took them both to the edge.

And then she was coming, hard and fast, Marley following only a moment behind her. His body stilled as she tightened around him. Then he was spilling inside her, calling out her name.

Telling her he loved her.

She could feel the thump of his heart against her chest as they slowly came down from their high together. He cupped her face with his hand, his eyes full of emotion as he gazed at her.

"I fucking love sex camp," he said. "And I love you."

"Sex camp?" She grinned. "Is that what we're calling this?"

"We're in a cabin." He kissed the corner of her lip. "And we're having sex. So I'd call it sex camp."

"I can't wait to hear our camp song," she told him.

"*Oops I Did It Again* by Britney Spears?" he said, making her crack up. "Or pretty much anything by Vanilla Ice."

"Old school." She glanced over at the half-empty tub of ice cream, melting by the side of the bed.

"By the way," she told him. "I'm calling shotgun on the left side of the bed."

"Why's that?" He frowned, pulling her against him. "I thought you slept on the right."

"I do usually. But you made such a mess of this side of the bed so I figured you'd want to lie in it."

He rolled dramatically over, pulling her with him so she was lying on his stomach. "It was worth it, wasn't it?"

"Yeah." She kissed him softly. "It was."

"Is everything okay?" Marley asked as Kate walked over to the hot tub, one of the complimentary bath robes from the cabin wrapped around her. He'd opened up the tub while she called home to talk with Shana and the kids.

"Yes. Surprisingly, Addy and Ethan haven't killed each other yet. And Shana hasn't tied either of them to their beds like she threatened. It almost sounds… peaceful."

"That's dangerous." He reached for her, pulling her toward the hot tub by the belt wrapped around her waist. "But good news."

"Very good news." She shucked off the robe she was wearing, revealing a black swimsuit. "Is it warm?"

"Pretty hot, yeah." He took her hand and helped her in. "But beautiful. Look at that." He inclined his head toward the mountains. The sun was setting, casting an orange glow across the peaks. Kate nestled into his arms and melted against him.

For a moment neither of them spoke. He was hyper aware of how soft her body felt against his. Of how her breasts were rising and falling with the cadence of her breath. Not in a sexual way – not yet, because they'd barely survived the two rounds in bed this afternoon – but in a way that made it feel like everything about them was in sync.

They fit together perfectly. That's what it was. And it gave him the kind of peace he hadn't felt in a long, long time.

She loved him. The memory of her whispering it when he was inside her made his chest feel tight.

Because he was so damn into this woman it wasn't funny. She was clever, gorgeous, a wonderful mother. And she made him laugh and smile like nobody else ever could.

"Want me to put some music on?" he asked her, kissing the top of her head.

"No, I like the silence." She tipped her head back to look at him. "By the way, how do you know all my favorite songs?"

"My Kate playlist?"

"Yeah."

"I just pay attention. And I might have asked Shana. I knew today was gonna be a tough one for you."

"You've made it surprisingly easy."

"Me and ice cream." He kissed the tip of her nose, wrapping his arms around her stomach.

"I want to tell Addy and Ethan next week," Kate said, tracing his hand with her fingertips.

"About us?"

"Yes."

His chest tightened in the best of ways. Because winning this woman's heart hadn't been easy. Not for either of them.

He smiled. "Okay. Want me to be there?"

"No, but I'd like you to come over afterward. Addy's six. She doesn't really get concepts without seeing them in action." She shook her head. "Before we left she asked James if he was going to die at camp because firefighters die."

Marley winced. "Ouch."

"She just… she's kind of fascinated by things but doesn't understand them. And I'd like her to understand that you're going to be around a lot more."

A smile pulled at his lips. "I'm all for that. I'm happy to come over. Or I can take you all out. Whatever you want."

"You're sure about this?" Kate asked him, turning his hand over to trace his palm.

"About what? Us? Yes, I'm sure. I've been sure about this

for a long time, sweetheart." Probably longer than he should have been, truth be told. All those runs past her house, all those attempts to make her life easier.

The way he'd told himself it was just about protecting her and the kids. But it had felt like so much more.

She lifted his palm to her lips, kissing it. "James said he's fine with it, too."

Weird how much that made him relax.

"And I think Ethan and Addy will be as well. They both like you a lot."

"That's good. Because they're gonna be seeing a lot of me." He leaned over to kiss her lips. "I like them a lot, too." Heck, he loved them, and not just because they were part of her. But because of who they were. He would do whatever it took to make sure they were safe and happy.

He cupped her face with his hands, kissing her softly. "How the hell did I get this lucky?"

"I'm the lucky one." She was smiling softly at him. And damn if he didn't feel it down to the tips of his toes. This woman was everything he dreamed he'd ever get. Strong yet soft. Determined and caring.

He'd move mountains for her. All she had to do was say the word.

Kate couldn't stop smiling. There was a warmth in her heart that hadn't been there for the longest time. Maybe it came from watching Marley cook dinner on the grill for them both, handling a huge ass steak like he was a caveman searing a mammoth leg for his woman.

Every time she tried to help him – she could make a salad, for goodness' sake – he'd insisted on her sitting back down. She'd spent the last thirteen years cooking and cleaning and taking care of her kids. A night off felt like a gift.

"I can't believe how quiet it is out here," she said, sitting on the porch swing, watching Marley plate the steaks. "Do you think there are bears?"

"Here? No." He grinned at her. "Do you think I'd be cooking meat with all this gorgeous aroma outside if there were bears?"

"Don't you fancy your chances against them?" she teased.

He gave her a 'what the hell do you think?' kind of look. "There's a saying; if there are two of you, you don't need to be faster than the bear. You just need to be faster than the other person. And I'm pretty sure I could outrun you."

"You wouldn't dare." She was laughing because she knew he'd be the first person to throw himself at the bear. Especially if it meant protecting her.

"Well, there are no bears here, so we'll never find out." He winked at her.

"You saved me from a snake," she pointed out. "Even if it wasn't poisonous."

"It was poisonous." Suddenly, he looked awkward. "Damn, forget I said that."

"The snake you found was poisonous?" Her mouth dropped open. "Why didn't you tell me?"

"Because I didn't want to scare you." He carried the plates over, putting one on the table in front of her.

"But I'm scared now," she pointed out.

"No you're not. The snake's long gone. And your house is snake proof, remember?"

"I mean, I checked it but…"

"So did I." He passed her the bowl of salad he'd made.

She tipped her head to the side, looking right at him. "You checked the house after I told you everything was fine."

"I needed some peace of mind, that's all. You did a good job."

"Thanks, I think. But I could handle it, you know."

"I know." His gaze was soft. "I know you can, Kate. It

wasn't that I didn't believe in you. I just sleep better knowing you're all okay."

Her breath caught in her throat. Being independent had been a hard fought battle. She'd gone from living with her parents to college, then only a few years later she was a wife and mom. These last few years had been difficult but maybe she'd needed them to prove something to herself.

That she could take care of her family alone.

But maybe, just maybe, she didn't have to. Or need to anymore.

Before she could say anything else, her phone started to ring, the shrill tones cutting through the silence of the country air.

Shana's name lit up the screen, a picture of her sticking her tongue out at Kate beneath it.

"Sorry." Kate grimaced. "She's probably having trouble getting the kids to bed."

"Take it. It's fine."

"Hi Shana," she said, answering the call. "Is everything okay?"

For a second there was no sound at all. As though the call hadn't connected properly. And then she heard a sob.

From her friend who never cried about anything.

"I'm so sorry," Shana cried. "Kate, I didn't know he was going to do that."

An ice cold shiver wracked through Kate's spine.

"What happened?" she asked, the blood draining from her face.

"It's Ethan. He's hurt. We're on our way to the hospital in the ambulance right now."

Kate's eyes met Marley's as panic overwhelmed her.

CHAPTER
Twenty-Six

EVEN WITH EMPTY roads all the way it would still take them two hours to get to the hospital. Kate couldn't talk, could barely breathe. All she could do was stare out at the dark night, peppered with yellow stars, and think about what a terrible mom she was. Ethan must be in so much pain.

And she wasn't there to comfort him.

It had taken Marley ten minutes to get all of their things into his truck so they could leave. She'd spent that time on the phone, talking to Shana, then arranging for somebody to watch Addy overnight.

All through the conversations, her stomach felt so tight she was certain she was going to vomit. Her hands were shaking, her breath was shallow.

Her baby was hurt.

She should have known that Ethan would have wanted to cook smores. The kid was obsessed with them. And Shana had told him no, because she didn't want to pull the grill out of the garage and get it all set up for just a few little sweet treats.

Of course, he'd taken that as a challenge, and he'd managed to connect the grill to the propane, then turned on the burners, and put some marshmallows on the rack, thinking he'd impress his aunt.

He hadn't banked on the garage filling with fumes. In his panic to take the marshmallows off the grill, he'd managed to catch his pajama sleeve on fire.

Shana had heard him scream and ran to rescue him.

Tears rolled down Kate's face. Marley reached for her hand, stone faced. She was never going away again. Not when her kids needed her.

Why hadn't she locked the garage? Or stored the propane tank somewhere else?

She turned to look at the man who only hours ago was her sole focus. His profile was sharp against the low glow of the waning moon. He was staring at the road ahead, his jaw tight. Apart from asking if she was too warm, they'd had no conversation at all since they'd left the cabin.

She couldn't gauge what he was thinking at all. Was he blaming her, the way she was blaming herself? It was all her fault, after all. She'd encouraged Ethan's obsession. Showed him how to set up and start the grill. She might as well have given him a loaded gun.

"I should never have left them," she whispered.

Marley didn't react at all. "This isn't your fault."

"Isn't it?" She blinked away the tears. "Ethan is my responsibility. He's hurt. This is absolutely my fault."

"Kate, it could have happened anywhere. At any time."

"But it didn't, did it?" She shook her head. "I should have been there. I would have known…"

He ran his tongue along his bottom lip, like he was trying to think of something to say. But there was nothing. How could there be? When Ethan needed her, she was busy getting it on with his father's friend.

She pulled her hand from his, lowering her face into it as she let out a sob.

"This is killing me," Marley whispered. "I just want to

stop and hold you. But I can't. I'm gonna get you to that hospital. Shana said he's hurt but okay, try to hold on to that."

"I'm trying," she told him, squeezing her eyes shut. "I really am."

"I know you are. And I know you're crying now because you won't be able to once you're with Ethan. I know how strong you are. How much you love your kids. Nobody ever doubts that."

Every word felt like a lie.

"We're less than half an hour away now," Marley told her. "We'll go straight to the hospital. Shana's with Ethan. You know she'll take care of him until we are there."

"I know." She let out a ragged breath. Because he was right. When they got to the hospital she'd be strong. She had no choice. That's what she did. Ethan needed her strength, he needed her to be calm.

She might have let him down today, but she wasn't going to do it again.

"What do you need me to do, Kate?" Marley asked her, as though he was searching for something he could hold on to. And she got it. He felt as useless as she did. He was a first responder. If he had been home, he would've been on call tonight.

He would have come to the house and helped Ethan.

"I just need my son to be okay," she whispered. "We both know what burns can be like."

"Yeah." This time it was Marley's voice that cracked. "But that hospital is the best. They'll take care of him. From what you've said, Shana got to him fast. Time matters in cases like his."

"Cases like his…" She winced at the words. "He's not a case."

"I know. I'm just trying to help."

"You're not." Oh God, she didn't want to snap like this. She knew he was trying to help. But right now she didn't have the emotional capacity to let him. "I'm sorry, I didn't mean that."

"It's okay." His voice was low.

"No it's not." She'd hurt him. "I really am sorry."

"You don't need to keep saying it, Kate," he snapped.

Her chest was so tight it was hurting. She blew out a mouthful of air but it did nothing to make her feel better. She needed to be at the hospital. To be with Ethan.

Addy was safe, she knew that much. Shana had left her with a neighbor when the ambulance arrived, and then Marley's brother had come to pick her up. She'd stay the night with him and his wife. Cassie had already messaged her to say that Addy was asleep and safe.

As for James, she'd already made the decision not to tell him what happened. Because she knew her oldest son would be beating himself up, too. She wanted him to enjoy camp. She'd tell him when she picked him up next week.

If Ethan was well enough to have been discharged from the hospital. *Please let him be okay.*

"Just hang in there," Marley said, his voice low. "You've got this, sweetheart."

But it didn't feel like she had anything. At all.

Marley dropped Kate off at the entrance to the hospital. She barely said a word as she got out, practically running to the door and disappearing into the building. He drove to the parking lot, easily finding a space and turning off the engine.

As he climbed out, the warmth of the night time air surrounded him. And he had to take a deep breath, because every part of him wanted to scream.

Watching her break down next to him as he drove as fast as he could without breaking the speed limit was excruciating. Seeing her blame herself when she had nothing to do with what had happened to Ethan was even harder.

If anybody was to blame it was Marley. He knew that deep in his soul. He was the firefighter. He should have given Ethan more of a warning about the grill. Discussed fire safety with him. They both knew about the kid's obsession with it, after all.

And he should have been here. He fucking promised Paul he'd take care of his family. Making sure they were okay.

Instead, he'd spent the past few weeks taking care of Paul's wife.

As soon as he stepped inside the sliding glass doors, he could smell that familiar, sterile, cold aroma. He'd been here way too many times – mostly when they had casualties from incidents they were called to.

But the time he would never get out of his head was two years ago. When he'd come in with Paul. They'd spent twenty minutes trying to revive him, as the ambulance rushed his body to the hospital.

But Paul never woke up. The memory of it swirled like nausea inside his body.

He looked at the one night clerk at the front desk, before he heard his name being called.

"Hey, Hartson," a voice called from the seating area.

Of course Tayto would be here. If he'd heard about one of Tayto's kids being here, Marley would have been waiting here for news, too. They were a family. Even with Paul gone, James, Ethan, and Addy were part of that.

"Hey." Marley nodded at his friend. "Did you see Kate come in?"

"Yeah, they took her straight to him." Tayto eyed him carefully. "You two were away somewhere, huh?"

He really didn't want to talk about that right now. Not when the guilt felt like chains weighing down his body. "Have you heard how Ethan is?" he asked.

"It's looking like second-degree burns. On his arm, nowhere else. Shana did a good job of responding. We should recruit her." Tayto smiled, but Marley didn't smile back. He just nodded and walked over to the desk.

"Hey." The clerk – Darren – smiled at him. Marley had been in enough times for the guy to recognize him. "We're still waiting for news on the kid. If that's what you're asking."

"Can I go see him?" Marley asked.

Darren looked awkward. "Not really. We have a two visitor rule at night and there's already two people with him. But if you sit with your friend I'll let you know as soon as we have news."

"Okay, thanks." He wasn't going to argue his way in. The last thing Kate needed was him making a scene.

But he didn't walk over to sit with Tayto either. Mostly because the thought of explaining himself to his friend made him want to hurl.

Yeah, I spent most of the day in bed with Paul's wife. While his kid got hurt. I'm a great friend, huh?

So instead he paced the hallway, trying not to think about the promise he'd made to Paul as he died. Not being able to think about anything else.

I'm sorry. So fucking sorry. I told you I'd take care of them.

And he didn't. He'd messed up so badly and he wasn't sure he'd ever be able to get over that.

CHAPTER
Twenty-Seven

THE DOCTOR'S voice was low as she talked to Kate and Shana in the treatment room. Ethan was asleep, thanks to the mixture of the painkillers they'd given him and the adrenaline rush from the shock of the burn.

"Your son is very lucky, Ms. Connelly," Dr. Golam told her. "It's looking like a partial thickness burn on his arm, around five inches in diameter." Kate frowned and he added, "A second degree burn. We'll need to monitor it to make sure the burn hasn't gone deeper than we thought, but if this stays the case then no skin graft should be needed."

Kate let out a long breath. Second-degree burns could be bad – she knew that much. But thankfully only his arm was affected. He'd be in pain for a while, and she hated that. She'd gladly step into a fire if she could save Ethan from the agony, but instead she'd take care of him for as long as it took.

"We've already done debridement under a mild sedation before dressing the burn. We'll keep Ethan overnight for monitoring, and assess in the morning if we will need to debride the wound again," Dr. Golam continued. "Once he's home, you'll need to clean the wound and change his dressing daily. A nurse will show you how this is done. If he's in pain, you can medicate him with ibuprofen or acetaminophen. If you give him a dose half an hour before you change the dressing that will help with his discomfort. If needed, we can prescribe him something a tad stronger."

"How long will he be in pain for?" Kate asked.

"Normally, the worst is past within one to two weeks. We'll want to check him regularly to make sure he's healing up properly. The nurse will schedule you an appointment with the burn clinic," Dr. Golam told her. "If you notice any discoloration or weeping from the wound, call us immediately. Also if he spikes a fever."

"Okay." Kate nodded. "What about activities? I'm guessing swimming's out." She knew he'd be bummed about that. Splashing in the community pool was his favorite thing to do during the summer. And it was the first week of school vacation.

"He will need to keep his arm dry and bandaged as it heals." The doctor smiled at her. "But honestly, he can do most things. He just needs to pay attention to his body. Is he right handed?"

"Yes."

"Well, since the burn is on his left arm, there's not a lot he won't be able to do."

That was lucky. If you could describe it as that. Because right now none of this felt lucky at all.

"Thank you, Doctor." She gave the doctor a smile as he left the room, before turning to Shana, who'd been listening silently.

"Not as bad as it could have been," she told her friend.

"Yeah, but I should have been watching." Shana looked pale.

Kate's guilt flared up again. Not just for leaving Ethan, but because her friend shouldn't be feeling bad. This was not Shana's fault.

"No. I'm not having that." Kate hugged her. "I'm so

thankful you were there. You did everything right. Thank you."

For a moment they held each other, the softness of her friend's embrace everything she needed. They'd been together through thick and thin and she'd never forget that.

"I promise to never make you babysit again," Kate told her.

Shana laughed. "Shut up. You know I love those kids." Her nose wrinkled. "But I need to use the bathroom now that you're here," she confessed. "I've been doing the pee dance for hours."

"Eek! Go!" Kate laughed and it felt good.

"You need anything while I'm out there?" Shana asked her.

"No, nothing. But thank you."

She watched as Shana left, sending up another thank you to the heavens for bringing her friend to her. She grabbed her phone to send a message to Marley letting him know that Ethan was okay, then walked over to the window to look out at the inky black night.

"Mom?"

Ethan was awake but his voice was groggy from the painkillers.

She turned to see him lying on the hospital bed, looking awkward with his arm wrapped in a gauze dressing.

She walked over to him, her face full of love.

"Hey sweetheart," she said softly, stroking his head. "How are you feeling?"

"I'm so sorry." His face crumpled, and it about broke her heart. "I didn't mean to ruin everything."

"You didn't ruin anything. Hush, it's okay." She leaned down to kiss his cheek. His skin was warm, soft. "Your arm will need to heal, but the doctor says you'll be fine in a couple of weeks." She'd save the fire safety talk until later. Not that she thought he'd need it – he'd learned from his mistake in the most horrific of ways.

Right now he needed to rest and heal. And his mom's love. "We're staying here tonight, and hopefully in the morning if everything is looking okay we can go home." she told him.

"It hurts a little," he whispered. "I was so scared."

Her heart tightened. "I bet."

"I just wanted to surprise Aunt Shana. Show her how good I am at cooking smores. With James gone, I'm supposed to be the man of the house." His face started to crumple. "Aunt Shana must hate me."

"Oh honey she doesn't." She cupped his warm face with her palm. "She was just worried, that was all. Scared, like you were. You're a little guy and you had a huge fright."

"You don't hate me either?" he asked, his voice small.

"Not at all. I love you so much." She kissed his cheek. "I'm so thankful you're okay. We're gonna get you home tomorrow and you can spend the next few weeks healing. I'm here, honey, I'm not going anywhere."

He nodded, still looking pale, his eyelids starting to flutter closed again. And as he fell back asleep, she sat down in the chair beside him, planning to never let go of him.

———

"Hey, how's Paul's kid?" Tayto asked Marley the next day. They were at the station, tidying up after the Junior Firefighters who weren't at camp had left. It was a smaller group, so they didn't start until after lunchtime. As it was, he wasn't supposed to be at the station today. In some other life he'd still be in the cabin with Kate, tidying up there, getting ready to leave. Probably having one last dip in the hot tub because it was too good to turn down.

But this wasn't some other life.

He'd driven Kate, Ethan, and Shana home this morning after Ethan had been released from the hospital. After he helped them get Ethan into the house, he carried her suitcase into the hallway, leaving the three of them, because the last thing they needed was for Ethan to start asking questions about why Marley was hanging around them.

So he'd left them and it had been the hardest thing in the world to drive away.

"He's doing good." Marley didn't look up. Truth was, his gut had been twisted all day. All night, too. Every time he thought of Ethan in that garage, catching on fire, with him and Kate so far away he felt like hitting something.

He should have been there. Hell, Kate should have been there.

If he hadn't wanted to fuck her with some kind of privacy, she would have been. And a little kid wouldn't be in pain. Wouldn't have some kind of scar on his arm for the rest of his life.

Some things were indelible. You could never reverse them.

It felt like the heaviest of weights on his shoulders.

"Paul would have been livid, huh?" Tayto continued. "Knowing one of his kids was playing with fire."

"Two." Marley's voice was monotone. "Two of his kids have been playing with fire."

Tayto blinked for a moment before recognition washed over his face. "Oh yeah, I forgot about James and that party. Jesus, it's been a long few months. You heard how he's doing at camp?"

"He's doing good." He'd called one of his contacts at the camp this morning. Just to be sure. And because Kate needed to know her other son was safe.

She was keeping it together remarkably well. Which only made him feel worse, because he wasn't keeping it together at all. He was getting that old, itchy feeling, needing to constantly move. Sitting still meant thinking and he couldn't do that.

"Hey, can you grab that hose?" Tayto asked. "I'll start reeling it in."

The end of the hose was on the far side of the yard. Next to the wall. Marley glanced up, his gaze landing on Paul's portrait.

And the guilt he'd been trying to keep down for so long felt like it was exploding inside him. His breath started to come faster as he thought of that day. He and Paul were talking about Kate. Because yes, he always had a thing for Kate, but he'd tried to hide it.

He loved Paul. He was one of his best friends. And he'd never do him dirty.

But you did.

He tried to blink back that thought. But it lingered, like the smell of hot concrete after freshly fallen rain.

A memory flashed into his mind. Paul had been telling him a story about one of Kate's library groups. Stitch and bitch, or something like that. And right as he was about to tell Marley the punchline, a smile already making his lips pull up, he'd winced, touching his head.

"Fucking headaches." Paul pressed along his brow. "Had this one all day. I'm telling you, don't get old. There's always something that hurts."

"You're not old."

"I feel it." Paul winced. "Kate tells me I need to slow down."

"You should go home," Marley had suggested. "I can finish up here. Turn your phone off, get some sleep."

"I…"

And then it happened. Before he could say anything else, Paul had crumpled to the ground, his head and body banging against the blacktop with a horrifying thud. He'd already been unconscious at that point, not able to put his hands out to soften the impact. And for a full ten seconds Marley had stood there, panic rising up in his body at the sudden change in his friend.

He'd been trained to respond. To be calm, to think things through logically. But when it was your friend who was the patient, everything changed. His mind was hazy as he dropped down to the ground, taking Paul's pulse, finding it.

But barely.

What's next? Check his breath.

Call the fucking medic.

He started shouting, fear rising through him, his hand on Paul's chest. "Breathe, buddy, just fucking breathe."

Everything was going wrong.

His whole body was shaking by the time the medic arrived and started asking questions, then Paul had stopped breathing.

They did CPR. Got him in an ambulance. Continued CPR because that's what they were trained to do.

"Stay with me," he'd said, his voice cracking. "Paul, you gotta start breathing. For Kate. For your kids. Fucking fight for them."

But he was gone and they knew it before they even reached the hospital. And Marley wanted to scream because this shouldn't be happening.

He should have been able to save his best friend. He was there. He should have done more.

Kate had lost her husband and her kids had lost their dad because of him.

"Hey Marley, you got the hose?" Tayto's voice cut through his thoughts.

"Yeah, I got it." His voice was raspy.

"Great. I'm reeling it in, start feeding it."

Marley pulled his gaze away from Paul's never-blinking eyes in the photograph and did as Tayto asked.

And as the hose reeled away, the guilt inside him grew and grew.

Before they wheeled Paul into the hospital, he'd kissed his friend's cheek. Promised him he'd take care of his family. That he'd never let his kids get hurt.

He'd let his friend down that day by not saving him. And this weekend he'd let him down again in so many ways it made him want to hurl.

And he wasn't sure how to deal with that.

The kids are all in bed. Want to play Romeo to my Juliet? – Kate xx

She hit send on the message and let out a low breath. She'd missed Marley so much today. After their trip together, even after it ended so badly, she'd felt so close to him.

Right now she needed his arms around her. To feel safe in them. It had been a tough day, getting Ethan settled and his medicine right. A couple of times he'd cried from the pain.

I'm on my way. – Marley

She heard the rumble of his truck's engine about ten minutes later. And it was a little confusing because he usually ran over so nobody saw his truck parked outside.

Maybe he was making a point. They were going to go official soon. She shouldn't care that his truck was outside her house all night. And right now she didn't. She just wanted to be in his arms again.

When she heard him start to climb up, her heart started thudding against her chest the way it always did. And at the same time her muscles relaxed. She'd been on edge all day. Ethan was a good patient, but he was understandably whiny and kept asking when he could go to the pool with his friends.

"Soon," she promised. "Let's get a few days of rest, then you can dangle your legs in." She'd already ordered a waterproof arm cover online, but she wanted him to take it easy. Even if his arm was covered, his friends were boisterous and a hit to his arm could cause him extreme pain.

So yeah, she was being a mom and putting her foot down right now. And putting up with Ethan's moaning was way better than him getting hurt again.

Marley climbed easily into the bedroom, his feet landing on her carpet with a thud, before he stood and ran his hands through his hair.

And of course her heart did a little loop the loop. Everything about this man set her on fire.

"Hi," she said softly.

His eyes caught hers. "Hi."

She was wearing a pair of short pajamas because the heat had taken it up a notch this week. She reached out her hand but he didn't take it.

"How's Ethan?" he asked.

"The same as when you asked an hour ago," she teased. "Asleep and fine."

Marley nodded, looking relieved. "Did you change his dressing today?"

"Yes." It was like being lectured by a parent. Kind of endearing but a pain in the ass. Still, she couldn't help but smile. "And I'll do it tomorrow, too." With every dressing change, she had to coat his skin with the ointment the hospital had given her. He hated it.

"Good." Marley pressed his lips together. "I took a look at the garage last night. There's some charring in there. I'll bring

Pres over next weekend and we'll make it like new. In the meantime, I'll get rid of the grill."

"Is it ruined?"

"I mean it's pretty damaged, yeah. But I assumed you wouldn't want it, anyway."

"There's no need for you to do that," she told him. "I can arrange for them to take it away when I buy a new one."

"You're still gonna have a grill after what happened with Ethan?" Marley's brows pulled tight. "Is that wise?"

She started to laugh. He was joking, right? "How else am I gonna cook burgers in the summer?"

But Marley wasn't smiling at all. "That thing hurt your child. It's irresponsible to have a grill near him."

She blinked, shocked by the turn in conversation. "I'm sorry?" Because clearly she hadn't heard right.

Marley pinched the bridge of his nose. "I'm not saying it right." He let out a low breath. "If Ethan's fixated on smores, maybe you shouldn't keep the temptation so close."

"That's not how it works," she told him. "You don't teach a kid how to behave by taking temptation away. That takes away their decision making. Ethan's learned his lesson. I'm pretty sure he's not going to be using the grill any time soon. Pain does that to a person."

"But why take the risk?" Marley asked her. "Why would you do that?"

She felt breathless at his question. Like he was calling her a bad mother without saying it. And yeah, it put her on edge, because she was already beating herself up about Ethan's burns. She didn't need him to do it, too.

"You want me to take the oven and fireplace out too?" she asked him.

"No, that would be stupid."

Oh boy. "So would not having a grill. I'm not removing things every time the kids do something wrong. Hell, there'd be no electrical sockets after they tried to put their fingers in them as toddlers. No baths after James slipped on the edge and cut his head open when he was six. We wouldn't have knives in the house, or stairs, because Addy once slipped down them. Did you know that?" Ooh, the annoyance was rising up in her. "You want me to take the stairs out, too?"

"That's not what I meant." Marley's voice was low, which was a good thing, because she knew hers was too loud. Too annoyed.

"Then what did you mean?"

He took a deep breath, his blue eyes on hers. "If you want burgers, I can cook you burgers."

"So you're to be trusted with a grill but I'm not?"

"Of course you're to be trusted. That's not what I'm saying. I just think, in the short term, we need to think about what Ethan needs."

"I think about what Ethan needs constantly," she said, her eyes flashing with annoyance. Weren't they supposed to be in each other's arms by now? In her bed even? Because that's what she'd wanted. What she'd needed all day, after looking after Ethan, answering Addy's questions. Trying to keep everything together. "I think about Ethan's, Addy's, and James' needs all the time, Marley. There's not a moment when I don't. So don't start lecturing me about what my kids need."

"Hush," he said. "You're gonna wake the kids up."

Her mouth dropped open. "Seriously? Now I'm not only a bad mother for having a grill but for waking my kids?"

"I never said you were a bad mother. I just thought we could talk about things in a calm manner. About how we can keep Ethan safe. That thing in the garage is a fucking death trap. Why would you want it anywhere near your kid?"

"Because I'm his mom and I know what's best for him. And if a kid does something wrong, you don't take away their choice about whether to do it again. You teach them how to make the right choice. That's how they grow into adults. And yes, I hate that Ethan had to learn his lesson in such a scary, horrific way. I hate it so much it makes me sick. But he's learned it, and if he still wants smores, then he'll get smores."

"You're making the wrong decision."

She jutted her jaw out, hurt by his words. But not willing to let him see that they'd caused her pain. Because dammit, he was wrong here. *Completely*. She knew her kids, she knew what they needed.

"Well, I'm his mom. And it's my decision."

Marley blew out a mouthful of air. "Just let me get rid of the fucking grill and be done with it."

"No." She knew she was being stubborn. But she was also right. "This is my house. They're my kids. I get to make the decisions."

Marley winced. "I get that."

"Do you? Just because I sleep with you doesn't mean you get to come into my house and tell me what to do. I'm in charge here. You're not my husband, they're not your kids." Oh, she was on a roll. A long, furious one. "You think I don't feel bad about Ethan getting burned? I got no sleep last night. I spent the whole night beating myself up because I should have been here to prevent it. And Shana's in pieces because she thinks it's her fault, too. We should never have gone to that damn cabin. Then none of this would have happened."

Marley's gaze didn't move from her face. But she couldn't bring herself to look at him. Maybe because she felt like she'd gone too far. Said too much.

She'd wanted him to hold her. To tell her it was all going to be okay. But instead he was making her feel so much worse than she already did.

"Maybe I should go." His voice was still low and calm. She hated that.

"Yeah, maybe you should." She crossed her arms in front of her chest, so aware of how little she was wearing. She felt hurt, exposed. And she had no idea where all of this had come from. She wanted to cry, but she wasn't going to cry in front of him.

She had some pride left.

"Kate..."

Letting out a low breath, she turned away, because yes, even though she was trying hard, she could feel the tears starting to sting as they formed in her eyes. "I'm tired. Please just go."

For a moment he hesitated, then she heard the shuffle of his feet. The thud of his body as he climbed back out of the window he just climbed into. And she stood there, her arms wrapped around herself as she listened to the sound of his feet connecting with the grass, and a moment later the slam of his truck door.

It was only when the engine started up, and his truck pulled away that she let herself collapse into tears.

What just happened? She had no idea. Everything had felt so perfect two days ago and now it felt painful. And she had no clue how she could even begin to fix things.

Instead, she crawled into bed, tears pouring down her face, her body curled into the fetal position, all too aware of the empty space on the mattress next to her.

CHAPTER
Twenty-Eight

HOW'S ETHAN DOING? – *Marley.*

Kate stared at the message lighting up her phone screen. No mention of last night. Of their argument or her tears. No apologies or recriminations.

He's fine. Watching TV and eating Fritos. Living his best life. – Kate.

And how are you doing? – Marley

Good, thank you. And you? – Kate

I'm fine. – Marley.

• • •

If she wasn't feeling so sad, their exchange would have made her laugh. It was so… polite. And yet meaningless. Yes, it was nice he was asking about Ethan. But then so had so many other people. Half of Hartson's Creek had either knocked on their door or called or messaged her.

Her freezer was stuffed full of casseroles that people had dropped off to show they cared. Marley's mom had brought one over this afternoon. And his sister-in-law had brought a little gift for Ethan and Addy along with some flowers for Kate.

"Mom?"

Ethan was looking up from the sofa. Addy was sitting next to him, curled against his side. Since he'd come home from the hospital the little girl had been sweetly protective of him, bringing him food and drinks and sitting with him while she let him choose the TV shows he wanted to watch.

Kate was keeping an eye on it. She didn't mind Ethan taking advantage for a day or two, but after that she'd put a stop to it.

"Yes, honey?"

"When's James coming home?"

"On Saturday, remember?" She smiled at her son. "That's when his camp finishes."

"That's when he gets to hear about your burn," Addy told him. "He's gonna freak out."

"Do you think he'll be angry with me?" Ethan asked.

Kate shook her head. "No, honey. He'll be worried. The same way we all are." She ran her tongue along her bottom lip. "Do you think you'll be up to coming into the library tomorrow?" She was scheduled to work a shift. Usually, she'd put Ethan in camp, because he hated sitting around. Addy, on the other hand, was happy going in to work with Kate, following her around, helping her shelve books.

"Can I bring my iPad?"

She nodded. "Of course."

"Okay then, sounds good." He gave her a smile.

And damn if she didn't smile back. She loved that kid even if he was a headache. "Maybe on Thursday we'll go to the pool?" she suggested and his face lit up. "If you promise to take it easy. Just dangle your legs in."

"I promise." Excitement pulled at his face. "Thanks, Mom."

"No problem."

He didn't even try to climb into her window that night. And she didn't send him a text asking him to, figuring that maybe they both needed the space. Truth was, she wasn't sure she could deal with arguing with him again. But he'd called to check in again on Ethan this evening.

Their phone call had been brief because she'd been trying to persuade her son to take a shower, but the kid who was desperate to get into the community pool was somehow deathly afraid of getting his arm wet in the shower. Even though the special waterproof cover for his arm had arrived and she'd showed him how to use it.

And now it was nighttime again. And she was alone with her thoughts, which didn't feel like a safe place to be right now.

She pulled his name up on her phone screen and stared at it for a moment. She hated this coolness between them, but had no idea how to make things better. Because she was still annoyed at the way he'd practically accused her of making bad decisions. About her own children.

She let out a long breath. She needed to get over this. Logically, she knew their heightened emotions would calm eventually. But it still hurt. And she felt so alone.

She turned her phone off and turned onto her side, willing herself to sleep.

It was an hour later that she woke to banging. She was groggy, unwillingly pulled from a deep, dreamless sleep. Her heart started to bang against her ribcage as she panicked that there was something wrong with Ethan.

But when she checked his room he was fast asleep. As was Addy when Kate cracked open the door to her bedroom. Maybe it had been a bird landing on the roof or something.

But then she heard it again. Downstairs. Running into her bedroom, she grabbed a robe and pulled it around her, before padding down the steps to make sure everything was okay.

The whole floor was dark and silent. She took a look down the hallway, in the living room and the kitchen, before heading back to the stairs.

But then there was that noise again. Coming from outside. She frowned and walked to the window, pulling the curtain aside so she could look out.

Marley's truck was parked on the road. But there was no sign of him. At least not until half a minute later when he emerged from the side of her house, carrying a blackened grill in his strong, thick arms, putting it onto the open flatbed of his truck.

Wait, what? He was taking her grill without her permission?

Seriously?

Oh boy, now she was awake. And annoyed. She hurried down the hall to the front door and pulled it open.

"What are you doing?" she hissed into the dark night.

Marley looked up. She could just about make out his expression in the moonlight. He looked surprised. A little guilty.

Caught red-handed.

"Just cleaning up some mess." His jaw was set tight.

She swallowed hard. "That's my grill. Put it back." It was stupid how much she cared about that grill. But it was hers. The black charred mess.

"It's unusable, Kate." He was looking at her like she was crazy.

"I know that. But it's still mine. You're stealing it."

He let out a sigh. "I'm doing you a fucking favor. Taking it away so you don't have to. You think Ethan wants to see it every time he looks out the window?" Because that's where the firemen had left it, in the backyard right outside the garage, under Ethan's window.

"Maybe he should," she whispered furiously. "It's a reminder not to do it again." And yeah, she just made that up, but seriously? He was actually taking their grill? After she'd told him not to!

Hell no. She was the one in control of her own home. She had to be.

Pulling her robe tighter around herself, she stepped outside, the concrete rough against her bare feet. "Put it back," she told him.

"What?"

"Put my grill back." Her eyes were wide with annoyance. "I'm serious, Marley. You think I don't know what you're doing here? You didn't get your way so you're trying to sneak around while everybody's asleep to do it? Should I call the cops? Will that help?" Not that she was serious. They'd think she was as unreasonable as Marley obviously did.

"Calm down. I'm just trying to take care of things for you." His eyes were narrow. "It's the only thing I can do right now. I can't sleep thinking about this fucking grill. I can't sleep knowing Ethan is hurt. It needs to be gone. Now."

"But it's mine."

"Why do you care about a burned out grill?" he asked her. "You said you'd buy a new one. Even if I think that's a bad idea."

She had no answer to that. He was right, she knew it. And yet she couldn't bring herself to say it.

"The grill was Paul's," she told him. "It was his, and you're taking it away."

Marley's face contorted like she'd stabbed him.

Had she really said that?

"I didn't mean it like that." She told him, reaching for his hand. But he stepped back, away from her touch. "I honestly didn't."

"Mom?" Ethan was standing at the front door in his pajama bottoms. "What's going on?"

Her eyes met Marley's. "Nothing, honey."

"Why's Marley here?"

"He's just leaving, sweetheart." She walked back to the house, shooing him inside the doorway. "You should be asleep," she said softly.

"I tried to find you. My arm hurts."

Her chest tightened. "Like normal hurt? Or worse?" she asked him.

"Normal. I just wanted a hug."

"You can have all the hugs. Go up to bed, sweetie. I'll come hug you to sleep."

"You won't tell James, will you?" Ethan asked.

"About what?"

"About me needing hugs."

Her face softened. "James needs hugs sometimes, too. We all do. He wouldn't tease you about it."

"Okay, but still don't tell him."

She ruffled his hair. "I won't. Now up you go. I'll be up in a minute."

"Thanks, Mom." He looked past her, out the door. "Is Marley taking the grill away?"

Oh, so he'd seen that. "Yeah, he just thinks it should go."

"I think it should, too." Ethan's bottom lip wobbled. "I hate it." He pulled out of her grasp and walked to the stairs, his movements heavy with the sleep he must have only just escaped from.

Kate took a deep breath and turned back to look at Marley, trying to remember why she was so mad about the damn grill.

He watched her stroke her son's hair and send him up to bed, before her shoulders lifted with a deep breath, as though she were readying herself for something. When she turned around the expression on her face was neutral.

At least compared to the anger on it only moments before Ethan interrupted them.

He'd messed up again. He was tired of doing it. He was downright tired. He hadn't slept for days.

But this argument wasn't about the grill at all. He knew it and she knew it.

It was an argument about who felt more guilty for Ethan's burn. And the fact was, she shouldn't feel guilty at all. It wasn't her fault. She wasn't the one who'd made a solemn vow to Paul before they'd taken him away. She wasn't the one who'd seen her husband die in front of him, because he didn't have the fucking skills to save him.

She was the one who suffered, though. And she was suffering again. And it was fucking killing him.

Everything that had happened was down to him. He'd broken his promise.

"You can take the grill," she said, her voice soft. "Take it all. I don't want to see it again."

And because they were both too fucking exhausted to argue, he fetched the rest of it from behind the house while she stood on the porch and watched. And once he'd closed the tailgate he walked up to the door, mostly because he couldn't leave without saying anything.

"Is Ethan okay?"

"He will be. He just wants hugs."

He nodded. "Then you should go."

"Marley..."

He looked up at her. "What?"

"What's happening here? Why did you show up in the middle of the night and take the grill when I asked you not to? Why didn't you talk to me about it?"

The breath he let out felt ragged. "Because I knew you wouldn't let me." The memory of last night, of her asking him to leave still stung. He'd deserved it. He knew that much.

She hadn't wanted him to take the grill. She'd made it completely clear. But the truth was, he couldn't sleep knowing it was near the house. He'd tossed and turned, thinking about it. Needing it gone. And yeah, he knew it made no difference really. Ethan wasn't going near that thing after the experience he'd just had.

But he needed to do something. *Anything*. Needed to make the world right again. And that meant moving the grill.

"I need to make sure you're all safe," he said. "Always."

She let out a low breath. "A grill isn't going to make the difference. We're a little battered and bruised but we're fine."

He shook his head. Didn't she understand? He had to do this. He had to do so much more. "I promised Paul I'd take care of all of you. And I haven't. James was at a bonfire. Ethan got hurt. You and I..." He shook his head. "I shouldn't have pursued you."

"What?" Kate asked, keeping her voice low. What was he trying to say?

Her eyes tried to catch his, but he wouldn't look her way. A shiver wracked down her spine.

"I can't love you and keep you safe," he told her. "Every time I try, things just get worse. Maybe it's a message. Paul wouldn't have wanted this."

Her throat felt so tight it was hard to breathe. "How do you know what Paul would have wanted?"

"You and the kids were his biggest joy. Nothing else mattered to him. Nothing. I saw him fall, Kate. I couldn't save him. It's my fault he died. It's my fault he's not here to take care of you. If he'd been alive Ethan wouldn't be hurt."

"He had an aneurysm," she whispered. "It had been there for years without him knowing. That's what the medical examiner said. It burst, nobody caused it. It was nobody's fault." She lifted her hand to wipe the tears away. And each one of them felt like another wound to his heart.

He'd never hated anybody as much as he hated himself right now.

"He knew, Kate," he told her. "He knew I was in love with you."

She blinked. "You were in love with me when Paul was alive?"

"I've been in love with you for years. And yeah, he knew. He would joke about it. He once told me I'd only get you over his dead body." Fuck, he'd only just remembered that. It had been after a fundraiser. A woman had slipped her number in Marley's pocket and Paul had asked him if he was gonna call her.

"Of course I'm not. She's not my type," Marley had answered.

"What is your type? You never date anybody long enough for me to figure it out?" Paul had winked. "Apart from my wife, of course. But the only way you'll get to date her is over my dead body."

How had he forgotten that memory? Right now it felt like he couldn't breathe.

"I have to go," he told Kate, as she stood there watching him, her brow wrinkled. "I'm sorry." His voice broke. "I can't do this."

"Can't do what?" she asked, sounding so confused it hurt to hear it.

"Us. This." He shook his head. "I have to go."

And then he ran down the driveway, climbed into his truck, and drove away before she could see him fall apart in a way that could never be put back together again.

CHAPTER
Twenty-Nine

"A FUCKING GRILL." Shana shook her head. "That's why he split up with you? The mother fucker. And that's the last you heard from him?"

"He hasn't messaged me today." Kate and Shana were behind the desk at the library. Ethan was in Kate's office, behind the closed door, watching a movie on his iPad. And Addy was rearranging the cardboard books in the baby section. The library was due to open in ten minutes. And because it was summer vacation they had a full program running.

"Have *you* messaged him?" Shana said, her brows furrowed as she leaned on the counter. "I don't get this. That man has it hot for you. Like boiling hot. Why is he acting like such an idiot?"

"I haven't messaged him," Kate told her. "And I'm not planning to. He's the one who walked away. I have some damn pride." And of course she went and spoiled it by letting her voice waver like she was on the edge of tears.

"And to think I actually told him I loved him when we were at the cabin."

"You what?" Shana asked. "What did he say?"

"It doesn't matter. Because it doesn't mean anything. He picked a fight with me, did exactly what I asked him not to, then he walked away from me. I'm not going to go running after him."

"Of course you're not." Shana reached for Kate's hand, squeezing it tightly. "You're worth so much more than that."

Yes, she was. Even if it hurt like nothing else had in a long, long time. She took a deep breath, checking the clock. Two more minutes then she'd have to be ready to face the public. It was baby and toddler reading hour first – something she'd created after having to juggle three kids during the summer herself, knowing how desperate she would be for something to entertain them.

She'd tell the stories to them as they played on the cushions, along with the puppets the fire station had donated after their last fundraiser.

That Marley had donated. Ugh, there was no getting away from the man.

At ten they had two law enforcement officers coming in to demonstrate how they protected Hartson's Creek. This was aimed at six-to-ten-year-olds. Ethan was already excited about that one.

Then at eleven they had research hour for the high schoolers. The ones who were trying to get ahead for the upcoming school year. One of the teachers from the high school would come in and along with Kate they'd help the kids with their searches on both the internet and in the non-fiction section to find the answers they were looking for.

And of course this afternoon they had the Stitch and Snitch Club. She was already dreading it. Even if they didn't know the latest update on her non-relationship with Marley, they'd still know that they gone away together for the night. And that she and her parents had joined his family for lunch the other Sunday.

Nothing got past the gossips of Hartson's Creek.

"Can you come over tonight?" Kate asked Shana. "If I promise absolutely no smores but lots of wine?"

She didn't want to be alone tonight. She needed her friend.

"Of course I can." Shana hugged her. "You say wine, I say when. You know this."

Flashing her a smile that didn't quite make it up to her eyes, Kate walked over to unlock the sliding glass doors at the front of the library. There were already a few moms waiting out there. Beyond the library was the town park, along with swings and slides, and a few more families that were making the most of the cooler morning before the temperature got too hot to be outside.

Because when the West Virginia sun shone, it shone humid. Unless it involved being in a swimming pool, everything that needed to be done outside was done in the early mornings or late evenings throughout the summer.

"Thank God," one of the moms said as the doors swooshed open. She was holding a baby, with a toddler by her side, whose face was red from screaming.

Kate smiled and took the little one's hand. "What's up, sweetie?"

"I'm hot." The girl's words were stuttered with sobs. "And I want ice cream."

"It is warm," Kate agreed. "But if you come inside you'll cool down. We don't have ice cream, but we do have stories. And if you take a seat over there, you can help me choose the first one." She pointed over at Addy, who at six probably seemed grown up to this three-year-old. "You see that girl over there?"

"Yes." The little one sniffed.

"That's my daughter. Addy. She'll find you somewhere cool to sit."

Mollified, the little girl ambled over to Addy, who looked pleased as punch to be given a task to do. Kate turned to look at the mom. "Why don't you and your baby go to the recliners?" she suggested, pointing at the chairs on the far side of the children's library. "I've set headphones at each chair. You can choose an audio book to listen to or just zone out, up to you."

"You have headphones?" the mom asked, her eyes wide with interest.

"Noise blocking ones." Kate winked. "I'll come get you when the reading hour is over."

More parents and caregivers started to pour into the library. Over the past few years she really tried to make it a hub of the community during the summer. Not everybody had pools or access to one, and being stuck in the house for two months was nobody's idea of fun.

"Okay," she said, forcing a smile onto her face as she walked over to where all the parents and little ones had gathered. Addy was with the little girl she sent over. Her daughter looked proud as punch to be a quasi-big sister for once.

Maybe she should encourage that more. As the youngest of the family, Addy always got babied. But she looked like she was glowing right now.

She'd think more about that later. The same way she'd sort out her life later. And then she wanted to laugh because nothing was sortable.

Thank God she was busy.

"Who's ready for an adventure?" Kate shouted out, forcing a smile onto her face. "Because I don't know about you, but I think we should go on a bear hunt."

Thirty little kids started cheering. And that's how her morning went.

As exhausting as it was, her busy morning meant she didn't have to think about Marley, their argument, or the fact that he sent her a message at ten o'clock that morning, with the same words as yesterday.

How's Ethan doing? – Marley.

Again, no mention of the grill or the middle of the night attempt at snatching it away. Or their heated discussion and his sudden declaration that he couldn't be in a relationship with her anymore.

And dammit, she wasn't going to answer him this time. If he didn't want a relationship with her, then he needed to stop messaging her. And she needed to stop caring.

By the afternoon her energy was waning. The Stitch and Snitch gang were firmly ensconced in the activities room, though she couldn't hear a lot of stitching going on. And yes, she'd put her ear to the wall to listen to them, because of course they'd heard about her argument with Marley in the middle of the night. Mary Cooper was telling them that the same neighbor who'd told her this story had seen Marley climbing Kate's wall at night.

So much for being discreet.

She'd been the topic of conversation for exactly two minutes before another stitcher started telling everybody about the hot new bearded man at the hardware store and suddenly they were all exchanging stories about leaking pipes and rusty door handles, agreeing that a trip to the hardware store was needed very fast.

"Okay, you two," Shana said to Addy and Ethan who were lying on the cushions in the toddler area, both on their iPads. "What do you say we go for an ice cream run?"

"Ice cream?" Addy said, pulling her eyes away from the cartoon she was watching. "Mom?"

Shana shrugged at Kate in a kind of 'sorry, not sorry' way.

"Sure, ice cream would be fine. If you both promise to be good." She knew Shana was trying to rebuild the easy friendship between her and Ethan again. And she knew that Ethan wanted that. "Why don't you go for sundaes at the diner," Kate suggested. "My treat."

"No, it's my treat." Shana rolled her eyes at Kate. "But sundaes do sound good. Want us to bring you back anything?"

"I'm fine." Kate flashed her a smile. It was almost three. When Stitch and Snitch was over, she'd clean up from the activities and get everything ready for tomorrow before locking up.

Not that she was working tomorrow – it was her day off. And Kate had promised Ethan and Addy a trip to the pool, which was going to be an experience in itself.

"You haven't eaten your lunch," Addy piped up. "It's still in the frigrator."

"Refrigerator," Kate corrected her. "And I'll eat it later."

Shana shot her a look. "Go eat now."

"No. I'm fine." She'd made herself some salad, but she wasn't exactly in a salad kind of mood. She wasn't in any kind of a mood. She just wasn't hungry.

"You have to eat, Kate," Shana whispered in her ear.

"I'll eat later," she promised her friend. "Now you guys go have some fun."

Ten minutes later the door to the activity room opened and one by one the stitchers filed out. A few of them hurried out of the library with breathy farewells, late to pick up their grandchildren or meet their husbands or whatever else they had planned.

A couple of others started to peruse the shelves, and the rest stood in the lobby next to the desk, carrying on their discussion about the new hardware assistant.

"I hear he's single," Gloria, one of the older stitchers, said. "Think he'd like a cougar?"

"The car or the cat?" one of the other ladies asked.

"Me, you dumbass."

Kate shook her head and looked down at her computer screen, trying to work out how many toddlers were booked in for reading hour tomorrow. Maybe that's why she didn't notice the sound of the doors opening. Or the fact that every single person in the library had stopped talking until she heard his voice.

"Kate."

Just one word in his deep voice was enough to send a shiver down her spine. And she hated that. She didn't have to look up from the computer to know who it was. Even if he hadn't said a word her body would have reacted to him being so close.

"Marley." She willed herself to look at him.

But she didn't smile.

Three of the stitchers who were about to walk out of the library changed their minds and walked back to join the audience watching them.

"I sent you a message," he said, his eyes catching hers. "Did you get it?"

Dammit, she felt like she was on the set of a soap opera. And then Mary grabbed her phone from her purse and actually started recording them.

"No recording in the library," Kate said to her.

"Spoilsport," Mary grumbled, putting her phone back in her bag.

Marley's brows knitted as he turned to see the gaggle of older women watching them. "Can we talk in your office?" he asked Kate.

"No," Gloria said, clearly wanting to hear what he had to say. "You argued last night in the middle of the road and I missed it. I'm not missing it again."

If this wasn't so excruciating it would be funny right now.

Maybe it would be, one day, when she was old and single and consoling Addy after some heartache.

"Follow me," Kate said to Marley, lifting the countertop so he could walk through.

And dammit, she was so aware of his presence as he walked into her office. He was in a pair of work jeans and those brown scuffed boots that did things to her body when she saw them. There was dust in his dark hair, like he'd just come from the construction site.

"Sit down," she said, pointing at the chair by the window. "I'll get rid of the crowd."

When she got back to the desk they were all huddled around it.

"Okay, the show's over," Kate told them. "You can leave."

"Are you two going to have sex in there?" Mary asked.

Kate rolled her eyes. "Of course not."

"Then why can't we listen?" Mary didn't look embarrassed at all at the prospect of being a peeping tom.

"Because my life isn't your entertainment." Kate took a deep breath. "I'm asking you as a friend, Mary. Please make everybody leave. I've had a horrible week." She shook her head, deciding to appeal to the woman's fairer nature, if she had one. "To be honest, a horrible few years. And I need to talk to that man without it going viral in the community. Help me."

Mary's face softened. She reached for Kate's hand and patted it with her own. "Leave it to me," Mary told her, a smile pulling at her face.

"I just got a message," Mary shouted loud enough for everybody to hear. "The sexy guy in the hardware store is so hot he's took his top off. Why are we all still standing here?"

And to Kate's amazement, Mary's lie worked, and everybody rushed out.

CHAPTER *Thirty*

MARLEY WASN'T SITTING in the chair when she walked back into the office. Of course he wasn't. The man could never do as he was told. And he couldn't sit still to save his life.

Instead, he had his back to her, his hands in his pockets as he stared out of the window toward the greenery of the town park. She took a moment to compose herself, trying really hard not to look at the way his muscles filled out the dusty fabric of his t-shirt. Or the way it was damp from perspiration.

Because he'd been working outside most of the day.

"They're gone," she told him, and he turned around, his blue eyes meeting hers. She took a deep breath. "And before you say anything else, I'd like to say something first."

He opened his mouth and she held up her hand.

"I mean it. Just listen, please. You owe me that much."

His brows pulled tight in the center of his forehead but he nodded.

Her heart was pounding against her chest. Not just because she was so close to the man who'd told her he couldn't do 'them'. But because every part of her hurt. It hurt to see him, it hurt to talk to him.

It hurt to love him right now.

"I don't want you messaging me anymore," she told him. "I don't want you to ask how my children or I are doing. You told me you were done. You're not my boyfriend anymore."

"Kate…"

"No! I haven't finished." Damn it, she was going to say what she needed to. "I don't care what promises you made to Paul. Paul's dead. And yes, that's the big, awful tragedy of all of our lives, but he's gone and he's not coming back. And although it's taken me a long time to accept it, I have. So whatever you talked to him about that day is between you and him. I don't need your protection. I don't need to be looked after. I don't want you to do that for me or my children."

He'd made his decision and now he had to live with it.

"And it was never about the grill," she told him. "You and I both know that. It was about guilt and you not getting over it. Well, that's on you. So please leave and delete my number, because I don't want to hear from you again." She blew out a mouthful of air. "And to answer your question, Ethan is fine. I'm fine. We're all fine. And that's all you're getting." She opened the door and stepped aside, ready for him to walk out.

"This isn't what I want." He took a step toward her, then thought better of it. "Let's talk. I care about you. I care about the kids. I promised I wouldn't walk away from them, remember? We're supposed to be picking James up on Saturday."

"I'm picking James up from camp, without you," she told him. "I don't need your help with that either."

"But I…"

"Go. Please." Her voice was firm. Because it was so clear that he wasn't here to say he'd been wrong. That he'd changed his mind. That he hadn't meant it when he said he couldn't do this.

"Kate." His voice cracked. "Don't do this. I want to be here for you all."

"I didn't do anything. You did." Her voice was monotone. For a moment he looked at her, and she had to tell her traitorous, injured heart to calm down.

He walked out of the office, and a moment later she heard the swoosh of the glass doors as he left the library.

And that's when she allowed herself to close the office door and break down.

"What the fuck is wrong with you?" Pres asked Marley later that evening after he'd told him about his encounter with Kate. Because he'd stupidly gone to his brother's house, thinking at least Pres would understand why he'd ended things with her.

Truth be told, he'd tried running his bad mood off, but he couldn't be alone with his own thoughts. They were way too dark right now.

And Pres had done something similar himself, after all. Unilaterally deciding that his now-wife Cassie should leave him for a job in New York. He'd given her an ultimatum, told her that unless she took the offer there'd be no future for them.

And yeah, it was a bit different. But still.

"I had to decide between loving Kate and protecting her and the kids."

"But why?" Pres asked. "That's what I don't understand." He led Marley through the house. Cassie was in the living room. She looked up from the sofa, her brows lifting as she saw Marley in his running gear. The TV screen was frozen, like she and Pres had been watching a show and she'd paused it so he could answer Marley's knock on the door.

The knock he was already regretting. He should have just gone home and drank himself to sleep. Or knocked his head on the wall until the thoughts didn't hurt anymore.

Something other than thinking his twin brother might show some kind of sympathy toward him.

"Everything okay?" Cassie asked, her eyes still on Marley.

"Nope. My brother's a dick," Pres answered. "Listen, this might take a while. We may have to finish watching this episode another night."

"Don't let me interrupt you," Marley said, sensing a chance to escape the prison he'd made for himself. But Pres grabbed his arm.

"You're not going anywhere." Pres glanced at his wife. "He broke up with Kate."

Cassie's mouth formed into a perfect 'o'. "I heard the rumors but I didn't believe them," she said, frowning at Marley. "I hope she's okay."

"I doubt it," Pres said, shaking his head. Then he looked at Marley. "The swing set. Now."

"You want me to sit on the swing set while you ream me out?"

"Nope. It's where Cass and I go when we want to yell at each other. It's far enough away from the house for the kids not to hear."

The swing set Pres was talking about was an old one. Rusting at the back of the yard before the mowed lawn disappeared into the trees. Marley walked toward it, feeling a sense of impending doom.

Pres was right behind him. They each sat down on a swing. It was a tight fit, truth be told. The chains bit into his hips.

"Okay then. Tell me why you think you can't love her and protect her at the same time," Pres said.

"Why? So you can shout at me and call me a dick? Let's just skip ahead, shall we?" Marley asked. "Because the sooner we do that, the sooner I can leave."

"Remember what you told me when I sent Cassie away?" Pres asked him. "That at least you could say you weren't the author of your own fucking misery?"

"I said that?" Marley frowned.

"Oh yeah. You said it. And you meant it. But Jesus, man, why the hell are you doing it now?"

"I'm not doing this for me." Marley's voice cracked. "I'm doing this for Paul. I made him a promise. To keep his wife and kids safe. I can't be with her and do it. The last few days have proved that."

Pres kicked at the grass, shaking his head. "Can you hear yourself? Christ, man. You had it all. Everything you wanted. Everything you deserved. You were happy. I could see it. And you actually decided that the misery was better. Because for some stupid fucking reason you blame yourself for Paul's death."

"I don't blame myself. I just… there should have been something I could have done." He tried to blink away the memory of Paul's body lying in the ambulance, lifeless.

"I get how traumatic it must have been," Pres told him. "More than anybody, I understand that. I felt guilt for years after I lost Delilah's mom. But you're the one who told me I needed to move on when I met Cassie. I needed to forget the things I'd lost and move toward the future with her."

"I know. And look how happy you two are together."

"And look how happy you were with Kate. Her kids adore you. You know that? And you adore them. I saw it that day at Mom and Dad's. You were born to be a dad. Whether to your own kids or somebody else's." Pres' eyes caught his. "Are you really willing to let all that go?"

"If it's what it takes to keep them safe, yes," Marley said, his voice sure.

Pres winced. "You're a stubborn asshole when you want to be."

"Takes one to know one."

"You gotta make peace with it, man," Pres told him. "With what happened to Paul. With falling for his wife and kids. Unless you do, you'll never be happy again. You know that, right?"

"Maybe I don't deserve to be happy," Marley mumbled.

"And there it is. The real answer." Pres lifted a brow.

Marley frowned. "What do you mean?"

"I mean you sabotaged your own happiness because you feel guilty. Because Kate was Paul's wife and you loved her before he died."

Marley's chest tightened. Mostly because his brother had hit the answer right between the damn eyes. But also because that truth made him feel sick.

"It was wrong. Falling for my friend's wife," he managed to say.

Pres' face softened as he looked at his brother. "You couldn't help loving her. You never told her or did anything about it, did you? When Paul was alive, I mean?"

"Of course not."

"Then what the hell is there to feel guilty about? If Paul was still alive they'd be happily married and you'd be…" Pres trailed off. "I dunno. A pain in my ass, I guess."

"Shut up." Marley shook his head.

"Can I put it in a different way to you?" Pres asked. "One that might actually get inside that thick skull of yours?"

"Sure, go ahead. Kill me with insults. They're nothing I don't deserve."

"I'm not killing you with anything," Pres told him, turning to look his brother dead in the eye. "I'm telling you something I feel deep in my fucking heart. As a father. A husband. A man who'd do anything for his family." His voice was deadly serious. "If something happened to me, if I died..." He let out a low breath. "I'd want Cassie to find somebody else. Somebody good. Somebody I would have had beers with, in another life. Somebody who will love my kids and fight for them until his last fucking breath. I'd want her to find somebody like you." Pres' voice broke. "And that's no word of a fucking lie."

His brother was crying. And Marley could feel the tears stinging at his own eyes. He didn't want them. He didn't deserve them. So he wiped them away and stared back at his brother's house, trying not to feel guilty about the fact he'd pulled his brother away from his wife to cheer up his miserable ass.

Not that it had worked.

"I didn't know Paul like you did," Pres continued. "But he was a good man. A family man. And I'm almost certain he would want the same thing I would. For his family to be loved. To be cherished. For them to be happy and taken care of. To have everything he would have given them if he was still alive." Pres blew out a mouthful of air. "And I'm not saying you're a replacement for him. Because you're not. You're you. But even if you don't think you deserve happiness, don't you think Kate does?"

"Of course she does." Marley's voice cracked again. That's all he wanted. For her to be happy. To be safe. For the kids to have a good life.

"Then think on this," Pres said. "If it's not you she's happy with, it'll be somebody else. And you'll be in this fucking small town, watching some other guy make her smile, make her laugh. Make her fall in love with him. Do you want that? Could you stand to live here and watch it happen in front of your eyes? Because I know for damn sure I couldn't."

Marley said nothing. Mostly because there was nothing he could say. Pres was right. Every single word he'd said was true. And each one of them felt like white hot pain searing through his body.

"You need to make your peace with the guilt," Pres told him. "And you need to do it fast. Because a woman like Kate doesn't come around very often." Pres moved his body laterally, swinging until his shoulder came into contact with Marley's. "And if you don't fix things, you're gonna regret it for the rest of your life. I guarantee it."

CHAPTER
Thirty-One

HE LOOKED LIKE SHIT. Not that he expected anything else after another sleepless night. Staring at his exhausted face in the mirror gave him a grim sense of satisfaction. Mostly because what he had to do this morning was the one thing he never wanted to do.

His house was silent as he showered and shaved, then got his clothes ready.

He ironed the shirt he hadn't worn for a long time. Polished his shoes until he could see his face shining in the leather. Then pulled on the dress pants and jacket firefighters only wore for formal ceremonies and memorial services. It was ironic that the last time he'd worn this was for Paul's funeral.

And now he was going to see his friend again.

The cemetery was quiet when he pulled his truck into the parking lot. There were a few people visiting graves, but no funeral services taking place. As he climbed out of the cab, the heat of the morning hit him square on the jaw.

But he wouldn't take off his jacket or loosen his tie. This conversation needed full dress.

Paul's headstone was just like the man. Plain and plain speaking. A white stone with the following engraved on it:

Paul Connelly. Beloved husband, father, and firefighter. Rest In Peace.

Marley's eyes traced the dates on the grave. Paul had been in his forties when he died. It was no time at all. Certainly less time than Paul thought he had left on this earth.

He had no time to make any last requests. No time to put his things in order. No time to say goodbye to the people he loved the most.

In the blink of an eye, he ceased to exist.

Marley laid his hand on the cool stone. "I have no idea if you can hear me," he said, his voice thick. "But if you can. I'm sorry. For everything. I'm sorry I couldn't save you. I'm sorry you don't get to see your kids grow up. Your son…" He swallowed hard. "James. He's a good kid. Becoming a man. Like his dad. And you'd be so damn proud of him. He's at camp right now. Junior Firefighter Camp. Remember when he was little and you used to chase him around the yard? The kid can run it in about five seconds now." A fleeting smile pulled at Marley's lips. "And Ethan. He's smart. So clued in. A little impulsive, maybe. You might have heard about his arm. I'm sorry about that. It's my fault, it really is, but I'm gonna make sure he gets better. Somehow."

A breeze ruffled through the trees, hitting his face, cooling it down. "And Addy. She was so tiny when you died. She's six now. As beautiful as her mom. I get the feeling she's gonna be a sassy one."

He dropped to his knees, knowing the grass would stain his dress pants. But not caring at all. He needed to be face to face with Paul for the next part.

Or with his headstone, anyway.

"And Kate…" He shook his head. "I think you'd be the proudest of her. She's so beautiful and strong and… of course, I'm biased. I'm in love with her. You know that. You always knew that. And I hope you know I never did anything about it. Even now, I'm fighting against it. Not because I don't want her but because I do. Too much. And right now I don't deserve her. I know that. But I want to deserve her. I want *you* to think I deserve her, too. Is that too much to ask?" He touched the stone again. "I'm sorry. Maybe it is."

Another gust of wind lifted his hair. It felt almost like a human touch. And yeah, he knew it wasn't Paul. He didn't believe in ghosts. Hell, he wasn't even sure why he was here.

It just felt necessary. Right.

He owed Paul so much. He needed to tell him that.

"I don't know if Kate will forgive me," he told Paul. "But I know I need to try to earn it." He swallowed hard. "It would be so much easier if you could give me a sign, man. A little thunder. A flash of lightning. Make the sun go out for a moment."

But there was nothing. Just the peacefulness of the cemetery and the blueness of the sky, peppered with little wispy clouds and the contrail of an airplane that had passed over so high it hadn't made a sound.

And maybe that's what life was. There weren't signposts pointing you in the right direction. You didn't get to know what the results of your actions were before you took them. You just had to navigate it, decision by decision, hoping they're the right ones. Knowing that some of them would be wrong, but you'd carry on anyway.

And yes, his decisions this week were so damn bad he felt like trash. He'd hurt the woman he was in love with.

He had to show her how damn regretful he was. Not for trying to protect her and the kids – because that was in his nature and he wasn't sure he could ever change that – but for thinking that overrode the decisions she made. For ending things with her because he couldn't deal with the guilt of not being there to protect Ethan when he needed it.

"I'm surprised to see you here."

He turned to see Mary Cooper standing there. The woman who'd been desperate to hear his conversation with Kate at the library yesterday was wearing a knit dress, carrying a bouquet.

"My husband's grave is over there," she said, pointing at a headstone two plots down. "I always leave a rose for Kate's husband when I come to visit Ralph." She picked a yellow rose out and laid it in front of Paul's headstone. "So have you pulled your head out of your sweet behind yet?"

It took him a moment to respond. Mostly because he wasn't sure he'd heard her correctly.

"My sweet behind?" he repeated.

"Voted the best ass in Hartson's Creek for the last five years running," she said, sounding deadly serious.

"By who?"

"The Hartson's Creek Stitching Society. At our annual awards dinner. You get beaten out for the best arms by your baby brother, sadly."

"You vote about male body parts at your awards dinner?" He didn't even know they had an awards dinner. Let alone that his ass had been a subject of it for the last five years.

"Among other things. And let me tell you," she said, waggling her finger. "You're currently running high in the charts for villain of the year for what you've done to our dear Kate."

He swallowed hard. "Well, I'm trying to rectify that."

Mary's lips curled into a smile and for a minute she looked like a sweet older lady. "You better do it right," she told him. "Woo her. Show her she's a prize. That woman deserves romance. You'd better give it to her."

"Romance?" He felt a little weak.

"Absolutely. And don't half ass it." She reached for his arm, patting it. "Ooh, solid. Maybe we need to rethink you losing out to Hendrix."

Jesus Christ, was he in some kind of alternate universe?

"Now stop talking to the dead and start thinking about the living," she told him. "You aren't going to get the answers you need here."

He was ready to leave, anyway. Not just because his conversation with Paul had been distinctly one way. But because he was sweltering in his dress clothes. And he was due on site, too. Pres had been understanding about his need to come in late, but the job still needed to get done.

But there was one thing that Mary was wrong about. He'd gotten the answers he needed here. Even if they'd been in his heart all along.

The community pool was a ten-minute walk from their house, so Kate hadn't bothered to drive there.

Ethan was sitting on the side of the pool in the shade, his arm protected by the waterproof sleeve she'd bought him, while his friends swam in the center, throwing a ball at each other and occasionally at Ethan.

She could tell he was itching to get in. She was proud of the way he didn't moan that he couldn't join them, or that he was getting the ball less than anybody else playing in the pool.

Addy was in the little pool, splashing with her friends while they talked nonstop about something that made them all giggle.

Kate had taken a book with her, but it was completely unread. Instead, her head had been full of thoughts as she'd watched her children play. Thoughts of James – who she'd see in two days, and how they only had a couple of summers left before he'd be going to college. Of Ethan and how she could keep him entertained with only one arm. Of Addy and the way she was so sweet and kept running to Ethan to make sure he was okay.

And even though his friends were there, watching him, he'd treated her sweetly back.

Her kids made her heart ache in the best of ways sometimes.

"Mom, I think I'm ready to go home when you are," Ethan said, walking over to the sunbed where she'd put all their things.

Kate blinked. Ethan never wanted to leave the pool. Neither did Addy, for that matter. "You sure?" She checked her watch. "We can stay another thirty minutes if you want?"

He shook his head. "Nah." He glanced at her book. "You look bored anyway."

"I'm not, it's fine."

"Seriously, Mom, let's get you home." He patted her shoulder and just that unexpected gesture brought tears to her eyes.

Was she so starved of kindness that her son taking note of her mood was enough to make her cry?

"Can you go get Addy?" Kate asked him, blinking the stupid tears away. They weren't about Ethan and he didn't need to see them.

"Sure."

Kate started to pack their things away as Ethan walked over to the little pool to talk to his sister. She watched him call out Addy's name and held her breath, half expecting the two of them to explode into their usual argument.

But instead Addy nodded and jumped out of the water.

And then took Ethan's good hand.

Dear God, had her kids been body snatched? Because they were walking around the pool hand in hand, like Ethan's friends weren't there, watching him.

"Everything okay?" Kate asked, her chest tight as they reached her.

"Everything's fine, Mom," Ethan told her.

Addy nudged him.

"Ask her," she whispered.

"I'm going to. Just a minute." Ethan shook his head at his sister.

"Ask me what?" Kate said, a smile playing at her lips. What were they up to now?

"Is Marley angry at us?" Addy said. "Because of what happened over the weekend?"

The shock of their question made her momentarily silent. She opened her mouth, but no words came out.

She took a deep breath. "No," she managed. "He's not angry at you. Not at all."

"He looked angry when he took the grill," Ethan said.

Had this been playing on their minds all week? "He wasn't angry with you. He was angry with me," she told him.

"Why?" Ethan asked.

"Can we talk about this at home?" she asked them. "Over a bowl of ice cream?"

"Isn't it almost dinner time?" Addy asked, looking confused. Because ice cream was never a treat before dinner. "And we had ice cream with Aunt Shana the other day."

"Yes, but it's hot and we need to talk, so we can make an exception."

"What's an expection?" Addy asked, messing up the word.

Kate tried to find the right way to explain it – and failed. "It's when you get ice cream," she finally said.

"Yay! I love expections," Addy says, clapping her hands together.

"Works for me." Ethan grinned.

It worked for her, too. Because at least she'd have time to think about how to explain the hot tempers of that night with the grill. That they both loved the kids – at least, she hoped they both loved the kids – and wanted what was best for them.

Her stomach felt tight at the memory. And at the thought that kept swirling through her brain. Her refusal to talk to Marley wasn't going to work. She needed to talk to him. To tell him that if he wanted to still see the kids that would be okay.

Their hearts were more important than hers, after all.

She passed Addy a ball to carry, and Ethan insisted on carrying Addy's inflatable ring with his good arm. Then Kate lifted the cooler half-full of drinks and the beach bag full of towels over her shoulder, letting Ethan and Addy lead the way out of the pool gate before they turned left to head toward home.

It wasn't just her kids who needed ice cream. She did, too. A whole sugary heap of it.

And yeah, it was probably going to ruin her dinner.

The idea had come to him as Marley was driving away from the construction site. They'd finished early because of the heat. And yeah, the only reason he wasn't driving straight to Kate's house was because he was taking Mary's advice seriously.

He needed to apologize. To explain. To throw himself at her fucking feet for being a scared ass who didn't deserve a woman like her.

But more than that, he needed to show her how sorry he was. And this stupid idea in his head kept growing.

So he turned his truck around and drove to the hardware store to get some of the things he'd need to pull this off.

It was weirdly busy. Who knew so many people wanted to do home projects in the middle of summer? He managed to push past a group of women who were asking the new guy for advice about leaky pipes and headed to the counter to pay for his supplies.

His next stop was the garden center. By the time he headed back into town it was late in the afternoon.

And enough time had passed. He drove straight to her.

He was going to lay it down, one way or another. Or rather, lay himself down. He wasn't guilty or afraid or fearful of the future. Kate's decision once she heard him out was up to her.

But he wasn't giving up without a fight. Not this time.

As he turned onto her road he could see the three of them walking toward the house. They were carrying inflatables and towels. The kids' hair was wet. From the pool, he assumed.

That made his heart feel a little lighter. Ethan was well enough to go to the pool – that was a good thing.

He slowed down, watching them walk up the driveway to the front door. Just looking at her sent tingles through him. She put the cooler down that she had been carrying and slid the key into the lock.

And he pulled into the driveway, making her jump.

"Marley!" Addy shouted when he climbed out of the cab. She ran down the steps, throwing herself against his legs. He lifted her into his arms. She was warm from the sun, damp from the swimming pool. And she had the biggest, toothiest grin on her face. "We missed you."

"I missed you too, kid." Even though it had only been three days, he really had. Before the weekend, he'd been ready to declare himself to these kids the way he declared himself to their mom.

Or he'd thought he'd been ready. Ironic, really, that he really was ready now. But he couldn't do it. Not yet.

Maybe not ever.

Ethan was more cautious. Marley's gaze sought him out and Ethan gave him a nervous smile.

"Hey," Ethan said.

"Hey man. How's the arm?"

Ethan lifted it up. "I went to the pool but I didn't get it wet."

"Great work. I'm proud of you."

That was enough to make Ethan glow. And fuck if that didn't make him glow, too.

And then there was Kate. She was hovering in the doorway, her wary gaze watching him.

"Kate." Just saying her name made him want to run to her and scoop her into his arms.

Wooage, man. Wooage. You got work to do first.

"Marley."

"I hope I'm not interrupting. I just need to borrow your kids for a while."

Kate blinked. "What? Why?"

"I'd like Ethan and Addy to help me with something."

"Oh." A look of disappointment washed over her face. Kate looked at her two youngest kids swarming around him. "Why don't you two go inside and get changed out of your swimsuits? Then Ethan, you can be in charge of getting the ice cream. Let me and Marley talk for a minute."

The mere mention of ice cream was enough for Addy to squirm out of his arms and run inside the house. Ethan was a little slower, but no less eager.

Marley walked up the steps, his eyes on Kate.

"Their dentist bills are going to be astronomical if I keep on like this," she said, shifting her feet.

"Summers are made for ice cream."

His gaze took her in. The dark hair, tied up into a messy ponytail. The thin straps of her white tank, the way the shorts she was wearing showed off the slimness of her thighs. Her skin, oh God, her skin.

"You look beautiful," he told her softly.

"Marley, I…"

"And I know I have no right to say that to you. I know that." His voice cracked as his eyes caught hers. "But there are a lot of things I want to say to you when the time is right and you're willing to hear them. But I'm guessing we have about five minutes before the kids are riding some kind of sugar high, and that's nowhere near enough time for me to say all the things I need to say."

Her expression was neutral. She wasn't giving anything away. And that was fine. He didn't want her to give him anything. He wanted to earn it. Like the prize she was.

"So let me start by telling you this. I'm a fucking idiot. And I'm so, so sorry. For the grill, for the argument. But most of all, for leaving you when you were at your lowest. For walking away when I always promised to be the one who stayed."

"Mom!"

Kate frowned. "I have to…"

"Yeah, I know. Can I come in? There really is a project I want to work on with the kids."

"Now?"

"It'll take a couple of hours, but yeah, now. If they want to."

"It's almost dinner time," Kate pointed out.

"We can stop for dinner. For drinks. For whatever."

"You know they'll be more of a hindrance than a help, right?" Her gaze softened. And damn, he loved that gaze.

"I'm counting on it," he said.

"Then come in."

Thank God. It was a first step toward his goal. But he still had a lot more to take.

CHAPTER
Thirty-Two

"WHAT'S HE DOING?" Shana asked Kate a couple of hours later, as the two of them stared out of the kitchen window at Marley and her kids.

"He just said it was a project," Kate answered, because she was none the wiser. The three of them had been working out there since they finished dinner. And no, she hadn't cooked him any, though she'd relented when Addy asked if she could bring him some sweet tea and a cookie.

Kate had tried really hard not to spy on them. She'd folded the huge pile of clean clothes that had built up over the past few days. Rinsed the swimsuits that Ethan and Addy had thrown on the laundry room floor in their excitement for ice cream and Marley.

But she kept getting drawn to the kitchen window. Desperate to see what was going on. She was certain Marley had caught her watching a couple of times.

And yes, every time his eyes met hers, she felt the connection.

"Wait, is that the grill lid out there?" Shana asked.

Yeah, that had been a surprise when he'd carried the charred lid into the yard. Although it wasn't charred anymore. He'd gotten Addy to power wash it off. Then he'd got to work with a welding iron, while Addy sorted out what looked like little shiny pebbles.

"Oh my God, is he making a sculpture?" Shana asked, her mouth dropping open.

Truth was, Kate still wasn't sure. All she knew was watching this big, beautiful man interact with her kids was killing her in the best and worst kind of way. "He said he was sorry," she told Shana.

"Was that it?" Shana wrinkled her nose. "You didn't accept it, did you? An asshole act like that requires a hell of a lot more than sorry."

"I didn't say anything. It was when the kids were changing out of their swimsuits. He talked the whole time. Said he's sorry, that he's an idiot." She let out a breath. "And he said I'm beautiful."

"Hmph," Shana said, clearly still not happy with his words.

"He wants to talk later, when we have time alone," Kate told her, watching as Addy started twirling around the yard, clearly getting bored after all this time helping her brother and Marley. Ethan, on the other hand, was still close to Marley, the two of them talking softly as they worked together, Marley instructing, Ethan following with his good hand.

She felt breathless. And there was something else. Hope. It felt like a warm glow in her heart.

"Will you talk to him?" Shana asked her. "Do you want to hear what he has to say?"

She looked at her friend. "Yeah, I think I do."

"Mommy, come see!" Addy shouted out an hour later. Shana had left about thirty minutes earlier. She'd only popped by to drop off a cake somebody had left for Kate at the library that day. It was getting late now. The sun was starting to fall behind the trees. The kids needed to take showers and get to bed.

But right now they were waiting breathlessly for her in the yard, huge smiles on their faces. "We made you a gift," Addy said, running over to her as she stepped out of the kitchen door.

"It's pretty cool, Mom," Ethan told her. "But we have to tell you the story behind it first."

"Where's Marley?" she asked Ethan.

"He's packing up the truck. Said we should be the ones to show you our hard work. So, Mom, remember the grill I hurt myself with?" Ethan said, sounding solemn.

Kate felt a twinge in her chest. "Yes, sweetie, I do."

"Well, I hated it. I really did. But Marley said that we can make good things come from bad. That we can turn things around and make ruined things better. So we made a planter out of it. Come see." He took her other hand, and the three of them walked over to the corner where the kids had been working.

"I chose the stones," Addy said, tugging at Kate's hand.

"And I helped glue them on," Ethan said proudly. "Marley let me use the hot glue gun."

The grill lid was transformed. The handle and dial were gone, replaced, she presumed, with some of the metal Marley had carried out of the truck. Then the whole outside had been enlarged into what looked like a six-foot planter. It was covered with a mosaic of glass stones that sparkled in the light of the waning sun.

Inside, they'd planted a cornucopia of pretty flowers. Yellow dahlias and pink coreopsis against the green and purple of Russian sage. You couldn't look at it and not smile.

"Good things come out of bad," Ethan repeated. "We can

make things better if we just work hard." He looked at her. "Do you like it?" he asked.

"Yes," she whispered, afraid she'd start crying again. "I really do. It's beautiful. You worked so hard."

"I don't hate the grill anymore," Ethan told her, his eyes bright as he looked up at her.

"Nor do I," Addy said, not wanting to be left out. "I love it now."

Kate hugged her kids, being careful not to squeeze Ethan's injured arm. "You're both so amazing."

"Marley did some of the work," Addy conceded. "But we did a lot too."

"Yes, you did. I'm so proud of you." She kissed her daughter's cheek. "If you go inside there's some juice waiting for you in the kitchen."

"Whoop!" Addy bumped her fist into the air and started running.

Kate turned to look at Ethan. "Your arm okay?"

"It's fine. You and Marley need to stop asking me that."

Of course Marley had been asking. She wouldn't have expected anything less. "And you're okay? With the grill?"

"Yeah. It was cool making the planter. I like working with Marley. He's not angry with us, he told us that. He's angry with himself. Or he was." Ethan pressed his lips together. "I told him I was angry with myself too, and he said that was okay. That sometimes we get angry, but it's what we do with the anger that counts. We have to work through it and leave it behind."

Her throat felt tight. "He's right."

"Yeah, I think he is." Ethan looked at her hopefully. "Can I have some juice too?"

"There's a glass inside waiting for you, too. Then it's time for a shower and bed, okay?"

Ethan nodded and walked back to the house. She watched

him until he opened the back door then took a deep breath before turning and walking around the side of the house.

Marley was still there, loading the last of his tools into the truck.

"Are you leaving?" she asked him.

"No, just putting everything away." His eyes caught hers. "But I can leave if you want me to."

"I don't." Her heart was hammering against her chest. "I need to change Ethan's dressing and get the kids to bed. And then I'm ready to listen, if you're ready to talk." And maybe she'd do some talking too. She felt like she needed that.

His gaze didn't leave hers. "I'm so ready."

"Would you like to come inside?" she asked him. "There's more sweet tea. You can wait in the air conditioning while I get them to sleep."

"I'd like that very much," he told her. And then he smiled and it sent a pulse of electricity to the tips of her fingers and her toes.

And she couldn't help but smile back.

"The kids want you to say goodnight to them," Kate told him. She was standing in the doorway between the kitchen and the hall. He was sitting in the kitchen in the dark, a half-empty glass of sweet tea on the table in front of him. His long legs were stretched out as he looked out of the window at the now darkening sky, watching as the stars began to pepper the fabric of the universe.

"Sure." He stood. "If that's okay with you."

"I think there'd be a riot if it wasn't." There was that half smile again. What he wouldn't give to make her smile like she did last week. Unguarded. Huge.

Like she didn't have a care in the world.

She stepped aside for him to walk past her, but not

enough that his arm didn't brush hers. He could hear her breath stutter at the contact, the same way his body clenched.

Damn, he liked that too much.

He went into Addy's room first. She was lying on her back, her eyes wide as though she was forcing herself to stay awake.

"Marley!"

"Hey." He sat on the edge of her bed. "Thanks for all your help with the planter. You did great."

"Mommy says I can water it every day to keep the flowers looking pretty." She smiled proudly. "It's my job."

"It's an important one," he said. "Keeping flowers alive is hard work. My mom is a big gardener."

"She is? Does she have lots of flowers?"

"Yeah, you saw them. When you and your mom and grandparents came for lunch at my parents' house, remember?"

Addy blinked. "Oh yeah." But she didn't remember at all and that was okay.

"She probably has a little watering can you can have. I'll ask her."

Addy grinned. "Thank you. Can I have a hug?"

Of course she could. He leaned forward and her little arms wrapped around his neck as she nestled her face against his. "Night, Marley."

"Night, Addy." His voice was low. "Sweet dreams."

Ethan was reading a book, holding it awkwardly with one hand when Marley went into his room. He looked up. "Thank you for bringing the grill back," Ethan said. "I wasn't sure I wanted to see it again, but I'm glad you did. It was fun."

"Yeah, it was." Marley nodded. "Thanks for your help with it."

"Can we build things again?" Ethan asked. "Together, I mean?" The hopeful look on his face touched Marley to the core.

"If it's okay with your mom."

"I already asked her. She said it was."

Weird how that gave him hope, too. Yes, it could just be Kate giving him her blessing to have a relationship with her kids. And he'd take that. But he'd still hope for more.

Marley leaned down to ruffle Ethan's hair. "There's nothing I'd like better. I was thinking maybe a water feature would look good in your backyard."

"Cool!" Ethan's eyes lit up.

"We'll talk about it soon. Now get some sleep. You did good work today."

"And all with one hand," Ethan said proudly.

"Imagine what you'll be like when you can use both of them again."

After he turned out Ethan's light and closed his door, Marley lingered on the landing for a moment. Knowing the woman who lit him up in every way was waiting downstairs for him. Giving him a chance to say what he needed to say.

More of a chance than he probably deserved.

His jaw was set as he walked down the stairs and into the kitchen. Kate was closing the dishwasher as he walked in. Slowly, she turned around to look at him.

"They're both on their way to sleep."

"Thank you." The soft tones of her voice did things to him. Made him want her all over again. "Would you like a drink? More sweet tea? Beer?"

He shook his head. "I'm good."

"Then shall we just go outside? If you still want to talk."

"I still want to talk." His voice was firm. He walked over to the back door, opening it for her, so aware of the slightness of her body as she brushed past him and walked through it into the night air.

It was still warm even though the sun had set. He followed Kate to the chairs at the far side of the yard, beside the planter they'd made.

"Catch." She threw something at him, and he put up his hand. A little bottle of bug spray landed in his palms.

"I put some on already," she told him. "You should too."

He did as he was told, spraying the pungent aroma all over him.

Then he looked at her, swallowing hard, because it was time.

"Are you okay for me to start talking?" he asked.

She nodded.

"Good. And thank you for agreeing to this." He took a deep breath, trying not to choke when a waft of bug spray got caught in the back of his throat. And he realized he couldn't do this with so much space between them. He turned in his chair and reached for her hand.

She gave it to him. And it felt like the best kind of prize.

"I'm so sorry I hurt you," he told her. "I'm so sorry I said I couldn't do this with you. Because there's nothing else I want in the world except you and your kids. What I said that night was unforgiveable. And yet I'm asking you to listen to me, and maybe forgive me. So I can prove to you that I'm worthy."

Kate squeezed his hand. Fuck, he needed that.

Kate's chest felt like it was being squeezed as Marley started talking. Mostly because she knew how hard it was for this man to admit weakness. To talk about his feelings.

But he was doing it. For her.

He looked down at his hands. "The last two years… since Paul… I've had one thought on my mind. Keeping my promise to him. Making sure you and the kids were safe. I thought that was enough, that by doing that my guilt would be eased."

"You shouldn't feel guilty." Her voice was thick. "Paul's death wasn't your fault. It wasn't anybody's fault."

"That was why I felt guilty. Such a painful, random act and it happened to a man with a wife and kids. When he was standing next to me, a guy who had none of that. Why him? Why not me?" Marley shook his head. "That's all I could think about. What kind of irony is it that the one man people wouldn't miss was spared and the man everybody needed was taken?"

Kate let out a long breath. "You would have been so missed. And Paul never would have wanted you to feel that way."

"I know. But I think I felt it, anyway. But I just concentrated on doing what I promised. Being a good guy, doing good things. Making sure you and the kids were safe and protected."

"You can't live your life paying a price for a deal you never should have made."

"It's a good way of not dealing with the pain, though." His eyes caught hers. "And then I'd feel guilty that I felt any pain, because I know it's nothing like the pain you and the kids have been through. And look at the four of you. You're thriving."

"So are you. And it's not a competition." Her breath was shallow. "You're allowed to feel pain. You're allowed to feel guilt. You don't have to keep beating yourself up over something you have no control over."

The corner of his mouth lifted. "You see, now you're consoling me."

"No, I'm just telling you a truth. It took me long enough to learn it. And you were there for me when I did."

He nodded. "And I'm hearing it. I'm hoping to feel it, too." He touched his chest. "In here." He stroked her hand with his thumb. "I went to see Paul today."

"I know," she admitted.

"You do?"

"I got a text from Mary. Said she saw you at the cemetery in full uniform."

"I guess it's impossible to keep secrets around here."

"She was just digging for gossip," Kate said softly. "How was it when you went?"

"I told Paul I'm in love with you. It felt right to be dressed in full uniform for the occasion." He looked almost peaceful for the first time in days. "I wasn't struck down by lightning so I figure he's okay with it." He smiled. "But what matters is you. I hurt you, and I hate that."

"It feels like you hurt yourself more," she told him. "And I wasn't exactly an angel. I don't know why I got so upset over a stupid grill."

"Because it wasn't about the grill. It was about my need to protect you overriding your right to make decisions. And it never should have. You don't need a protector, Kate. Though I'm gonna admit I'll find it hard not to be that guy. What you need is a partner. Because you've got this on your own. You're already winning at this."

"It doesn't feel like it," she admitted. "It feels like I'm losing more than I'm winning."

"Maybe that's why you could use a partner," he said softly. "To show you how wrong you are. And I have no right to ask, but I'm going to, anyway. Because I want that partner to be me. I want to be yours in every way possible. With my heart, my body. My fucking soul. It's all yours. It has been for a while now." He lifted her hand up, pressing his lips against her wrist. "Maybe I'm the one that needs a protector."

"From what?" she asked, her voice thick. Because this man of few words was killing her with so many. And she knew he meant every single one of them. He was used to actions, to communicate by doing things.

Hell, the planter they were sitting next to was a testament to that.

"From myself, I guess." He smiled at her and it was devastating. "From my own bad decisions."

"You only made one of them." She nodded at the grill. "And it's back now."

"Is it?"

Even though his hand was in hers she still felt the distance between them. It was too much. She needed to be closer.

She needed to feel him.

"Can I sit with you?" she asked.

He pulled her over. Instead of shuffling so she could sit next to him, she landed on his lap.

He let out such a contented sigh she felt warmth rush through her.

And maybe she hadn't thought this all the way through. Because now that they were touching she felt the need again. Like an ache that never truly went away.

She squirmed in his lap and this time his groan wasn't so contented.

"Kate…"

"Sorry." Though the smile she gave him wasn't sorry at all.

He cupped her face, his eyes intent on hers. "I want a second chance," he said. "I want us. I want our family. I want to be the one to put all the smiles on your face and wipe all the tears away. I want to protect you and have you protect me. I want to take care of your kids and listen to them argue and moan. I want them to become the teenagers that hate us because we're the parents that are always making out in the kitchen when they're around."

She laughed, because the image of it was so strong. Marley pulling her in for a kiss as she cooked dinner and a teenage Addy and Ethan did their homework, while James wrinkled his nose at their antics.

She ached to have that. To have *him.* To get back on the

road they'd started to walk together. The one that twisted and turned but led to the most beautiful of sunset-lit horizons.

"I want that too," she whispered. "So yes. Yes, please."

"You forgive me?"

She nodded, emotion making her chest feel like it was going to burst. "Yes, I do."

"Okay, but you need to know. This isn't it. Operation Woo is just beginning. Because every day with you feels like I've won something I want to be worthy of. And I'm never going to stop letting you know that you're the biggest and best prize any man can have."

"Operation Woo?"

"It's a Mary thing."

"She's been quite the busy woman." She held up her phone. Two more messages from her appeared on Kate's screen.

"She really has," he agreed, his warm eyes on hers. "Let's keep her in suspense for a little while longer, shall we?"

"It'll be my greatest pleasure." Kate put her phone down. And his gaze softened in that way she remembered all too well. She could feel him swelling beneath her, see the way his eyes were darkening. The need in them reflecting her own desires.

"Are you going to kiss me now?" she asked him.

"Just working up to it." His gaze dropped to her mouth. "This one means something. A lot of something."

"What does it mean?" she asked.

"It means I'm here, Kate. I'm in this thing. We're in it together. It's serious. You know that, right? I'm serious about you."

Her heart did a little loop the loop. "I'm serious about you, too."

"Thank God." He cupped her face with his palm, moving his own face closer, until she could feel the warmth of his breath against her skin. She was holding her own, the anticipation of his mouth making her body start to tingle.

And when his lips met hers, they started a fire inside her skin. Everything about his kiss was heated. The way he angled her head, the way he plundered her mouth, the way his tongue felt like it was making love to hers.

She wrapped her arms around his neck, kissing him back, loving the taste of him. How had they almost thrown this away? Not kissing Marley Hartson would have been a stupid waste of the rest of her life.

"Mommy?" a little voice called out from the upstairs window. "Are you two kissing?"

She started to laugh, because if he hadn't realized before how intrusive kids could be in a relationship, he sure as hell was about to find out.

"We're just talking very close to each other's faces," Kate called back to Addy. "Now go back to sleep."

"Okay," Addy said, closing the window.

Marley was grinning at her. "I'm guessing sex is out for the next fifteen years."

"You're going to have to get used to climbing up my drain pipe," she told him.

"I'll do whatever it takes to be with you," he said, suddenly serious. "But eventually, when the time is right, I want us to be together. A couple. Married. A family. You know that, right?"

"I want that too."

His smile was big. "Good." He kissed her again. A soft one, but so, so sure. "I love you, Kate Connelly."

Her warm eyes met his. "I love you right back."

Epilogue

"MOMMY!" Addy called from the backyard. "You can come out now."

Kate's lips twitched. How many times had she heard those words this summer? The long, balmy days were drawing to an end – school was back in session next week – and she felt a little pang in her heart.

Despite starting out as the worst summer ever, it had quickly morphed into the best. After their heartfelt talk, she and Marley had agreed to start their relationship again. The following week, with James at home, they'd told Addy and Ethan that they were dating.

Not that Ethan and Addy had blinked an eyelid. As far as they were both concerned, Marley was their best friend as well as Kate's new suitor. And the three of them – or four once James was back – were thick as thieves, plotting ways to 'woo' Kate.

She was now the proud owner of a fountain creatively made from old metal tire rims that Marley had found and painstakingly shaped into flowers with Addy, while Ethan and James concentrated on the plumbing. There was also a 'remembering tree', as Addy called it. This one was made from rusted metal struts, and as big as a real tree, with fronds that cascaded down like a weeping willow. It was where the kids could go when they were sad about Paul. Not that she'd seen any of them under there recently.

More and more there were smiles on their faces when they talked about their dad, or when Marley regaled them with a story about him.

But this last project was a secret. Whatever it was, they'd been carrying it in and out of the garage each night so she couldn't sneak a peek.

They didn't trust her, and she got that. Because she totally would have snuck out to see what they were doing if given the chance.

"Okay, I'm coming," she called out.

"She's coming," Addy shouted.

"Yeah, we heard her." James' low voice sounded amused.

He'd had a fantastic time at junior firefighter camp. When she'd picked him up with Addy and Ethan – Marley had stayed behind because they were short on volunteers that weekend thanks to a bug that was sweeping through the station – he'd looked like he'd grown up. Like a man.

She'd never felt more proud.

Another bonus of camp? He'd decided he definitely wanted to go to college before becoming a firefighter. "A lot of the instructors said a college education is a good thing," he told her breathlessly, like she hadn't been saying the same thing to him. "They think I should go."

Next year she and Marley would take him to tour some colleges. Then during his senior year he'd apply. He was growing fast, her first son. And she was so happy to see him bloom.

She opened the door to see all three of her children waiting for her. Addy was jumping up and down with excitement. James just smiled at her as Ethan took Kate's hand.

"Mom, we all made this," he said solemnly. "But you get to decide if you want it."

She turned to see the structure built at the center of the grassy lawn. This time it was a pergola, formed from whatever iron Marley had managed to find, welded together in a circle then painted white. There were pink flowers twisted around the iron from the base to the circular roof, making it look like it belonged at a wedding venue, not in their backyard.

And then she saw him. Marley. Wearing his dress uniform, on one knee in the center of the pergola, a ring in his hands.

"We planned this," Addy said, her voice an octave higher than usual. "We kept it a secret, didn't we, Marley?"

"Yeah, we did." He winked at her.

"He's going to ask you a question, Mommy," Addy said breathlessly.

"Add, let him speak," James said, scooping his sister up in his arms. "Remember what we planned?"

"I remember. I just want it to happen now. Please." She was jumping with excitement.

Ethan was still holding Kate's hand. His arm was healing well, thank goodness. The doctor was pleased with his progress. He had to keep it covered until it was completely healed, and once it was, he'd have to wear sunscreen all year round.

But he was playing ball, going swimming, doing all the things he loved doing. And last week he and Marley had gone to choose a new grill. They'd talked about whether to get one at all after what had happened. But it was Marley who suggested they let Ethan choose. The two of them had gone out for the day, and come back with a small but perfectly formed gas grill.

And last night they'd cooked smores on it and Shana had come over, cuddling Ethan and telling him how proud she was of him. And even though he'd squirmed as she kissed his cheek, he'd looked secretly happy.

Now her youngest son was leading her over to the pergola, like he was a proud father walking her down the aisle. Then he took her hand and gave it to Marley, before stepping back to join James and Addy.

"Go on then," Addy shouted.

Marley's eyes caught hers and they both smiled. Damn, she loved this man so much. "Kate, James, Ethan, and Addy," Marley said, looking at each of them in turn before bringing his eyes back to Kate's face. "This summer with you has been the happiest few months of my life. I love every single one of you more each day. I smile when I wake up because you're part of my life, and I pretty much sleep as soon as my head hits the pillow because you all wear me out so much."

Kate laughed, because this was so true. He was constantly running around the yard with them. Sure, he went home each night – or at least he'd pretend to.

Half of those same nights he'd climb in through her window like the teenage delinquent wannabe he was.

"And I want you. Every one of you. To be mine." His voice cracked. "To be my family. And that doesn't take away from your dad, because you'll still be his, too."

He looked at Kate. "Kate, will you do me the absolute honor of my life by agreeing to be my wife?"

A tear rolled down her cheek. "Yes, please."

"Do you agree?" he asked the children. "Do you agree to be partially mine, too?"

"Yes!" Addy squealed. "Yes!"

"I do," Ethan said solemnly.

James just smiled. And that was enough to tell her what she needed. Marley would be more of a friend than a father figure. But that's what her oldest needed right now.

He'd come along at the right time, this man they hadn't

realized they needed. He was the final piece of the jigsaw puzzle of their lives. He completed them.

Marley stood and slid the ring onto her finger. It was so simple yet so perfect. An emerald, cut square, in a white gold setting. She lifted her hand to look at it before Marley pulled her into his arms. His mouth was warm and soft as he kissed her. "Jesus Christ, I'm gonna sleep for a hundred years after this one," he told her.

"I'll run you a bath," she said. "And you can consider me officially and completely wooed."

"Oh no," Addy said, running in a circle around them. "We're still doing Operation Woo, right?"

Marley laughed against her mouth before breaking the kiss, his hand still on her waist, like he couldn't bear to let her go. "Of course we are," he agreed. "Operation Woo is a lifelong thing."

She looked at the yard. At the planter and the water feature and the tree and the pergola. "Isn't the yard getting a little full?" she murmured.

He lifted a brow. "We're gonna need a bigger yard."

Yeah, they did. But they'd bring those woo tokens with them. The way you always brought the past and made it prettier with the present.

"I like the idea of that," she murmured, as he pulled her against him, his lips soft as they kissed her brow.

"Me too." He slid his hand down her side. "I love you so damn much."

She lifted her face to look at him, her smile full of the kind of radiance you can only have when you truly feel happy.

"And I love you right back."

"Mommy!" Addy shouted, pulling at Kate's hand. "I'll get to be a bridesmaid. I'll get to wear a dress."

"Yes, you will." Kate grinned at her daughter's excitement.

"You want me to go do the next thing?" James asked, his eyes meeting Marley's.

"Yeah, you'd better." Marley smiled at him.

"There's another thing?" Kate asked. What on earth else could there be? She had a ring, she had a pergola, she had more metal yard décor than she could ever know what to do with.

But then James was walking around the corner of the house. "Okay, you all," he was shouting. "You can come back now."

And then a crowd of people started to file into their backyard. Shana was first, running over to Kate and demanding to see the ring. Followed by some of her friends from the library, and Marley's family – his mom hugging her tight and telling her how happy she was for the two of them.

Before she knew it their yard was full of everybody she loved. Even her mom and Carlton had made the trip to celebrate. According to her mom, James had called them last week. They were staying with Marley's parents, and she was loving staying the night with a rock star.

Everybody had brought food and drinks, and Addy was telling them where to put things, while James, and Marley, along with his brothers and cousins were carrying out chairs and tables for the makeshift party.

And every time he walked past her, he had to touch her, just the way she'd pictured it would be. The way she needed it to be.

"You two are disgustingly romantic," Shana said, smiling approvingly. "Is it really a surprise? Didn't you suspect a thing?"

"Nope." Kate shook her head. It was a shock, truth be told, that they could all lie to her so convincingly. Addy and Ethan were definitely going to cause trouble when they hit the teenage years.

Before she could say anymore, the Stitch and Snitch brigade filed in, carrying homemade cakes and a quilt they'd embroidered for Kate and Marley. "To hide the honeymoon stains, dear," Mary told her with a wink. "On the mattress."

"Thank you," Kate said solemnly. "I'll treasure it always."

It was another hour of congratulations and talking to friends and family before she found herself alone with Marley. He slid his arm around her waist as Pres started playing his guitar and Cassie started singing. Couples slowly started to dance around the pergola he'd made for her.

"You want to dance?" Marley asked her.

"In a minute," she said. "But for now I just want to stand here with you. And marvel at how perfect a night can be."

"You think it's perfect?" A smile played at his lips. The man got so happy by making her happy.

"Yes I do." She nodded. "I have one question for you, though."

"What's that?"

"What would you have done with them all if I'd said no?"

Marley grinned and took her hand, lifting it so he could kiss the sensitive skin at the back of her wrist. Then he kissed the finger with his ring on it, as though he still couldn't believe his luck.

"I tried not to think about that," he told her. "I prefer hoping for the best instead of fearing for the worst. But I guess if you'd said no, I would've sent Shana around to comfort you, then I would've taken everybody else to the Moonlight Bar and paid for us all to get steaming drunk."

"I like the hope better," she whispered.

"So do I." He pressed his lips to hers. "And by the way, my parents and your parents are taking the kids tonight. So I *hope* you're ready for some loving."

Her body tightened at the thought. "We have a free night?"

"All night." He nodded slowly, his gaze full of intent.

Her lips split into a grin. "Then bring it on."

The End

Dear Reader

Thank you so much for reading THAT ONE HEARTBREAK. If you enjoyed it and you get a chance, I'd be so grateful if you can leave a review. And don't forget to check out my free bonus epilogue which you can download here: https://dl.bookfunnel.com/xpr18tizm0

The next book in the series is THAT ONE NIGHT, Hendrix's story.

WANT TO KEEP UP TO DATE ON ALL MY NEWS?

Join me on my exclusive mailing list, where you'll be the first to hear about new releases, sales, and other book-related news.

To sign up just put the following address into your phone browser:
https://www.subscribepage.com/carrieelksas

I can't wait to share more stories with you.

Yours,

Carrie xx

Also by Carrie Elks

THE HEARTBREAK BROTHERS NEXT GENERATION SERIES

That One Regret

That One Touch

That One Heartbreak

That One Night

THE HEARTBREAK BROTHERS SERIES

A gorgeous small town series about four brothers and the women who capture their hearts.

Take Me Home

Still The One

A Better Man

Somebody Like You

When We Touch

THE SALINGER BROTHERS SERIES

A swoony romantic comedy series featuring six brothers and the strong and smart women who tame them.

Strictly Business

Strictly Pleasure

Strictly For Now

Strictly Not Yours

Strictly The Worst

Strictly Pretend

THE WINTERVILLE SERIES

A gorgeously wintery small town romance series, featuring six cousins who fight to save the town their grandmother built.

Welcome to Winterville

Hearts In Winter

Leave Me Breathless

Memories Of Mistletoe

Every Shade Of Winter

Mine For The Winter

ANGEL SANDS SERIES

A heartwarming small town beach series, full of best friends, hot guys and happily-ever-afters.

Let Me Burn

She's Like the Wind

Sweet Little Lies

Just A Kiss

Baby I'm Yours

Pieces Of Us

Chasing The Sun

Heart And Soul

Lost In Him

THE SHAKESPEARE SISTERS SERIES

An epic series about four strong yet vulnerable sisters, and the alpha men who steal their hearts.

Summer's Lease

A Winter's Tale

Absent in the Spring

By Virtue Fall

THE LOVE IN LONDON SERIES

Three books about strong and sassy women finding love in the big city.

Coming Down

Broken Chords

Canada Square

STANDALONE

Fix You

An epic romance that spans the decades. Breathtaking and angsty and all the things in between.

About the Author

Carrie Elks writes contemporary romance with a sizzling edge. Her first book, *Fix You,* has been translated into eight languages and made a surprise appearance on *Big Brother* in Brazil. Luckily for her, it wasn't voted out.

Carrie lives with her husband, two lovely children and a larger-than-life black pug called Plato. When she isn't writing or reading, she can be found baking, drinking an occasional (!) glass of wine, or chatting on social media.

You can find Carrie in all these places
www.carrieelks.com
carrie.elks@mail.com

Printed in Great Britain
by Amazon

51875914R00182